Torn B

"Like Melville and Conrad, Inverness can graphically capture the passion and danger of the sea and bring the heart pounding experience to his readers in the safety of their living rooms."

J.P.
Novato, Ca
***

"Inverness is a remarkable writer and story teller. His knowledge and firsthand experience at sea pours out in every word."

S.P.
Glen Cove, NY
***

"The first time in years the reader can experience life at sea without the fear of getting sick and drowning."

M.S.
Middletown, RI
***

"Torn Between Destiny and Desire crosses generations, cultures and oceans as the story unfolds."

D.K.
Vero, FL
***

"The second of three entwined stories of the van der Waterlaan family and the shipping dynasty they control. *Torn Between Destiny and Desire* is rich with intrigue, romance and twists. Readers will find they can't put the book down."

T.V.
Amsterdam, Netherlands
***

"*Drawn to the Sea, Torn Between Destiny and Desire* and *The Gentleman Pirate* ... read all three. You'll be glad you did."

J.F.
Newport Beach, Ca
***

Other Books by Rex Inverness:

Drawn to the Sea
The Gentleman Pirate
Two Warriors Collide
Bonnie Mae
The Cursed Seven
Lobsta
Leviathan
Death of a Liberian Seaman
The Accidental Heir

MV2

Maritime Fiction Novels
Bristol, Rhode Island
02809

Torn Between Destiny and Desire

While visiting Rotterdam Ian Blokker is drawn to a bronze statue standing in a city park and as he approaches his world is tossed upside down. The tarnished yet striking face looking down is the grandfather he never knew. Later that day fate strikes again as an elegant woman flanked with bodyguards and handlers approaches her limousine and sees him.

Ian apparently looks exactly like her dead son and she nearly faints. He almost does too, when he learns she's his grandmother and he is the heir to massive wealth, power and a life of entitlement. In that moment his life changes forever.

Not even a month later Ian is speeding across the Atlantic sitting beside his newly discovered grandmother aboard her lavishly appointed private jet. He thinks it's to meet his Dutch family but the crafty woman has something far more cunning in mind.

Knowing death is near she races against time, her final objective, carefully maneuver and prepare Ian to assume command of her dynasty. The innocent boy from Rhode Island has no idea what lays ahead. His destiny now includes high intrigue, politics, cut-throat competition, and even murder. Will he survive?

Rex Inverness

Dedication

To my wife… whose incredible patience and understanding allows me to write and pursue my dreams.

Acknowledgements

Thanks to Bradley Van Vleck for the cover art and John Sewell who read my draft manuscripts when no one else would.

Chapter One
Another World

At twenty-one Ian faced a personal crisis. In the course of just a few weeks everything in his life had changed.

It all started when he accidentally discovered his father's family and learned their dynasty was one of the largest and most powerful in the world. Up until then he was a rather normal American boy raised by his mother and her friend in a quiet New England town. A handsome and athletic young man, he, by fate or destiny, aspired to become a merchant seaman like his father.

His decision had been a difficult one for his mother to embrace. After all, it was the sea that carried Ian's father away to an untimely death somewhere in the Pacific Ocean.

Ian attended the merchant marine academy and it was during his first sea year he accidentally came across a statue standing tall in a Rotterdam city park.

As if by fate, the statue led him on a search to learn more about his father and his Dutch family – that quest changed his world forever. A quick succession of discoveries and he became aware of his family's privileged status and the heavy burden accompanying it. Then in a freak series of events he was at exactly the right place at the right time and met his Dutch grandmother. The story

8

continued to develop at an ever increasing pace. After their abbreviated visit, Ian received letters and pictures further developing the history of the van der Waterlaan family, and the wealth, privilege, power, and burden they carried and with each image and sentence he read the foundation to his once normal life crumbled.

The sole heir to one of the top ten wealthiest families on the planet, his head spun. Still in an emotional whirlwind he and his mother were flying over the Atlantic to the Netherlands in a private jet sitting on fine leather seats, near an elderly woman, he had come to learn was his grandmother.

His mother had met the family matriarch for the first time just moments before the jet sped down the T.F. Green Airport runway.

The aircraft fuselage was configured for the requirements of the van der Waterlaan family. A comfortable sitting area was located in the middle of the plane, with a separate area forward where the staff and security personnel traveled. Forward was the galley and storage compartments. Aft was a plush and comfortable bedroom where Madam van der Waterlaan often rested her tired body during the frequent long trips she made.

Not this time! She was alert and attentive as she sat comfortably bracketed by her grandson on one side and his mother on the other.

For the last twenty years, Madam van der Waterlaan lived her own private hell after word of her son's death. His ship, the doomed bulk carrier, *Amore Islander,* had broken in two in a Pacific typhoon, and the words in his final letters haunted her. She thought, *he was ready to come home and assume his rightful position at the head of the family dynasty. He was in love with this woman on my right and this is my grandson. Why did you get on that ship, Ian? My dear son, why?"* Her eyes began to water slightly.

Her son was the only heir, or so she thought, which made his loss all the more devastating. It wasn't until recently she'd become aware she had a grandson. She knew it was divine intervention which led to their accidental meeting, in front of the Lutz Theater in Rotterdam.

Now she felt alive and her spirit rekindled. At least long enough for the young man to ascend to the throne of van der Waterlaan Transportation Industries and Holdings Corporation; an international consortium and the fourth largest privately owned of its kind in the world. She thought to herself as they spoke. *The circle continues, young Ian. You'll fill the gap created by your father's untimely death.*

She smiled as the pleasure and comfort of the thought poured over her like a warm shower. She sipped her champagne while the stewardess kept a discreet eye from the corner of the room. Her only purpose was to ensure the madam and her guests wanted for nothing and she was good at her job.

Up in the cockpit, the pilots quickly attained altitude, trimmed the jet, and pointed down the first leg of the great circle course back to Schiphol Airport. The co-pilot spoke to the captain, "Six hundred knots thanks to an unusual tail wind … at this rate we should be there in just under six hours."

"Good, thanks Fritz," the pilot said. He reached for the intercom and called back to the phone in the cabin and relayed the estimated travel time to the stewardess who in turn walked over to Madam van der Waterlaan and whispered into her ear. The madam thanked her and asked for more champagne. The request was quickly filled and the newly poured wine bubbled wildly in the crystal glasses sitting on a small but ornate table positioned between the woman and her guests.

Madam van der Waterlaan could hardly contain herself and she asked an endless number of questions of Ian and Susan. She wanted to know every detail to help her fill in the last twenty years of her life.

The two were comfortable with her and freely answered her in sufficient detail to satisfy her curiosity and the six hour flight seemed like mere minutes. The three only stopped to sip their wine and nibble on an endless array of tasty snacks served on silver trays.

The jet sped to its destination while the skies gradually changed from day to dusk and then dusk to night. No one except the pilots noticed. The staff sat in the forward part of the airplane and gently rested in their seats.

Ingrid, the pretty stewardess, tended to her employer and her guests and the conversation continued without pause.

Back in Swansea, Massachusetts, unknown to Susan, her partner was lying in the arms of another. Both spent from the uncontrollable passion they'd unleashed, and now both in the after-glow were racked in guilt. After a few moments of uncomfortable silence, they turned towards one another in their disheveled bed and looked into the other's eyes.

In the cheap hotel room, their lust erupted once again, and in their rapture, they released hold of their conscience, their bodies, and their souls. Again spent, guilt reemerged to fill their tormented minds and so the cycle continued.

All the time, Susan and Ian moved further and further away and deeper into the grasp of the van der Waterlaan family.

Chapter Two
Breathe

The pilot called back to Ingrid, "The plane will enter the landing pattern for Schiphol in fifteen minutes." With the precision and skill which had made Captain Hans Dieter the most lethal and respected fighter pilot in NATO, he maneuvered the plane to the ground with the finesse of putting a sleeping baby into a crib without disturbing it.

The landing was so smooth the passengers hardly noticed the plane had transitioned from flight to rolling down the runway on its landing gear except for the noise and bumps they sensed compliments of the imperfections of the heavily used runway.

Captain Dieter decelerated the aircraft and took the off-ramp to taxi the jet to the private van der Waterlaan hangar. As the plane turned off the main runway, the staff in the front compartment of the plane began to prepare themselves. The security men strapped on their weapons straightened their ties, and put on their dark glasses. Each consciously looked at themselves as they walked by the full length mirror on the door separating the staff from the plush spaces Ingrid meticulously managed for Madam Margareta van der Waterlaan.

Hans van der Molen, the madam's personal secretary, discreetly entered into her private space as the plane approached the hanger. He was an excessively handsome man with blond hair, blue eyes and an athletic build. His clothes were immaculate and his grooming impeccable. He held a finely bound notebook where he kept Madam van der Waterlaan's schedule and the many notes he made for himself to ensure her comfort and satisfaction.

"Madam, we'll be in the hangar in another minute or so. I've cleared you and your guests through Dutch Immigration and Customs. Carl has the limousine waiting for you. Would you prefer to spend the night in Amsterdam or the country estate?"

Ian and his mother looked at each other, *Amsterdam or the country estate ...?* They smiled in disbelief.

Margareta thought for a moment, looked at the dark veil covering the sky and she realized for the first time she was quite exhausted. She looked at her guests with her blue eyes and then up at her secretary. "We'll stay in the city tonight, Hans. Please make arrangements for us to have dinner shortly after we arrive."

"Yes madam!" Hans clicked his heels, spun around, and left the room to make arrangements.

Ingrid stepped from the shadows and said, "Is there anything else you desire before you depart?"

They in turn nodded and politely said "no." Ingrid smiled, left the owner's cabin and walked to the front of the plane and knocked on the cockpit door.

"It's me," she said,

The co-pilot opened the door and hollered for her to enter. She nodded to him and then eyed the pilot. "Madam and her guests have all their needs met. They are ready to disembark."

Captain Dieter grinned. "Great, mission accomplished. Thank you, Ingrid." He glanced at the co-pilot who was making notes in the flight journal, and then gave her a wink.

She made a hand gesture to her mouth, as if holding a glass, and mouthed the word, "Champagne?"

His eyes lit up and he nodded. "Yes, but first I have to put this baby to bed."

The co-pilot was still logging copious notations.

Ingrid shot a wink back to him and whispered, "After that, you can put me to bed." She blushed and darted her eyes at the co-pilot who seemed oblivious. Blowing a kiss at Captain Dieter, she made her way back through the staff, as they busied themselves preparing to disembark.

The bodyguards were the first to leave the plane. They moved into their pre-assigned positions and looked around the hanger. Each person in the hanger had been screened by the ground security staff while they waited for the jet's arrival.

The head of the traveling security team walked over to a similarly dressed man and discussed something for a moment. The traveling security leader raised his left wrist to his face and said something. Ian watched the whole thing through the jet window. A moment later, there was a knock on the door and Hans reemerged. "Madam, we're ready for you. The limousine is parked in front of the stairs and your luggage is in the trunk. Please let me help you, madam."

"Thank you, Hans, but that won't be necessary. I'll have Ian help me if I need it." She smiled and Ian came over to her chair and stood ready to offer assistance as the proud old lady stood.

Though exhausted, the matriarch of such a large dynasty, and her years of performing, had taught her to stand tall and erect, proud and proper, no matter how tired she felt or how troubled she was at the time. It was theater and she had loved to entertain as a young woman.

She was a picture of stately beauty and elegance. The fact she had just spent six hours seated in her jet hadn't diminished her appearance one bit. Her hair was surprisingly well-groomed, her make-up flawless and her clothing without wrinkles. She stood for a moment and then moved gracefully towards the exit.

Hans stood at the door and stepped ahead of her as she approached the door. One of his duties was to walk down stairs ahead of her to lessen any injury should she stumble. They descended the stairs slowly and once on the ground he moved aside to walk behind his employer, or if requested by her left side.

Protocol was a must in the dynasty. He was good with the rules and expectations. He had learned working for Madam van der Waterlaan had many more perks than quirks and the money was amazing.

Ian and Susan waited at the top of the ladder until the madam and Hans were safely at the bottom and moving slowly towards the awaiting limousine. Ian recognized the long black Mercedes Benz. It was the one he'd sat in less than a month ago during his chance meeting with his grandmother in front of the theater. It had been the first time he'd ever been in a limousine and he remembered it well.

He motioned to the car and turned to his mother. "Mom, there's the limousine Hanna and I told you about."

The driver had the door open for the old lady long before she approached the car. She politely addressed Carl, her driver, and he bowed and welcomed her back home. By now, Susan and Ian had caught-up with their hostess.

Hans politely directed them to the other side of the car where a large man in a dark suit and sunglasses stood looking around the hanger for the slightest thing out of place and then he opened the door for them to enter. The instant they were in the limousine, the bodyguard closed the door behind Ian and resumed his vigilant security posture.

Ian looked at his grandmother and asked, "Madam Grandmother, why do you have so many bodyguards?" An innocent question about an obvious situation ... Margareta looked into the eyes of her grandson and wondered how long it'd be until he accepted the reality of his station by birth. It was too soon to start down the road, or she may scare her guests away.

Margareta was a clever woman and the master at manipulation and control. She knew she'd have to be patient and work carefully to position the boy and his mother so there could be only one outcome ... That would come with time.

She spoke in a kind and warm voice. "Ian ... security is one of the many burdens people of wealth and power must endure. There are, unfortunately, a number of people, for any number of ill-conceived reasons, who try and hurt or even kill the affluent. As a van der Waterlaan you and your mother will learn you're not average people."

She stopped and realized she had just about gone too far too soon.

She smiled and watched Susan and Ian for any indication they sensed anything more than she wanted them to. Satisfied, she looked at Carl through his rearview mirror and said, "Carl, to the Herrengracht, bitter." Sitting in the limousine facing his employer Hans called the house and let the staff know the madam and two guests would be arriving in forty minutes and dinner should be ready twenty minutes later. Watching his efficiency and thoroughness, Susan thought, *He's not bad to look at either.*

Carl maneuvered the car out of the hangar and started down the road to the perimeter security gate around the international airport. Margareta called to him, "Carl, stop the car for a moment." He brought the car to a stop on the dark road.

Expansive lush green grass fields stood on both sides of the otherwise empty road. Behind them was the glow of light visible from the open hangar. The jet shined under the bright halogen bulbs as the mechanics looked over the aircraft.

Madam van der Waterlaan reached over and with her diamond adorned index finger pushed the switch to lower the window. The bodyguard in the passenger seat fidgeted and appeared antsy, "Madam, this is very dangerous to stop and expose yourself."

"I just want to breathe the Dutch air …" She turned to her grandson and said, "Ian, smell the air. It's clean, crisp and Dutch. There is nothing like it in the world." After a long moment, she rolled up her window and nodded to Carl.

He gradually accelerated the car and drove on to the security gate. As the car gathered speed, the bodyguard seemed to relax a little. Ian and Susan watched everything with wide eyes, they were in another world. A world, not only defined by location, but by a whole different set of rules and expectations … the likes they had never experienced or frankly even knew existed.

Only a handful of people had ever known what it's like to be one of 'those' people. This wasn't rock star or movie star rich… this was something way beyond that. As the limousine cleared the gate, it was met by two police cars that took their stations, one in front and the other behind the limousine, their lights flashing and the sirens announcing the oncoming motorcade.

Madam van der Waterlaan looked at the lights of the city and then to her grandson. Her mind was sharp and she had an important plan requiring a solid strategy and supporting timeline. Ian would one day, and soon, lead the family, control its fortune, and maneuver its powerful scepter. Then she could join her husband and son for eternity, in peace with the knowledge their dynasty was in good hands.

As Margareta considered her plan, Susan was in a nearly out-of-body experience. She watched everything around her, both inside the car and the images as they flew by the window. She thought of her lost Liberian Seaman. *So this was your life, my love. I wish we had more time together. This is so much. You came from such a foreign world of wealth and power. I never knew. Why didn't you tell me? Why did you run from this life? Why?"* She quietly asked the memory of Ian van der Waterlaan, her one true love and the father of her son.

Young Ian was overwhelmed by the day's events too. He considered the words his grandmother had spoken moments before. *Ian ... security is one of the many burdens people of wealth and fame must endure. There are, unfortunately, a number of people, for any number of ill-conceived reasons who try and hurt or even kill the affluent. As a van der Waterlaan you and your mother will learn you're not average people and will never be again. I just want to breathe the Dutch air ... smell the air, it is clean, crisp and Dutch. There is nothing like it in the world.*

Something or someone gnawed at his sub-conscience. He recalled the image of his father's ghost aboard the *American Spirit.*

Chapter Three
Surrounded by Wealth

The police sirens drowned out the normal sounds of the city with their alternating two tone warning. The blue lights made the fast moving motorcade visible to pedestrians and motorists alike as it maneuvered by cars pulled over to make room on the narrow roads.   The motorcade continued at high speed along a prearranged route to avoid traffic and confuse those who would do harm to the van der Waterlaan family. Of course, this was by design and had long ago become second nature to Margareta and her staff. Her guests were completely unaware of these precautions.

The cars entered Amsterdam and headed over the concentric canals, a unique feature of the city, towards its center.They passed over bridges and moved along cobblestone roads. The buildings were tall and closely spaced together. They were clearly very old, yet well maintained.

Ian and his mother were exhausted but their excitement kept them riveted to the sites outside the car. It was their first time to Amsterdam. They both thought the shops and homes were so much more impressive in person than they appeared in the pictures in a number of books and websites they'd read in preparation for the trip.

Madam van der Waterlaan looked through the darkly tinted windows. She never tired of her city in part because she loved Amsterdam and the people who lived there. She was lost in thought as she gazed at the lights and the store fronts.

Hans was busy with his Blackberry and jotting down information into his notebook. Carl was calmly maneuvering the large car through the narrow streets with the precision of a grand prix race driver and the bodyguard in the passenger seat kept a vigilant lookout for any indication something was out of the ordinary.

His shoulders and neck were held in a stiff position. He allowed a few seconds to himself and thought, a *massage by the Korean masseuse on the Rosenstraat would be nice. She always finishes with a happy ending.* He smiled to himself and reengaged in his surveillance and security duties, his fingers trailed over his Glock nine-millimeter pistol hung under his left arm, and well-hidden by his tailored jacket.

As the limousine crossed the Herrengracht there was an abrupt change in the scenery. The tall, narrow houses of most of the older part of Amsterdam were replaced with large free-standing mansions with ever increasing opulence and beauty. The limousine slowed and turned into a short driveway between two tall stone and iron walls.

The police cars continued along the main road, turned off their flashing lights and sirens, their detail complete.

The large iron gates stood commandingly before the momentarily stopped limousine and reminded Ian of the massive gates at his school back on Long Island. They were large, heavily constructed, and ornately fabricated and possessed beauty, strength, security, and sheer intimidating mass. The doors opened and several men in dark suits with sub-machine guns were visible roaming the grounds.

The driver brought the car around to the front of the mansion and stopped. A nanosecond later, he was opening the door for Madam van der Waterlaan. She acknowledged his effort with a kind, but distant smile, and gave him her hand as she slowly rose out of her seat. Her body was tired and her back was stiff. The matriarch and a proper lady, her discomforts would remain hidden from all who observed her.

She stood near the car door for a few seconds to compose herself, then she smiled and walked towards the house staff as they waited in a line on the steps for her arrival. She greeted each one by name and said a nice thing or two to each of them as she made her way towards the entrance.

At the top of the marble steps, she turned and addressed the staff. The house staff were still at their receiving stations, the security and transportation staff busy with their respective duties. Madam van der Waterlaan cleared her throat and then in a clear and theatrical voice said,

"One and all … I would like to introduce my only grandchild and the last male heir of this magnificent family -- the family van der Waterlaan. Please make Ian Blooker-van der Waterlaan welcome. Anything he or his lovely mother, Susan Blooker-van der Waterlaan want -- tend to it immediately."

Then she turned to Hans on her left and nodded to him. She turned to Ian and Susan, "Herr van der Molen will show you to your rooms. We'll meet in the parlor in twenty minutes."

With that, she turned and walked into the great house with two uniformed young women in tow. The madam was home and everyone understood she was the center of gravity, and their job was to please her.

Hans turned to Ian and Susan and his face softened. He produced a genuine smile and said, "A bit overwhelming isn't it? I felt the same way when I was introduced to this family by Ian." He bowed his head, faced Susan and said, "You appear tired from the long trip, though it doesn't minimize your kindness, purity or beauty."

Susan blushed.

"Please follow me to your suites," he spoke in perfect English.

They followed him as he ascended up two flights of stairs then led them down a long open corridor. Ian and Susan walked behind Hans but their heads were swiveling around as they looked at classic paintings lining the large walls. Massive furniture was present throughout the house, but the size of the rooms allowed these large items to look proportional. The tables had exotic and expensive vases and statues on them. Not a thing was out of place. "It must take a staff of a hundred to keep this place so clean," Susan said under her breath.

Hans stopped in front of a pair of French doors which opened into a large suite. "Ms. Blooker - van der Waterlaan, this will be yours." He walked in and showed her the suite of rooms and private bath for her exclusive use. "Ma'am, I took the liberty of having clothes purchased for you. They are in the closet and bureau. If there is anything you require, please let me know. Forgive me, but you are expected in the parlor in fifteen minutes. Please wear a dress and be punctual. Madam van der Waterlaan likes it that way."

"Yes" she said. Han clicked his heels and turned facing Ian.

"Now your room young man ..."

He proceeded down the hall to another set of French doors. These doors were open in anticipation of a guest. Ian's room was decorated in darker colors and favored a masculine taste. Unlike the colorful and bright room for his mother with an abundance of flowers and festive pictures, Ian's had several mounted animal heads and antique guns and swords mounted on the walls.

Hans addressed Ian, "Junger ... your grandmother is expecting you in the parlor in fifteen minutes. Please dress and present yourself on time. You should wear a coat and tie. You'll find I have arranged clothes for you. Coats, ties, and slacks are in the closet and more casual clothing can be found in the bureau to your left."

Hans clicked his heels and spun around and disappeared down the hallway. He knew more about these guests than just their clothing size.

Chapter Four
Welcome Home

With only fifteen minutes, Susan and Ian moved quickly to wash, dress, and prepare themselves for dinner and wondered what was in store for them. So far, the day had been full of 'firsts' in endless succession. With only moments to dress, they would have enjoyed a nice long bath or hot shower, but there wasn't time, they were expected to meet prior to dinner. They assumed it would be a formal affair, *Will I remember the proper sequence for using the forks and knives on the table?* Susan thought to herself, and all of a sudden, she wished she could just sneak out for a burger and fries.

In their rooms Ian and Susan found hand towels, soap, and everything imaginable in the bathroom. They washed as best they could in the limited time.

Ian was first to finish. As he left the bathroom, he thought he'd never seen a bathroom so large and well-appointed. The home he grew up in Bristol, Rhode Island was larger than most and in one of the better parts of town, but nothing came close to what he saw here.

He walked over to the closet and opened the doors. Ian stood back and laughed. There were a dozen sport coats, six suits, and two dozen slacks on one side and at least twenty buttoned-down shirts on the other side. Half of the shirts were heavily starched and brilliant white, the others were assorted colors, but all of the finest quality. Below the hanging clothes, neatly paired together on the shoe rack, Ian noticed ten pairs of shoes ranging from dress shoes to sneakers. "Holy Shit … I don't have these many clothes at home." He opened the bureau and it was full of shorts, undershirts, socks, and casual clothing.

He looked at his watch and said to himself, "gitty-up partner or you'll be late." He grabbed a white shirt, dark slacks and a black tie with diagonal light and dark blue stripes and thought, *this must be the van der Waterlaan family colors.* He tied it around his neck and tightened-up the knot, and remembered the colors reflecting back at him in the mirror were also the ones he'd seen on the family jet.

He looked at himself, grinned, and puffed out his chest a bit. His blonde hair was combed off his forehead, his eyes clear, although he was tired. He gazed in the mirror, thanked his academy training for teaching him to make himself presentable in just a few minutes.

He wondered if his father had dressed like this when he was a young man … when he lived in this house.

Ian clicked his heels as he'd seen Hans do and smiled at himself in the mirror. He spun around, copying Hans once again, and moved to the door. His athletic frame strolled fluidly down the corridor to his mother's room. He'd escort her to the parlor and dining room. *Where ever that is,* he thought.

Down the hall things weren't going quite as smoothly. Susan had used her face cloth and soap to clean herself. Her blond hair appeared to have a mind of its own after the long trip and she got more and more frustrated as it refused to cooperate with her brush. Finally, she gave up and pulled it back in a ponytail and said, "Damn it."

Susan moved to the closet, and when she opened the doors, she nearly fell over. Her closet was full of the most beautiful dresses, slacks, and blouses she'd ever seen. The colors were exactly the kind she'd have chosen herself. She thought, *Amazing, the madam has such an insight to what I like, and at the same time, appropriate ... and expensive.* She thumbed the fabric.

Susan was sensitive to the time as she rifled through the dresses remembering Han's advice to wear a dress. She found one made of fine, red cotton with a flower pattern.

As she reached for it, a knock on the door caused her to jump. "Just a moment," she called.

Ian spoke through the door, "Mom, it's me … I'm here to escort you to dinner." He smirked a little and stood at the door.

"Just a moment, Ian, I'm putting on a dress."

"Okay"

As she slid it on, she was relieved by how well it fit. She thought, *how's that possible? They even have my size perfectly correct.*" She smiled at the reflection in the full-length mirror and thought about her deceased lover, *Ian, I wish you were here. I need you to help me navigate this life. I'm excited and scared... your world is so very different from anything our son or I have ever seen. I love you more this day than I ever have ... God I miss you and wish we were together.*

She left her private thought and said to her son on the other side of the door, "Ian, here I come ready-or-not…" and she opened the French doors.

She stood there, a vision of beauty. Her hair up in a casual ponytail, her dress and shoes confirmed she was a lady of class, wealth and distinction.

"Mother you're beautiful," Ian said, as he held out his arm. She reached out and intertwined their arms. She beamed, "Thank you. You're so handsome! I've always been proud to have you as my son, but right now, especially so."

Down the hall, the butler watched from the shadows, nodded his head, and smiled. He mumbled, "They'll fit in nicely."

Ian turned to his mother, "Mom, where do you think the dining room is?"

"Ian ... hell if I know!" They laughed. "This is so overwhelming, this morning we woke up in Rhode Island and now we're on the other side of the world. I feel like I'm on the adventure of a lifetime!"

"Me too, mom, I'm glad we're experiencing this together. I keep thinking I'm in some kind of crazy dream."

Figuring the parlor was on the first floor, they moved towards the stairs and tried to memorize objects and pictures so later they could find their rooms without assistance. They continued arm-in-arm and made their way down to the first floor.

As they stepped off the last step, they were met by an older gentleman wearing a tuxedo and a dour expression. "I'll escort you to the parlor, please follow me." He clicked his heels, spun, and headed down a large corridor.

The two of them looked at each other, smiled, and followed a comfortable distance behind the butler. As if on cue, they started to skip. The butler acted as if nothing was happening out of the norm. It was a happy and uncontrolled moment for mother and son.

They abruptly stopped their skipping and giggling as the butler walked around the corner and stood at the double door entrance to a large room. They peered inside and saw a dining table that seemed a mile long. At one end, the table was prepared with three settings. Ian and Susan froze and their jaws dropped. The walls had gold leaf and exquisite old paintings adorned them. Two candles burned near the prepared side of the table. The place settings consisted of a number of fine china dishes and three crystal wine and water glasses reflected the light. The silverware was perfectly polished to a brilliant shine.

The butler cleared his voice. "This is the dining room where you'll have your mid-day and evening meals with the madam of the house." He gestured them forward. "Now please follow me to the parlor, Madam van der Waterlaan would like you to join her for a drink before dining."

He clicked his heels, spun around, and led the way to an adjacent room. He stood at the door as straight as a board and knocked on the door frame, "Madam … Master Ian Blooker-van der Waterlaan and his mother Ms. Susan Blooker-van der Waterlaan, my lady …" Again, he clicked his heels and bowed slightly from the waist.

"Thank you, Herbert. We'll dine in ten minutes." He bowed again and disappeared around the corner. The madam looked at her grandson and his mother and motioned for them to sit in the comfortable chairs on either side of her. She sat near a large fireplace. The glow from the flames radiated around her, giving her an ethereal appearance.

Ian and Susan still stood arm-in-arm. Embarrassed, they dropped their arms and sat in the chairs, soaking in the heat of the fire.

The old woman had a crystal tumbler with an amber liquid swirling around in ice. "Would you like a drink before dinner? I like my Scotch before I eat." She pointed with her chin to a pretty young woman standing behind the corner bar.

Susan spoke first. "Madam may I have a glass of red wine, if it's no trouble, please?"

"Of course, my dear, you may have anything you desire. Do you have a preference? We have a large wine cellar. I'll have Herbert escort you there in the morning so you can let him know your favorite wines. But for now, what varietal can Maria pour for you?"

"Is anything open?"

The matriarch's eyes focused hard on Ian's mother and Susan became uncomfortable, then slowly the woman's face softened, and she spoke in a gentle voice, "You're a van der Waterlaan, you'll always have whatever you want and never worry about whether it is already opened or not." Then she offered, "My dear, may I recommend a California Cabernet from the family winery?"

Susan said, "Yes, madam, that would be fine. I hope I'm no trouble."

"My dear, you're no trouble. You're the woman my son loved and the one he wrote so fondly of. You helped him find his way back to us. I will always love you for that and so much more." Then she looked at Ian and smiled, "and you, my dear young man, what would you like?"

"Grandmother, may I have a Pepsi or Coke, please?"

"Of course"

Maria delivered the wine and Pepsi in crystal glassware, and slipped away. Ian sipped the cold drink and stared into the roaring fire. Susan sipped her wine and recomposed herself, then said, "Madam, after dinner, I would like to call my friend Maria and let her know we made it here safely."

"Fine, dear, please use one of the phones in the house. We don't use cell phones, they can be monitored. Our phones are secure. That reminds me, Herbert will provide your new cell phones with important numbers preprogrammed. Ian, your lady friend in California, Hanna, such a lovely woman, her number has been added to your new phone."

"But grandmother, there is nothing wrong with my cell phone," Ian protested.

"Ian, please indulge this old woman." Ian slumped his shoulders and bowed his head.

Herbert presented himself at the door and announced, "Madam, dinner is served."

"Yes, Herbert … Thank you. Ian, will you help me up from this seat? It is very comfortable but difficult for me to get out of."

"Yes, grandmother."

She stood with a little assistance, and after a few seconds, glided easily to the dining room. The feast sat on the table and the air was filled with numerous savory aromas. Herbert held the seat for his employer as she settled into the throne at the head of the table. Ian followed suit and held his mother's chair. They shared a smile as

Susan gently sat down. Ian took his place on the other side, next to his grandmother.

Madam van der Waterlaan looked left and right, and reached out towards Ian and Susan. "We'll hold hands and say grace." Ian took his grandmother's hand and thought, *her hand is cold, fragile and delicate.* Then he reached across the table to his mother and he thought, *her hand is warm and strong – what a contrast.*

Susan complied and took the old woman's hand in her left hand and her son's in her right.

The matriarch said, "Bless us, oh Lord and these thy gifts which we are about to receive from thy bounty, through Christ our Lord." Then she continued, "Please take care of my Hans Christen and Ian who are in your kingdom. Thank you for the gift of my grandson and his lovely mother, my son's one true love and his soul mate here with me tonight. Look out and guide them in your name, Amen."

Two servants appeared and served the meal. A slow and carefully orchestrated affair, an hour and a half later, the guests were full and ready for bed. Susan and Ian excused themselves and walked back to their rooms.

Madam retired back to the parlor and sipped another glass of Scotch. She walked over and sat down in front of her dear friend … her cherished three quarter grand piano. Long ago she named it Monika, and she began to play Beethoven's Moonlight Sonata with unharnessed passion. The feelings poured out of her heart and soul.

She had things to sort out in her mind. She stared into the fire, the flawless classical music erupted from her and the stirring sounds filled the house. She gently rocked on the piano bench long into the night while she considered the possibilities and challenges which lay ahead.

Susan called Maria and the phone rang until the answering machine picked up. Susan thought, *that's odd, it's eight in the evening. It's not like her not to be home.* The beep on the answering machine announced it was recording, "Hello Maria, Ian and I are in Amsterdam. You really won't believe it. Ian's family has a wonderful home. I'll tell you more when we talk. Love you." Susan put the phone back on the receiver.

In the other room, Ian dialed his girlfriend's phone and she picked up on the second ring. He filled her in on the trip and the things he'd seen so far. "I wish you were here with us. I love you Hanna," he said.

"I love you too, Ian ... be safe and come back to me in one piece."

"Good night."

"Good night."

With the calls made, Ian and his mother crawled into their beds and listened to the music fill the great house and filter into their rooms. The music was hauntingly beautiful and more than just harmonious sound. It was the outpouring of the artist's soul. They were exhausted, lying snug in their beds and the music held each of them in its grip.

They thought, *what's next?*

Chapter Five
There Was More...

The next morning Ian and Susan were awaken by a gentle knock on the door and a uniformed servant entered the room with a silver tray containing a bone china cup and saucer, a silver coffee service, all presented on a fine linen cloth. The staff member set the tray on the table near the bed without looking at Ian or Susan and said, "Breakfast will be served at seven o'clock. Madam van der Waterlaan would like you to dress in casual clothes, you'll be moving to the country estate this morning. Is there anything I can get for you?"

The embarrassed guests both declined, wondering what the new day would bring. They sipped their coffees and imagined the possibilities.

After coffee, they washed and dressed in casual clothes as instructed. Wiggling his toes in his new shoes, Ian thought, *how could they have known exactly what my size is?* Ian headed over to his mother's room and knocked on the door. "Mom, are you ready?"

"Yes, dear, please come in." Ian entered and eyed his mother in a cotton dress hemmed above the knees. The bright colors and floral print complimented her complexion.

"Wow, mom, you're beautiful."

35

"Thank you, Ian," she said as she spun around in several slow circles, her dress slightly fanning outward as she moved. Then she turned to him and kissed him on his cheek. "You look very handsome too, my dear." They blushed and walked together out of her room towards the sun room where Madam van der Waterlaan ate her breakfast.

Ian turned to his mother while they walked, "Did you hear grandmother play the piano into the night?"

"Yes, it was the most beautiful thing I've ever heard." Then she changed the subject and said lightheartedly, "I wonder what we're going to see and do today?"

Ian said, "Me too."

As she spoke Susan's mind flew across the ocean and she thought of Maria at home, *I wonder where Maria is. I hope she's alright.*

They found the breakfast room easily and Madam van der Waterlaan was already seated having coffee and orange juice.

She was dressed in silk slacks and a colorful blouse with a heavy necklace and many expensive rings on her fingers. Her wrists adorned with large, gold bracelets. Susan blushed and looked down at her feet, "I am sorry, madam, I fear I may have under dressed. I'll change immediately."

"Oh no, not at all, my dear, on the contrary, you look beautiful and are dressed perfectly. Forgive this old woman," as she motioned towards herself, "nowadays I must compensate with clothing and jewelry for the beauty you still possess. Please, you two sit and join me for breakfast."

Breakfast was remarkably normal. It was informal and although it was served by the staff, it was a basic affair much like in their own home. There were eggs prepared to taste, bacon, sausage and toast. The orange juice and coffee were on the table, and without requesting it, Ian's mother was served a mug of hot tea just the way she always enjoyed it in the morning.

Ian said, "Grandmother, we heard you play the piano after we left last night. It was the most beautiful music I've ever heard. Would you play for us again? Mother and I would really appreciate it."

The old woman looked at him. "Ian, I have only played for myself since your father died. It is my private sanctuary. I'm flattered, but I don't perform any longer." Ian looked down at his plate as if he had been scolded. She looked hard at her grandson. "For you two, I'll make an exception. But we have many things to do and see today." Ian's face lit up.

The sun was shining and its brilliance filled the room with warmth. The conversation was light and pleasant and just as the meal came to an end, Hans van der Molen walked in.

He was also dressed casually in a sweater, cotton slacks, and suede leather shoes. "Madam, would you prefer to drive or fly to the country estate?" he asked. Ian and Susan looked at each other and smiled.

"Hans, I'd like to fly and tell Captain Dieter I'll want to make some detours on the way to see Rotterdam and Amsterdam from the air before we fly to the estate."

"Yes, madam, is there anything else before I tend to affairs?"

"No, Hans, thank you."

Hans clicked his heels, this time with the soft suede shoes it was inaudible, and he turned and left. Ian smiled and thought, *Humm, even Hans, I was beginning to think clicking heels is a requirement to be Dutch.*

"Excuse me for a moment," Madam van der Waterlaan said. "I need to check on something." She rose from the chair, Susan and Ian nodded.

When she was gone, Ian and Susan whispered back and forth. Susan said, "I really like her. She is so kind and elegant! I'm surprised I feel so comfortable around her, but I do."

"I agree. I like Hans too. For some reason, I trust him. It's weird, I barely know him."

Susan giggled. "I know it! There's something about him, he reminds me of your father. Ian was rough and rugged and Hans is suave and sophisticated, but they are alike somehow. Maybe it's their honest nature showing through?"

Ian was about to reply when his grandmother returned and said, "Let's walk together." They strolled through a large glass and wrought iron door onto a raised marble patio to the steps that descended to the garden. "This is my favorite place. It's very therapeutic."

The madam cleared her throat and began to tell her guest about her husband, referring to the pictures she had sent to Ian through Captain van der Meer. She spoke for twenty minutes as she mindlessly walked through the garden and examined every flower and plant as she told her story. Soon they were seated on a marble bench in front of a statue of Venus. Hans came around the corner and she momentarily stopped.

"Madam, the helicopter will be here in two minutes. May I escort you to the landing pad?"

"Yes, Hans." She turned to Ian and Susan. "I'll continue the story later today."

The sound of the approaching helicopter could be heard in the distance. A moment later, the sleek bird was visible, painted identically to the jet they'd flown in the day before. The white fuselage with diagonal light and dark blue stripes was striking to see.

The pilot made a perfect landing on the helipad. The door on the side of the helicopter opened and Ian recognized the flight attendant from the day before standing there securing the steps for Madam van der Waterlaan.

Over the noise and prop wash of the idling helicopter, Ingrid greeted her employer and helped her up the steps, Hans was right behind her to protect her from falling, Susan and Ian followed. Ingrid assisted the madam to her chair and strapped the waist belt.

From the cockpit Captain Dieter looked over his shoulder and greeted his employer and discreetly looked at Ingrid as she bent over to open a bottle of champagne. He turned back to his instruments and looked over to his copilot Fritz. "Looks good over, here how about you?"

"Looks good here, skipper," Fritz responded.

Ingrid checked to make sure Susan and Ian were seated and their belts secured. She looked at her employer who smiled and said, "Let's go!" Ingrid nodded and touched Dieter on the shoulder, he turned to look at her and then to his instruments. Seconds later, the helicopter powered up and took flight. Ingrid poured champagne into glasses and presented them to Susan and Ian. The helicopter was less stable than the jet and the vibration and motion impacted her ability to serve like she would have liked to. Glasses in hand, Madam van der Waterlaan called for a toast then looked out the window and began to tell her guests about the sites below.

Occasionally, the madam turned to the pilot and gave him directions, "Hans, head to the east to the Amsterdam harbor." During the flight they saw the important sites in Amsterdam and Rotterdam, including the buildings the family business had built. After an hour, the madam was getting tired. She leaned forward and asked the pilot to fly directly to the country estate.

Holland was small and densely populated. Only the most wealthy and powerful families had country estates and none compared to the compound the helicopter headed to at full throttle, two hundred meters above the green field below. Soon, fields were replaced with wooded forests.

The green forest was abruptly interrupted by a large castle-like structure centered on a large grassy field. Along the perimeter stood an imposing fence and security patrolled the wall. The helicopter made a quick approach to the landing area and the captain set the helicopter down with the same finesse he'd landed the jet the day before.

Ingrid opened the door and secured the steps as the security detail approached the now idling helicopter. Madam van der Waterlaan was assisted from her seat and as she stood, she thanked the pilots and Ingrid for the safe flight and led her guests to an awaiting car. Security kept a close eye while Hans escorted the three to the car. Once the madam and her guests were in the black car, the security detail seemed to relax.

Captain Dieter powered up the helicopter and lifted off to return to the hanger at Schiphol. He smiled and focused on the horizon. He was now flying at fifty meters off the deck at one hundred and eighty knots.

When they landed, Fritz rolled his shoulders. "That was a helluva ride, captain."

"Sorry, Fritz, I was in a bit of a hurry."

Fritz glanced at Ingrid and back at Captain Dieter. "Can't say I blame you, I'm anxious to get back to my wife and kids."

"Understood, I'll tell ya what. Go ahead and take off, I'll attend to the log and everything else."

Fritz jerked his head. "Are you serious?"

"Ja, thanks for your assistance today. You're a good man."

Fritz glanced at Ingrid. "Okay, you two … have fun." He shot Captain Dieter a wink and climbed out of his seat and grabbed his flight bag.

When Fritz was gone, Captain Dieter eyed Ingrid. "I was hoping we could repeat last night."

She grinned, "My apartment, let's say in an hour?"

"Perfect"

Ingrid sighed. "Damn you, Captain Dieter. You can turn me on without even touching me."

The captain leaned back in his seat. "Oh, I intend on touching you, Ingrid … all over your sweet little body."

Chapter Six
The Country Estate

The car pulled up to a large home resembling the castles Ian had seen in his middle school European history books. The building was a massive structure, it was old and well-maintained. Built of large stone blocks, an engineer of exceptional skill had to have been responsible for their assembly into walls, floors, and ceilings. Lichen grew on the old stone adding to the ambiance of the home.

The castle stood in the center of a large open field offering little cover to an approaching army. Ian remembered the large wall securing the perimeter which stood back from the tree line about fifty yards and was well patrolled. This was a fortress for the queen, his grandmother.

In the past two days, Ian had become numb to the presence of security and their constant routine of ant-like business, visible, but hardly noticeable.

The driver brought the car up to the circular driveway wrapped around in front of the entrance and, as had been the case at the Amsterdam house, the staff stood side by side leading along the steps from the castle's large open entrance down to the driveway. Each one, in an impeccable uniform, stood straight like soldiers on the parade field.

The driver stopped the limo in front and rushed around to open the door. He assisted the madam to her feet, the subtlety of his help assured it would not to be noticed by those watching. A woman of her pride and unbending demand for protocol and dignity would never allow herself to be publicly seen needing help.

She smiled warmly and lightly squeezed her delicate hand around his. In a near whisper, only he could hear, she said, "Thank you, my dear friend. Only you seem to understand I can never let age defeat my pride."

He stood tall and in a professional voice heard by those standing around the limousine, he said, "Yes madam, it's a wonderful day in the country. Welcome home, my lady," and he clicked his heels with the pride of a German general. She smiled, discreetly took a deep breath and walked briskly towards her staff.

She addressed each member with a kind word and asked about their families. She had a remarkable memory and could recite the names of her staff's spouses and children. She genuinely cared about her employees. Well, most of them.

Anyone who crossed her would be hung from the yard-arm at dawn. No exceptions, including her family. It was her kindness and concern, yet her unwavering demand for perfection which made her a fair, but firm employer and formidable adversary in the business world.

Though her brother was the face of the corporation and ran much of the day to day affairs, she was the power and the strategist behind the dynasty and many an opponent would attest to her skill after they realized they'd been out maneuvered.

As the lady of the house addressed her staff and slowly made her way up the stairs to the entrance, Ian and Susan climbed out of the limousine on the other side. A security guard holding their door open.

Hans positioned himself one step down from his employer, ready if she fell. Ian and Susan walked slowly well behind the activity centered on Madam van der Waterlaan.

When she emerged at the top of the stairs she cleared her throat and again introduced Ian and Susan to the staff, "One and all ... I'd like to introduce my only grandchild and the last male heir of this magnificent family, the family van der Waterlaan. Please make Ian van der Waterlaan welcome. Anything he or his mother Susan van der Waterlaan wants tend to it immediately." She turned to Hans on her left and nodded to him. She turned to Ian and Susan.

"Herr van der Molen will show you to your rooms. We'll meet in the garden in twenty minutes." She turned and walked into the great house with two young women following behind her.

Hans escorted Susan and Ian into the castle, up several flights of rough and uneven stairs worn by hundreds of years and millions of steps. The castle was darker than the city home and there were many things adorning the monstrous structure making it feel like a medieval castle of knights and maidens. Shields, swords, lances, and coats of armor lined the massive walls. There were few windows and the dampness in the air gave the place both a rustic and powerful feel.

There was no doubt this was the power base for the dynasty. From here, the decisions driving subtle and substantial shifts in the markets of the world were made and put in play. From this place of power and security the van der Waterlaan dynasty reined.

Ian thought, *why would she bring us here?* He felt a chill crawl up his spine. *Dad, was this supposed to have been your's to command? Why am I here? Quite frankly, I'm a little scared.*

Hans stopped in front of a heavy wooden door and pointed into the room. "Ms. van der Waterlaan, this is your room. There are clothes and bath items in your closet and bathroom. Please let me know if you require anything additional and I'll attend to it immediately." He clicked his heels but the soft shoes deadened the effect and Ian smiled to himself.

Hans spun around and looked at Ian. "Follow me if you will, sir." He strode back into the hallway and proceeded twenty feet or so and stood in front of another heavy wooden door. "This way, sir," and he motioned with his hand and followed Ian into his room. "I hope you'll find everything to your liking. Your clothes and shoes are over here and the bath is located through the door to your left. Please remember Madam van der Waterlaan expects you and your mother in the garden in a few minutes. Is there anything else you require, sir?"

"No, sir, thank you."

Hans fiddled with his cuff links and his face grew crimson. "I'm flattered, but sir, please don't call me, 'sir'. Please call me either Hans, or if you'd prefer Herr van der Molen. I'm an employee and you're a member of the family I work for."

"Sorry, I'll try and do better ... Herr van der Molen. There's just so much mom and I have been exposed to in such short order. I'm ... well, quite frankly, overwhelmed."

"Sir, I can understand. If there is anything I can do to assist you in making sense of this, please let me know and I'll do what I can to help. Will that be all, sir?" Hans asked.

"Yes, thank you." Ian said. Hans clicked his heels and this time he smiled at Ian and said under his breath for only the two to hear, "Damn these soft shoes," and they both smiled. Hans spun around and walked out the door.

Hans stopped and spun around again, causing Ian's head to snap in his direction. "Forgive me for my forwardness, sir," Hans said, "but I know exactly how you feel. It seems like only the other day your father, my best friend, brought me into the van der Waterlaan family as a young man." The lines around his eyes crinkled when he gave Ian a half-smile. "I remember how over the top it felt and how uncomfortable and on edge I was while I learned to survive in this most unique of existences." His gentle eyes grew sharper when he said, "You, junger, are now a part of the ultra-wealthy and powerful."

Ian didn't have a chance to respond before Hans clicked his heels again and spun and strode away.

Chapter Seven
The Country Gardens

Ian and his mother found Madam van der Waterlaan in the garden. She was wearing a large sun hat and dark glasses. In her delicate hands she held a pair of gardening gloves, pruning shears, and a piece of canvas about three feet square.

The old lady made her way to a large rose bed thirty yards beyond the large steps connecting the patio to the expansive garden. The rose bed contained over a hundred varieties of flowers, many of them in full bloom.

She looked over her shoulder as the two made their way to her. "You're just in time – I'd like to cut some roses for the house."

Ian thought, *what a complex lady. She's a powerful woman, is respected, no, revered by everyone around her. She's a gifted musician, she holds her God near her, she's daunting and without doubt ruthless and yet she finds pleasure in the simplest of things like cutting flowers. Who is this woman?*

The madam carefully slipped her hands into her gloves and began to harvest roses, placing them on the canvas she'd spread with care on the ground nearby. As she cut the first flower and gently placed it on the canvas she started her story.

"This was the home I was raised in. My father had this rose garden planted for me back when I was only ten years old and these flowers have always provided me pleasure. These varietals have been brought from around the world. See this one, Ian? This rose was named after your father. The rose was officially named the same day he was baptized. I loved your father so much," and tears came to her eyes.

She wiped them away, with the back of her glove, and continued the story, "This was my father's home and it had been in his family for generations. His people were wealthy landowners who had great holdings in Holland, Europe, Indonesia, and the Caribbean. He was landed and had title and lineage."

"As you may imagine, my brother, Johan, and I grew up with many opportunities, but also were separated from other children. The isolation came with the other burdens of the privilege and Ian they can be profound." Ian and Susan gazed at her with solemn expressions.

"It was really not an issue for us until the war. The Nazis came and destroyed our country. The Germans stole or destroyed everything. I was fourteen when the war came to Holland."

"My father was killed by an SS officer wearing a black uniform with skulls on the lapels. He shot my father four times in front of my mother, brother, and me right over there," and she pointed towards the field.

"The Nazis occupied our home and forced us to move into the servant quarters. For years, my mother and I lived in fear of being assaulted by those filthy monsters."

"During the four years of the war, my only freedom and comfort was the piano. I was fortunate to have been educated by one of the finest pianist in Europe before the war and the older, but still usable, instrument in the servant's quarters became my only true friend and somehow we survived."

"Then, in May of 1945, the Americans and British came and liberated Holland and drove the Nazis out."

Susan and Ian shook their heads in wonder. "Wow," Ian murmured.

"It was a glorious day and we celebrated and looked optimistically to the future. Your great grandfather was gone but his wealth and property were gradually restored as we recovered from the war. Little by little, we learned to move forward without our father. Our mother stayed behind at this home while Johan and I moved to Amsterdam to attend the recently reopened university where I studied music and he focused on business."

It was there, I met your grandfather. He was a few years older and bigger than life. He was full of energy and drive. He was a young businessman who saw opportunity in the Dutch ruin. He was from a wealthy family but not landed or of title. It didn't matter, I fell in love with him anyway."

"We married against the advice of my mother and uncles because he wasn't from a noble family but I didn't care. He proved them all wrong and he quickly ascended to prominence in the business world. By the time your father was born, your grandfather Hans Christen van der Waterlaan had increased the family fortune ten-fold and the van der Waterlaan holdings were in the top twenty-five in the world. He had used part of my father's wealth to seed his ambitions and made my family exceedingly wealthy. At the same time, he provided a fortune and a wonderful

49

living for us. God only knows what might have happened had he not been murdered in Rotterdam."

"After he was murdered, I asked my brother Johan to run the day to day affairs of the corporation and be the front man. I, however, became the 'wizard behind the curtain' and have continued all these years. I'd always wanted to hand the reins over to your father."

Her eyes grew tired and she looked at her grandson and said, "Ian, I'm tired and want you to take over control of the business. There'll be education, mentoring, and we'll create a staff to guide you until you're completely ready. I'll groom you to succeed and succeed you will. It's a competitive and dangerous world and you'll become the master."

Ian's eyes grew saucer-like, as Susan's face paled.

The madam looked over at Susan and gently said, "Susan, you'll have an important role in this dynasty as well. As the love of my son's life and the mother of the heir, you'll be a visible part of the family."

The old woman stood up over the roses she'd cut and looked off into the distance and then at Ian and Susan. "Ian ... love, will you gather the flowers and let's retire to the parlor for some tea?"

She took Susan by the arm and they walked towards the steps and slowly made their way up to the patio. Ian followed behind. He wasn't sure he could handle many more revelations like he'd been bombarded with for the last two days.

They entered the parlor and a neatly dressed servant brought over a tea service and set it in the center of the circular table then began to pour and serve tea. The madam was served first, followed by Susan, and then Ian.

The three watched as the tea was poured and presented. Then, without a word the servant was gone. The three looked at each other and sipped their tea, each lost in their own thoughts.

Chapter Eight
The Story Continues

Madam van der Waterlaan looked up from her tea. "I can only imagine the last few days have been mind-numbing for the two of you. There is so much I want to share with you and so much I want to know about you and your lives, I can believe, you must, at times, feel overwhelmed." She took a dainty sip. "I want nothing more than for you to learn about your family and to connect with them, their heritage, and enjoy what is yours as a member of this noble house."

"I want to learn as much as I can, grandmother," Ian said, the sincerity ringing clear in his voice.

The woman set down her tea cup and her lip began to slightly tremble as she said, "My seemingly urgent desire to accomplish so much so quickly is driven by my failing body. I must give you the tools and experience to thrive in this world. I hope you'll accept my help and love as we groom you for the ride of your life. If you accept this, you'll never want for anything as you ascend beyond your wildest dreams." She turned to Susan. "Susan, this is all yours as well."

"Oh my," Susan said, her cheeks pink and glowing.

"Regardless of your decision to stay or return to your lives in America, this will always be your family, the name, the heritage, the title, and the destiny."

Ian and Susan nodded.

"I'll pray and hope you'll see your future here and commit to commanding the dynasty." After she finished her outpouring to her grandson and his mother, she looked old and tired.

Ian saw it first and with a concerned look said, "Madam, grandmother are you alright?"

"Yes, my dear … having you and your mother come into my life has been the most precious gift I've received and I struggle with wanting so much with the limited time remaining. My old body can't keep up with the demands of my heart and mind."

Susan came over to the madam with a look of concern on her face.

The older woman leaned forward and said, "You see, since your father died, I've spent my life running the business without passion, love, or close friends. I focused on creating the most powerful consortium the world has ever known. I guess gathering power became my supplication for the feelings of compassion, caring, and kindness. I'd become cold and calculating, working long hours, and taking what I could and watching the losers suffer what they would."

She sipped her tea and continued, "Then one evening, Ian and Hanna came into my life. Our chance meeting threw my life into a tail spin and I remembered what it was like to love and care and my heart re-awoke. Now I feel alive once again but unfortunately my body will not rejuvenate like my soul, heart, and mind have done. In short, I race the clock and selfishly want to enjoy every minute with the two of you."

In an instant the older woman seemed to recover and Susan's face relaxed as she moved silently back to her seat.

The madam said, "Forgive me for burdening you with so much so fast. I'm tired and will take a nap. Please make yourselves comfortable and enjoy the house and grounds. Feel free to look around. I'll ask Hans to check in with you and provide anything you'd like. See you later this afternoon."

Just as if they knew, two young ladies came into the room, and on either side of their employer, assisted her to her feet. She seemed more unsteady than before. They helped her turn around and maneuver out of the room. The madam turned and said over her shoulder, "My dear, call your lady, Hanna. I know she misses you. She is welcome here with us if you'd like," and then she turned to Susan,

"My dear, you are always welcome in my home for as long as you desire. My son made a good choice falling in love with you. You're a wonderful and special woman with purity and honestly. It's so refreshing, had Hans Christen and I been lucky enough to have had a daughter, I hope she'd have been as wonderful as you, my dear."

Susan's eyes welled up in tears and she stood and walked over to the woman and embraced her and said softly, "Thank you, madam, you are incredibly kind and I love you very much."

"Thank you, dear, now it's time for me to rest." The madam walked away with the escorts bracketing her on either side. Susan stood there watching her host shuffle down the long corridor. This was no longer the elegant lady they'd seen for the past two days, she was walking slowly, slightly hunched over and her feet slightly dragged over the stone floors.

Ian and Susan returned to the large expansive gardens and walked well into the green fields reaching out to the perimeter a distance from the garden limits. This was the first time they had been alone for any length of time since Rhode Island.

They took the opportunity to discuss what they had seen and felt with incredible candor. It allowed them to compare observations, feelings and gut instincts. Little did they know the madam sat in a chair by the window of her bedroom and watched them as they strolled and talked.

The matriarch said out loud, "Good ... look at you two talking as a mother and her son should. I wish Ian and I'd been as close." A tear came to her eye and she moved to her bed. "I fear my time is coming to an end soon."

As the lady restlessly slept in her castle, her staff and security worked for and protected her, her grandson and his mother walked the grounds engrossed in conversation as they wrestled to understand the nature of the world they found themselves in.

Some distance away, two men in dark suits and sunglasses with automatic weapons over their shoulders followed them. By now, the presence of security was becoming second nature. After all they were van der Waterlaans or so they kept being told.

Several hours later, the two returned from their walk. They were exhausted and made their way back into the house, headed to the kitchen for a glass of water or lemonade. They entered the large stone house and their ears registered the beautiful sound of a Chopin nocturne.

The romantically influenced music was nearly angelic as played through the hands and soul of Margareta. It filled the large house with a richness and beauty that caused them to stop in their tracks and listen to the sounds as they poured over them like songs from heaven. Oblivious to the fact Ian and Susan had returned from their walk, the madam rocked gently back and forth as she skillfully massaged the keys in an endless combination of perfectly choreographed cords.

Drinks in hand, Ian and Susan returned to the sun room where they sat and listened to the music as it cascaded down the stairs into the entire house for over an hour. After the nocturne was completed there was only a moment of silence and then the first movement of Beethoven's Moonlight Sonata filled the air. The atmosphere in the home instantly changed to a somber and church-like feel. The beauty and emotion flowed from the musician's soul pouring out through the body of the instrument. Everyone in the home privately bathed in the music she provided until it abruptly stopped. That instant, everyone in the home froze and wondered why.

A few moments later the madam came down the stairs and greeted Ian and Susan. Susan offered, "We heard you playing the most beautiful music. The sound is magical as if heaven sent. Thank you, for the privilege of listening to you, madam."

"Susan, my dear, you are too kind. Let's take a drive in the country and see the sites." Ian and Susan both knew the car would have already been brought around to the front of the house and the necessary preparations made for what seemed like an impromptu idea. Nothing can be completely impromptu when there is a logistic and security tail like the one that followed Margareta van der Waterlaan. Hans waited by the front door with the butler.

Madam walked towards the men and they both clicked their heels and bowed slightly at the waist. Hans fell in front of his employer as she approached the large stairs leading down from the house to the awaiting car. He walked slowly to stay only a step ahead of her. They approached the awaiting car and the driver opened the door as security watched everything around like birds of prey. The security detail had keen eyesight and they saw each movement and every detail.

The four of them climbed into the rear of the black sedan and leaned back in the soft leather seats. The driver and security officer climbed into the front. Through the sliding glass window separating the driver from his passengers, madam leaned forward. "Take us out into the country and head towards the German border. Make the trip a scenic one. I'd like to travel for no more than two hours, Raul."

"Yes, my lady." The driver said as he looked at his employer in the rear view mirror. He'd been her driver for forty years and had come to the country house as a young man seeking employment. He worked hard and was an honest and humble man and Hans Christen and Margareta liked him and trusted him.

He was the driver the day Hans Christen was murdered in his boardroom and he remembered the day vividly. He was waiting to take the three of them to the theater following the fated meeting.

He never forgave himself and felt there must have been something he could have done to prevent the murder.

He didn't for the life of him know what but he felt guilty just the same. Every time he looked into Madam van der Waterlaan's eyes, the pang of guilt struck his heart.

Of course, he had always been in love with her but would never tell or offer the slightest clue of his heart's secret.

She had suspected it just the same and never let on she knew his secret.

Chapter Nine
A Drive in the Country

The madam sat quietly in the limousine for the first twenty minutes looking out the window deep in thought. Ian and Susan looked through the tinted windows absorbed in the sites while Hans explained the area and provided the names and history of each of the places they saw. They saw forests, grassy and tulip fields, canals and rolling hills that would eventually connect to the larger mountains over the German border.

The madam would occasionally look over at him with an approving smile. He continued with an occasional glance over to his employer to ensure his descriptions were to her satisfaction.

Susan, especially interested, looked at him as he spoke and she realized she was falling in love with the handsome and articulate Dutchman. Something within her was beginning to stir. It had been years since she'd felt this way and wasn't sure it was even possible any longer. She looked out the window and drove the thought out of her head.

She'd still been unable to contact Maria back in Bristol. If she couldn't get a hold of her tonight, she'd call her parents to check in on her and make sure she was alright. Susan reengaged with Hans as he continued to provide information about the sites they saw passing by.

59

In the front seat the driver focused on the road and the security officer kept his eyes on the road, roadside and the forests for anything of potential danger. At ten minute intervals, he spoke into his left wrist where he had a small concealed microphone, providing their location and status to security headquarters.

After about an hour the madam began to grow tired of the trip and said, "Raul, head north west to the North Sea please. Take us to the Molen Haus."

"Yes, my lady."

Then she turned to Susan and Ian and in a gentle voice said, "I'd like to get some stroopwafels and tea. I think we have been in the car long enough."

Ian asked, "What is a stroopwafel? "

"It is a cookie made of two waffles with a caramel center. They are quite delicious."

Susan spoke up, "Your son loved them and used to bring them to Sarah and me in Tampa years ago."

"Oh yes, my dear, I've been so remiss, not asking about your daughter, Sarah. She lives in California, married and has two children, correct?"

"Yes, madam, but how did you know?" Susan asked.

"Please don't worry about something so trivial, my dear," the madam said indicating the topic was closed as she looked out the window.

Susan tilted her head, squinted her eyes, and Hans leaned towards her and said, "The madam, after learning about young Ian, had some discreet people confirm her intuition. You certainly can understand a woman in her position has to be careful."

"I guess," Susan said absentmindedly as she was swimming in Hans' blue eyes. She knew she was falling fast for this man and, she had no right to, she was spoken for. But in his eyes, she felt safe and protected. He wouldn't let anything happen to her or her son, she was sure.

The Molen Haus came into view and Raul maneuvered the limousine to the front door. The security officer climbed out and surveyed the area. Satisfied it was safe, he nodded to Raul and Raul climbed out and walked around to the door his employer would exit the car from. He opened it and discreetly helped her to her feet. All the time, the security guard watched for signs of trouble. With Madam van der Waterlaan and Hans out and moving towards the restaurant door, Raul strode around to open the door for Ian and Susan. They were on their feet, thanked the driver and moved swiftly to catch up with the madam.

The owner of the restaurant saw the limousine pull up and he knew who it was. Margareta had been a regular customer for so many years the owner had a special table he kept for her in the corner; much to the satisfaction of her security detail. Fritz, the owner, came up to greet his guest while his wife, Trudy, came from the kitchen wiping her hands on her apron, her blonde hair slightly pulled out of the bun she wore, flour dust accented her cheeks.

Trudy smiled broadly and in a high pitched voice said, "Madam, welcome, welcome, welcome! I have some stroopwafel coming out of the oven at this very minute and our strudel is excellent today, if I may say myself." She blushed and slightly curtsied.

Madam smiled at Trudy, shook Fritz's hand and asked about their two children. Fritz assured her they were fine and happy in their own lives. She turned towards Ian and Susan, "Fritz and Trudy Shoemaaker, I'd like to introduce my grandson, Ian van der Waterlaan and his mother Susan van der Waterlaan. They're visiting from the United States and I want to introduce them to stroopwafels and tea."

"And so it will be done," Fritz said with a smile and led them to the table. Security had already looked around and under the table just in case.

They dined on piping hot waffles. The pastries were round, thin and exquisite. As a plate full of waffles was consumed, another plate arrived.

After consuming four or five plates piled high with waffles and several cups of tea, they bid the owners farewell and headed to the car waiting out front.

They prepared to enter the limousine, but first, they looked back at Fritz and Trudy, waved and said, "Thank you." The security officer was the last to enter the car, satisfied the area posed no threat.

"Raul, please take us back to the country house," Margareta said.

Raul looked back in the rear view mirror and nodded as he spoke, "Yes, my lady. " He gazed at her with an admiring smile on his face and then, as if startled, snapped his eyes towards the road and began driving in the general direction of the country estate.

Margareta spoke of her childhood and the things she and her brother Johan did as children. She spoke lovingly of her parents and how her father had been such a good man and tried to help his Jewish friends and employees escape the country when the Nazis revealed their intentions to annihilate the Jewish race. "It was his activities to save those poor souls that led to his murder by the SS officer in front of his family. The memory still burns in my mind."

She gazed out the window for a few seconds and said, "It's ironic it would be a Jew who would murder my husband years later." When her eyes misted over, Ian grabbed her hand and gave it a squeeze.

She continued, "My mother was a kind and strong woman emotionally. It was her strength which allowed the three of us to survive the Nazi occupation and rebound after the war. Unfortunately, the war and the pressure of protecting her family and their holdings made her old before her time. She died of consumption shortly after Hans Christen and I were married and before my brother married."

"Oh, how sad!" Susan said, shaking her head.

Margareta nodded. "Speaking of my brother, he'll be coming to the country estate tomorrow. I know he's looking forward to getting to know you. He's been my best friend and confidant since I lost your grandfather, Ian.

Johan is the person who runs the company and is the face to the world all these years. He's a good man, but like me, he's getting tired too."

She continued to speak openly and lucidly about her youth and the war and how it greatly influenced her. The hour it took to return to the estate was consumed by her memories and random thoughts and recollections of family.

As she talked, Ian and Susan focused on her. Meanwhile, Hans' eyes roved over Susan's face and what he could see of her shapely legs. Susan glanced at him and her eyes widened. He jerked his head away and peered out the window. A half-smile came to her face and her cheeks burned a bright red. She lowered her eyes for a moment before turning back to the madam.

The car pulled up to the security perimeter and barely slowed down as the gate opened in anticipation of their arrival. Moments later the limousine pulled up to the building.

Raul and the security officer opened the doors and Margareta, with Hans, Ian, and Susan made their way up the stairs. The butler stood there waiting to greet Madam van der Waterlaan and receive any instructions.

Greetings made, there were no instructions. Hans followed his employer towards the office. Madam van der Waterlaan turned and addressed Ian and Susan, "Relax and enjoy yourselves. The house is yours. I must tend to business for a while. I'll see you for dinner at eight tonight." She turned and moved towards the large room down the corridor. There were several men in dark suits and briefcases already seated inside.

Ian and his mother looked at each other and together agreed to retire to their rooms for a nice bath and time alone. Ian wanted to call Hanna in California and his mother needed to hear Maria's voice to counter her romantic feelings for Hans van der Molen.

Ian and his love spoke for thirty minutes in happy and excited voices. Susan reached Maria and told her of the wonderful things she'd seen and experienced. Maria was quiet and distant.

"Are you alright Maria? You sound different."

"I'm fine, it sounds like you're having fun." Maria said and then cut the conversation short, "I have to go. Goodbye, Susan."

"Goodbye, Maria." Susan said and the phone went dead.

Maria hung up the phone and leaned over and kissed John as they fell back into their warm bed. Their writhing bodies entwined once more. Though they were racked with guilt, they continued to consume one another.

Maria thought, *this will not end well.*

Chapter Ten
Private Business

The next day, Susan set down the phone, Maria wasn't home again, and Susan was sure something was wrong. She couldn't put her finger on it but it gnawed in the back of her mind like a dog working over a discarded ham bone tossed from the kitchen.

Susan thought, *was it she missed me? Was something wrong with her business? Was it something with her or my parents and she didn't want to tell me? Maybe I should go home to be with her?"But then again, I can't leave Ian here alone either.*

Susan lay back on the bed in her room and her mind swirled around in confusion. An endless number of questions ran around in her mind and there were no answers to a single question until her parents came to mind.

"I'll call my parents and see if they'll check on Maria for me," she said to herself in a soft voice. She sat up on the bed and dialed her parent's number. It rang twice and her father picked up the phone. "Hello," he said. Tears came to Susan's eyes as she heard the strong and confident voice of her father. He was the bedrock she could always lean on. "Hello, dad,"

"How are you and Ian doing in Holland?"

"We're fine. The van der Waterlaan's live an incredible life with jets, helicopters, limousines, and servants. We're in the country home where Ian's grandmother grew up. It's a castle … It's all so beautiful. We'll tell you all about it when we come home. Yes, dad, we're fine and having a wonderful time. Please don't worry about us," then she got to the purpose of her call,

"Dad, I called Maria a number of times and the phone just rang. I finally got a hold of her yesterday and … well … I don't understand, but I think something is wrong. Would you and mom check in with her and make sure she's alright?"

"Of course, sweetheart, we'll call her this evening and check in with her. I guess we should have been more sensitive about Maria because she hasn't lived in an empty home since you came home twenty years ago. Don't worry we'll take care of her if she needs anything, we're here. Now don't you worry, have a good time. Your mother and I send our love to you and Ian."

A couple of comments about the weather as only New Englanders do and the conversation came to a close with, "I love you, sweetheart"

"I love you, dad." The phone went dead and Susan lay back down on the bed relieved she'd called and he was there to talk with her. As she laid the phone down she thought about him and how glad she was they'd reconnected. It was so cold and lonely without a father's love for those years long ago.

Just as she was thinking about how her life had taken a number of strange turns, there was a knock on the door. "It's me … mom." Ian called through the door.

"Come on in, honey." He walked over to his mother still sitting on her bed. She could see he was very upset. "What's wrong, son?"

"Hanna broke up with me. She said, 'we were too far apart and it just wouldn't work'."

"Oh, Ian," Susan reached out and held him as he sat down next to her.

"What happened, mom?" Ian asked as his eyes filled with tears and he began to cry. He buried his face in her shoulder. "Why?" he asked again.

Susan just held her son close and let him cry. "Ian, you'll be alright, you'll be alright." After ten minutes, he was spent and put his head down on the bed and fell asleep.

His mother covered him and moved to a chair near the bed and watched her son as he worked through the disappointment and confusion. *I wonder what the real reason for Hanna calling off their relationship was.* She thought about it until she nodded off in the chair.

While the drama unfolded in the bedroom and Ian worked through his first heartache, Madam van der Waterlaan was in her office with members of the board of directors. The meeting was confidential and the purpose and outcome would be kept quiet until the moment the snare was secured around the neck of the unsuspecting hare.

There was a major corporate consolidation effort afoot, subtle but hostile all the same. For the last three years, Margareta had her eyes on the holdings of Angelo Nappolini. His World Bulk Carriers Shipping Company and his holdings in many of the major ship building yards around the world had become a competitor in the Pacific transportation network of bulk products. There was more and only she knew the connection.

Margareta had discreetly approached him three years ago with an offer to work together to leverage their tonnage capabilities to drive the market in favor of the transportation providers. It was a simple scheme. With the two major bulk ship owner operators carefully reducing the available ships and tonnage available to the cargo owners, the price per ton of cargo carried would rise and so would profits. With van der Waterlaan/Nappolini control over the market, small bulk ship owners would be pushed out.

Nappolini was nearly the same age as Margareta. He was a man of principle and though he'd never had a son, had groomed his nephew Michael to continue the family business Angelo's father had started with two American surplus ships after the First World War. They shared the same high regard for honesty and integrity.

Angelo had declined the offer and continued to compete on the open market against the slightly larger van der Waterlaan fleet. His shrewdness and business acumen allowed him to continue to expand his market share and was perceived as a threat to be dealt with.

In a cunning and carefully orchestrated series of acquisitions, Margareta was ready to close in around her handsome opponent. Yes, it was business, but it was personal. It was Angelo who had built, and was the original owner of, the ship her son died on.

Angelo had long since sold the ship to a succession of owners until Y.G. Yang, a Hong Kong ship operator, had purchased the old ship and renamed it the *Amore Islander*.

Margareta had already destroyed Y.G. Yang years before by hostile takeover and her security people had discreetly ensured those culpable for the conditions leading up to the sinking, as she alone judged, were eliminated. Nappolini was the last on her private list to even the score for her lost son.

As the meeting broke up, she was certain everything was finally in place for the 'check mate' move in her private game and her son would be avenged.

Ian and Susan slept in her room until there was a knock on the door, "Ms. van der Waterlaan." It was the familiar voice of Hans van der Molen. Susan was the first to hear the knock on the door. She walked to the door and opened it. Hans politely clicked his heels and slightly bowed. "Ms. van der Waterlaan. We'll be joined for dinner this evening by the Madam's brother, Johan. Dinner will be in an hour. Would you be so kind as to inform young Ian?"

"Of course Hans," she blushed as she had called him by his first name… and she continued, "Ian is resting in my room. He got some bad news from home. His girlfriend just broke off their relationship."

"Oh, I'm sorry to hear that." Susan raised an eyebrow when he didn't look surprised. It was almost as if he *knew* it had happened. "Is there anything I can do for you?"

Susan considered the offer and wondered what he'd be like as a lover, then looked in his eyes wanting to say one thing but said, "No, thank you. I assume dinner will be formal."

"Yes, young Ian should be in a suit and you a formal dress. I'll pick you up here in an hour." He clicked his heels, spun around and moved away.

As she closed the door, Ian sat up on the bed and looked at his mother. She said, "Ian, dinner will be in an hour. We'll dine with your grand uncle tonight. You should wear a suit and Hans will escort us." Ian rubbed his eyes and stood up. "I guess I'd better get in the shower and clean up. Mom, thanks for being here for me, I love you."

"I love you too, Ian," she said as he moved towards the door. Susan fell back on the bed and thought about Hans van der Molen before she moved into her bathroom to prepare for dinner with Ian's relatives.

Chapter Eleven
Family Dinner

Just as they'd become accustomed, Ian and Susan waited for Hans' knock on their doors. Susan thought to herself as she heard the rap on the door, *Right on time, Herr van der Molen. Come to think of it, Ian's father was always that way too...*

She opened the door and without thinking about it produced a pretty smile as she greeted her escort. Hans looked at Susan and she responded by spinning around in front of him. "Ms. van der Waterlaan, you look stunning ... simply stunning, if I may be so bold."

"Thank you and of course you may ..." and they shared a smile.

A moment later they stood in front of Ian's room and Hans knocked. Ian opened the door before Hans spoke through it. Ian was in a dark suit, white shirt, the family tie, and a pair of patent leather shoes. Hans and Susan looked at the handsome young man who looked every bit the heir to a throne. Hans spoke, "Sir, your grandmother will be very proud of the way you look. Now shall we?" Hans spoke, and turned abruptly.

Susan took his arm and the three of them walked towards the stairs making their way down to the dining room and the parlor where they would meet the madam and her brother. At the foot of the stairs the butler stood to escort them the rest of the way to dinner. Hans excused himself and Susan asked, "Won't you be joining us?"

"No, not tonight, my lady, good night," and Hans bowed at the waist and was gone.

The butler got their attention with a slight cough and led them towards the parlor. This time he just stepped aside and Ian and Susan walked into the dark room.

A fire was burning in the fireplace and the madam was sitting in a chair in the corner sipping on her Scotch. There was an older gentleman sitting next to her and it was clear the two were very close as their conversations were light and happy.

Madam van der Waterlaan waved them in with familiarity and set down her drink. With some effort, she stood. The gentleman next to her rose to his feet as well.

"Johan ... I'd like to introduce my grandson, Ian van der Waterlaan and his mother Susan van der Waterlaan. Ian and Susan this is my brother, Johan van Winkle."

Johan carefully approached Susan and gently lifted her hand to his lips and kissed her as he bowed slightly from his waist. "It is a pleasure to meet you, my dear lady. Margareta speaks so highly of you. I can see she is right." Then he smiled and looked over to his sister. "Like always, I might add," and he winked.

She waved her hand at him and said in a soft voice, "Johan, you flatter me to no end."

Then Johan looked intensely at Ian. His tired blue eyes bore into the boy's soul. Ian stood there and felt as if he were naked, for all-the-world to see as his grand uncle's scrutiny continued. Then the old man's face softened and his eyes lit up with happiness. He turned to his sister,

"Margareta, you're right he is a perfect copy of his father at this age. It's remarkable!"

"Junger," he addressed Ian "It's my sincere pleasure to make your acquaintance." He clicked his heels, walked up to the young man and gave him a hug. "Welcome to the family and welcome home," he said with Ian in his arms.

From the shadow came a young lady with a silver tray with glasses of champagne. She served Margareta, Susan, Johan, and Ian in order.

Johan took the opportunity, raised his glass indicating a pending toast, cleared his throat and said, "Dear sister, we love you. You've always been there for me and everyone who has come into your world, and to young Ian and his charming mother, welcome to this wonderful family. Hold on for the ride of your life." He toasted and laughed. Margareta just looked at him with a look of, "I'll get you for that," and they all laughed together.

There was lighthearted conversation in front of the fire while they nursed their drinks. When they were ready, the butler presented himself and in a deep voice announced, "Dinner is served, madam, mein herr." He turned and walked towards the dining room where the food had been carefully served.

They sat, Madam van der Waterlaan at the head and, as she had done at each evening meal, she held her hands out and the seated took each other's hands forming a circle. She closed her eyes. "Bless this food, we are about to receive from thy bounty. Please look after my Hans Christen and our son Ian and Johan's wife, children and grandchildren. Please protect Ian and Susan and give them health and happiness, Amen." The wine was poured and the soups and bread were delivered on cue to the table.

Susan hoped Hans would slip into the room. She knew she was falling for him. She looked around as the food was presented and the conversation focused on Ian.

The walls were made of large stones chiseled into blocks carefully stacked on top of one another. The room was darker than the dining room in the Amsterdam home. The walls were covered with old tapestries and paintings.

The furniture was heavy oak with ornate carvings, albeit crude. It was clear the furniture had been part of this home for hundreds of years. The linen was fresh and clean and the candelabras burned brightly bringing both warmth and light to the meal.

The table was fastidiously prepared and the food presented with talent and care. It was a perfect experience and the food kept coming. It was another hour and a half before they finished and returned to the parlor.

The young lady who'd served them champagne earlier in the evening was still standing by the bar. She had madam's drink ready when she came into the room and the glass was set on the table next to her favorite seat in front of the fire. Johan was a brandy drinker and his neat pour was on the table next to the seat he occupied on his not – too -- often visits. Unlike his sister, this place was not a sanctuary and he never felt comfortable since his childhood. He'd come when his sister beckoned and hardly any other time. He'd decided, if he outlived her, he'd sell the place. There were too many bad memories within these walls for him. As Johan thought, the young lady walked over to Susan and Ian and asked for their drink choice.

Susan asked for a Bailey's and coffee and Ian ice water. In a few minutes, their drinks were delivered, they settled into seats near the fire, close to the brother and sister. Johan began to tell his stories of their youth in the house and of his family. Ian and Susan listened intently as he spoke. It was interesting for Ian and his mother and clearly therapeutic for Johan to share. Madam said nothing as she looked into the fire and sipped her Scotch. After Johan finished, they politely bid each other good night and retired.

As Ian and Susan left the parlor and headed to their rooms, Johan and Margareta spoke quietly for a moment. Johan said, "I like the young man and I agree he'll make an excellent heir."

"Thank you for your support and assurance, Johan. I love you, my brother," Margareta said as she kissed him on the cheek. He smiled and left the room. As much as he dreaded spending the night in the castle, he would for the sake of his sister.

He moved off to his room knowing he'd be busy the next day. His helicopter would come for him at twelve to fly him to Rotterdam. A few short meetings and he'd be on the jet headed to Rio de Janeiro by four in the afternoon.

Alone with the young maid, Madam van der Waterlaan asked for another Scotch and she shuffled to her piano in the corner of the room near the back wall. She dropped heavily onto the bench and for a long moment sat quietly as if reintroducing herself to a dear friend.

The piano, which she called Maggie, was as close to her as her Monika waiting in Amsterdam. She set her drink and crystal coaster on the piano. Madam reached over and took a sip, set the glass down, and her finger reached out for the ivory and ebony keys. It wasn't until the music poured out of the body of the instrument that she recognized she was playing the Piano Concerto No. 2 by Rachmaninoff. His moving and powerful music was fitting for the way Margareta felt at the moment. She'd carefully planned and orchestrated a strategy down to the final move she'd put into play. The aim was to destroy a man she respected and even loved over the years. The moment to act was a long time in coming, yet she was conflicted. The reason for her revenge was long over and now she had a grandson. She should look forward not back. Her prey was not responsible for the loss of her son and she knew it but she couldn't let go.

Margareta played on … It was a piece her instructor before the war had composed. The vision of her instructor, Sergi Rachmaninoff, came to her. A tall Russian composer who'd fled the Soviet Union and then the Nazis. He made his way to America where he died. Margareta had not only learned to play the piano from the gifted artist, but to play with the passion providing a third dimension to the sound.

She had a gift few musicians are blessed with. The music continued to pour from the instrument as she carefully massaged the keyboard. Her mind wasn't on the music, it just flowed from her soul. She thought about the fine Italian gentlemen she was about to destroy. Angelo Nappolini would never know what hit him and he didn't deserve it. The final move was in play as the music poured from her soul.

She played for hours while tears ran down her cheeks.

The other secret she carried was too horrible to consider …

Chapter Twelve
His Father Remembered

The next morning, Ian and his mother made their way to the breakfast room and were met by Johan. He was already seated, reading the morning paper and sipping his coffee when they walked into the room. He stood and held the chair for Susan and kissed her on the cheek and smiled at his nephew. "Good morning, junger."

"Good morning, Uncle Johan" Ian said and the men sat at the table. The staff brought Susan her tea in a large mug and Ian orange juice.

Johan set down his paper. "Margareta is under the weather this morning. She played her damned piano until God only knows when and now she's sick. She loves the piano more than life itself, I think. You know, before her husband was murdered she was one of the best pianist in Europe -- and the world for that matter. Her music was light, happy and full of a joyful soul. Then after Hans Christen was gone, she rarely performed and her music changed."

"When your father died at sea her music took on a darker tone. Her soul pours out in her music. I hope your coming into her life will help her return to happier times. We'll hear it in her music before we'll see it in her heart. Trust me, junger." Johan smiled at Ian and winked at Susan as she held her mug between her hands, absorbing the warmth through her palms.

The young stewardess came into the room and asked for breakfast preferences and just as quickly left the room to retrieve meals.

Johan continued his conversation from last night and told of his family, his children, and their children, and then briefly about the accident in the Swiss Alps in nineteen ninety-four.

His wife, son Johan Jr. and daughter Trudy, and their families were on holiday staying in a cabin on a mountain side when an unexpected storm erupted. In its violence it brought down a mountain of snow that engulfed the cottage and in a matter of seconds destroyed his entire family. His face showed his pride as he spoke and the sadness he lived with each day.

Ian looked at him and thought, *Uncle Johan, you're a kind and simple man. You're honest and open and so much different than your sister who was smart, manipulative, cunning, and cold. How could you have managed the large family holdings and successfully avoided being out-maneuvered in the board room?*

It was clear Johan was cast into a roll not suited for him, but then again, had survived and the business expanded and its power base influenced international commerce and politics. Clearly, Margareta was the 'Oz' pulling all the strings behind the curtains.

The meals were served and the hungry trio consumed the food placed in front of them. As they finished Ian asked his uncle, "Uncle Johan, would you tell me about my father? I know so very little about the man responsible for bringing my mother and me here. I'd like to know everything you can tell me about him."

Johan looked at Ian and then at Susan and after a moment looked into Ian eyes. "Ja, junger... Let's walk in the garden." Then he looked at Susan with questioning eyes.

She said, "You two run along, I'll stay behind and read a book."

The two men rose from the table and made their way to the glass doors out to the marble patio and the garden beyond. They walked to the stairs and down onto the lawn near Margareta's rose garden. Margareta looked down at the two of them from her room high above. Her face was swollen and her eyes red from the night before.

Her restlessness had followed her into her bed and she hadn't slept. She was conflicted as she'd never been before. She'd destroyed men and businesses with regularity, and without a single second of remorse. *Why now?* She watched the two men walk by her beloved roses and move off into the large field.

Susan rose from the table just as Hans came around the corner. She walked out of the room as he walked by and they collided. Neither was hurt, just startled and embarrassed. "My lady, I am so very sorry, are you hurt?" His expression showed concern but it soon changed to one of a man who landed in an opportunity to see the woman he desired.

"No, Hans, the truth is I was just thinking about you."

"Really, I was thinking about you too," he said softly.

"Do you have time to walk with me?" Susan asked

"Yes, my lady. Where would you like to go?"

"Oh, I don't care where, I would like to walk and talk with you if it's okay," she said looking down at her feet. She was flirting and she hadn't even noticed until now. They smiled and walked out the front door into the large green fields facing forward of the house.

Susan was glad they'd be out of ear shot and wouldn't have to worry about bumping into the men walking in the back fields. She wanted to take Han's arm as they walked, but the fields were open and she thought they were being watched closely from a distance. She was correct.

Back in the fields behind the castle Johan started his story, "Junger, so you want to know about your father do you? Well your grandmother became pregnant shortly after she and Hans Christen were married. In fact, it was barely nine months after the honeymoon," and Johan gave Ian a wink and a smile.

"Your father was a happy boy and always busy. He loved to play outside and loved to build things from kits and from scraps. He loved to laugh and tell jokes. He was your grandparents pride and joy."

Your father seemed to understand there were times he could be a kid and others where he needed to be a van der Waterlaan. He was a natural to assume the reins from your grandfather when the time was right. Unfortunately it didn't work out that way."

"Your grandfather's senseless murder sent shock waves through the family and your father was forever altered. One day he was a happy, loved, and cared for child, and the next his world was upside down."

"The fact he saw his father murdered as he ate ice cream standing next to his mother melted away his youth."

Johan looked away for a moment and continued, "Your grandmother was a wreck and became a recluse. Prior to the murder, she was a famous musician and socialite. Then all at once, her light just faded and she focused her energy on running the business.

"She leaned on me, too, and brought me into the business as CEO to run the day to day affairs, and be the man at the helm for the entire world to see. But it was and has always been Margareta who ran the business." Johan reached for his pocket and retrieved a handkerchief and wiped the sweat from his brow, folded it carefully and shoved it into his trousers. Ian could see the story troubled his uncle as he drew a deep breath and continued,

"As she became more involved in corporate politics and maneuvers, your father was alone for longer and longer periods. My wife and I tried to bring Ian into our lives, and have him spend time with his cousins Junior and Trudy, our children." His face went sad for a moment.

"Ian, Junior, and Trudy became as close as any cousins and Ian thrived on family closeness. I argued and pleaded with Margarita to be more engaged in his upbringing but she was more interested in building the empire. As a result Ian grew up with access to anything he wanted except the love of his mother."

Johan's voice changed as he said, "Your father was a smart man and extremely handsome. You favor him more than you could possibly imagine. As he reached young adulthood, things changed for the worst. I don't know if it was to get even with his mother for abandoning him emotionally or the temptations which accompany wealth or maybe a little of both but your father became a world class playboy and family embarrassment."

"My father was a playboy?" Ian said in hollow voice. He'd never imagined his father like that. He swallowed hard and looked at his uncle with an inquisitive expression.

"He was always in trouble with the law and the media because he played outside the social norms. Fast cars, too many beautiful women, drugs, alcohol and exorbitant bills became his reputation. He was killing himself, I'm sorry to say."

"Then in an effort to bring him back into the fold and groom him to take over the family business, Margareta and I encouraged Ian to go to sea with Captain Adriaan van der Meer, who had been an early business partner of your grandfather, a close family friend and senior sea captain."

"Yes, you met him recently, Ja? That plan backfired and Ian continued to go to sea, not as a career, but as an escape from the pressure and reality of accepting his destiny."

"Finally Margareta and I agreed that Johan Jr. would be the heir and began to groom him. That was, until he and his family died in the snow storm. Your grandmother and I found ourselves completely alone. Your father died at sea and my family wiped from the earth in a few seconds. All we had left were each other."

"Your grandmother sought revenge for the loss of her son and it fueled her for years. I buried myself in the work and together we continued to build an empire for naught. Just because we could and it kept us busy. Neither of us wanted to retire and enjoy life. We were bitter that our lives had been stolen by fate."

"Then one fateful day, Margarita runs into you and the whole world changed … Changed for the better, I might add."

"Knowing we have an heir gave us both a reason to live again. If you could only understand how important it is for your grandmother and I to know you're here and there is now a possibility we can turn over the dynasty to a family member has given both of us a reason to go on."

"Margareta will approach you in time. Be prepared, you'll be expected to fill the role intended for your father and I know you'll make an excellent heir to the van der Waterlaan dynasty."

Johan looked at his watch and stopped. "Junger, I must return to the house. My helicopter will be arriving in thirty minutes and I need to prepare."

"Oh, one more thing before I leave. Your father really loved your mother. He and I spoke often of her. She helped him realize there was more to life than what he had let himself evolve too and he was returning little by little to the point he could consider marrying your mother and return to the family to assume his title. Unfortunately, he died just as he was prepared to bring your mother and sister, Sarah, to Holland."

"Knowing how she struggles in California, I think we should consider asking her to move here and join the family soon. She'd be safe and secure and well-cared for, I assure you, junger. Enough, I must go."

Johan turned and headed towards the house as Ian considered all the information he'd just been overwhelmed with.

On the other side of the house, out near the perimeter of the compound Susan and Hans talked. They walked into the woods and found themselves hidden in the shade of the rugged trees, Hans stopped and faced Susan. She turned and leaned forward, gently raised her chin to his as their lips met and they embraced.

Chapter Thirteen
The Accident

At the prearranged time, Captain Dieter brought his helicopter in for a landing on the grass behind the castle in the same location he'd delivered the bird several days before with Ian aboard. This time, however, Ingrid was not aboard and a middle-aged woman emerged from the helicopter. She was dressed formally and it was immediately apparent she was Johan's executive assistant.

She greeted him as he approached the idling bird, its prop wash molested the grass, flowers and bushes nearby with the violent wind. She handed him several letter-sized envelopes and yelled into his ear over the noise of the machine. He nodded and climbed into the helicopter and in moments the bird sprang into the air, pivoted in place and raced off at tree level. Surely, Johan was more of a thrill seeker than his sister.

Moments before Susan and Hans had returned from their walk and joined Ian as he watched his uncle in a suit walk down from the castle to the helicopter. Johan waved and smiled to the three of them, then looked at his approaching secretary.

Ian noticed he was no longer the easygoing gentleman he'd walked with in the garden -- he had transformed into a business tycoon and everything about him was professional and all business.

Margareta watched from her bedroom high above the theater of activity. She had worked hard to transform her younger brother into the powerful and respected man he was. It had taken a long time and a lot of coaching and subconscious mentoring, but he was the respectable and feared face of her dynasty.

His presence distracted her opponents and allowed her to quietly out maneuver them. Johan got the credit, but they both knew who the brains were in the family.

Ian turned to Hans. "Johan said he's going to meetings in Rotterdam and then will fly to Rio de Janeiro. What will he be doing in Brazil?"

"Business ... the van der Waterlaan family has business interests around the world. Maybe when the time is right, you'll start to escort your uncle and learn the business." He looked over at Susan and smiled. She smiled back, but an alarm began to ring in the back of her mind. *Would Ian be given a choice when the time came?*

In a few moments the helicopter was gone and chirping birds in the garden replaced the mechanical noise of the flying machine.

Johan and his secretary prepared for the meeting and were focused on the papers sitting in front of them as Captain Dieter flew low and fast. It was unusual that both Fritz and Ingrid weren't aboard the helicopter. Fritz was sick at home and Ingrid was away on holiday with her mother. Normally, there would be two experienced pilots in the cockpit, but today Dieter brought his son. He'd just finished pilot training and was legally qualified, but only had a handful of hours of rotary wing experience.

It was a clear day and the visibility was unlimited, in pilot's jargon. Dieter confirmed all the instrument readings were where they should be. He looked over to his son and was about to say something when there was a loud crash and the helicopter began to shutter, smoke poured from the engine compartment.

Dieter struggled to regain control over the violently wobbling helicopter, the nose pointed ever higher above the horizon. Johan and his secretary looked at each other and instinctively held each other's hand.

Dieter, the season combat pilot, kept his cool as he worked through the protocols drilled into pilots during their training. When they all failed, he tried a few more as time and altitude bled away. He fought the bird until the end.

Moments later, the helicopter crashed into an isolated grass field. Fortunately for all aboard, they died, or at least the coroner said, immediately on impact.

The business world buzzed with sadness and entrepreneurial curiosity as word the CEO of van der Waterlaan Transportation and Holdings Corporation had been killed in an accident.

His obituary filled a full page in the Amsterdam and Rotterdam papers. He was prominently posted in the business journals and papers around the world while the business world held its breath to see what would happen to the fourth largest privately held company in the world.

Captain Dieter would be buried with full military honors. His son and Johan's executive secretary were "oh by the way" and their funerals quiet and small.

Word got back to the van der Waterlaan castle within minutes of the crash. Hans was the first to be notified by the Dutch Aviation Authorities that the helicopter was missing and an SOS message had been sent by the pilot. Search and rescue assets were dispatched and more information would be presented to the family, for obvious reasons, before being released to the media.

Hans had just left the company of Ian and Susan when he received the call. He walked up the stairs of the castle to the madam's room and nodded to the security agent standing in front of her door. The large, muscular man in a dark suit holding a submachine gun nodded back. Hans knocked on the door and waited for her to ask him to enter.

When he walked through the door, she was sitting by the window. He clicked his heels and with sober and sincere concern he relayed the call he had just received from the authorities. She looked up at him and asked several questions with little emotion on her face. Her final comments to Hans, "Cancel the meetings at the home office and postpone the meeting in Brazil. I'll reschedule it after Johan is buried. Oh, and Hans, I'll tell Ian and Susan over dinner tonight. No reason for you to do the onerous task."

"Yes madam, as you wish," Hans said, "Shouldn't we wait until there is more information about the ..." he caught himself, then continued, "the helicopter and if your brother and the crew are okay."

She considered his counsel for a moment and said, "Good point, we really don't know what happened just yet do we." She shared a sinister smile with Hans and his skin crawled.

"Yes, madam," he turned and walked for the office where he'd cancel the meetings Johan was to chair and say nothing to the employees on the other line about why.

Susan, unaware of the accident, had retired to her room and moved between a comfortable chair looking out a large window onto the grounds and her bed. She struggled with the two things troubling her. Was everything okay with Maria and she couldn't deny she was falling in love with Hans. She'd committed herself to Maria yet she found this Dutchman irresistible.

She loved Maria in her own way but the way she felt about Hans was the same way she'd felt about Ian's father twenty years ago.

Chapter Fourteen
Pieces Move into Place

It took the Dutch authorities four hours to find the crash site and recover the bodies and another twenty-four hours to confirm the identification of the victims, but Margareta knew the story.

In the privacy of her office she made several discreet calls. The Dieter family and Johan's secretary's family would never be told the name of the benefactor who covered all the expenses nor would they know the name of the anonymous donor who provided them each a million Euros to ensure they were cared for the rest of their lives. Hans knew how to do things like that and do it without the slightest trail. Even INTERPOL couldn't locate the source. It was done through an off-shore account, laundered and provided via a discreet third party with no ties to the family, van der Waterlaan. Hans had done it a number of times at the insistence of his employer. She was ruthless, but possessed a conscience.

Johan was another story. His untimely death would be celebrated and the proper ceremony would be conducted. It would be as if a head of state had passed and Margareta insisted on nothing less. Flags were flown at half-mast throughout Holland. Businessmen and diplomats from around the world would come to the funeral and offer Margareta condolences.

The evening of the crash, Ian and Susan were given the news about Johan in the parlor. Margareta informed them of the disturbing news as they gathered for their evening drink before dinner. She mustered up sufficient drama to make the story believable as she told of her brother's death only hours before in a helicopter crash.

Ian and Susan were numbed and hurt by the news. They had both considered Johan a good and honest man and wanted to get to know him better. He knew so much about the family and the business and, of course, Ian's dad.

The dinner was quiet and somber. Few words were exchanged. Ian and his mother retired without following Margareta into the parlor, where she sipped her drink and played her piano.

She played Tchaikovsky, his symphony #6, another dark, classical arrangement written by a troubled Russian composer who nine days after performing it for the first time committed suicide. The pain and sorrow poured out of the piano as Margareta played well into the night. The dimly lit room was full of shadows and demons only she could see.

Elsewhere in the house the staff finished their chores and Ian and Susan lay in their beds thinking of Johan and the others who had died. The music filled the rooms and subconsciously influenced all who listened.

It was a sorrowful night in the castle van der Waterlaan. Only three people alive knew the whole story, and by midnight, there would only be two. Those two would never tell.

The next morning, the newspaper was full of the accident and speculation of the future of the van der Waterlaan dynasty. The television pundits carried on about the accident and the mysterious mechanical failure terminally crippling and destroying the aircraft. An initial report indicated the aircraft had been properly maintained and the mechanical failure was unprecedented. There, of course, would be a thorough investigation, but at this point the accident was not attributed to pilot error or anything considered criminal.

Buried in the last page of the paper, where most people never even look, was a story of a murder. It occurred sometime during the night. A man was shot in the back of the head in his hotel room. It turns out the victim used a falsified name to rent the room on the Rosenstraat in Amsterdam and the police had quickly turned the case over to INTERPOL to track down the name and country of origin of the corpse. He had no apparent ties to Holland so the authorities were happy to turn over the case.

Margareta was busy making arrangements and running the company and for the next four days was rarely seen by Ian or Susan. Hans was kept close to the madam's side during the whirlwind of activities.

They never spoke of the accident, but focused on managing the consequences of the accident. There were board members needing reassurance and clients needing hand holding. There were the clients in Brazil who needed to be addressed. Madam van der Waterlaan was a strong woman, but these were difficult times and dark circles appeared under her eyes.

The turn of events took its toll on Ian, as well. His broad shoulders hunched over a bit when he realized, by some fluke, besides his eighty-year-old grandmother, he was the sole heir of a family who controlled tremendous wealth and power.

TORN BETWEEN DESTINY AND DESIRE

He had wanted to return to the *American Spirit* next week and resume his education and training to work at sea but returning to sea and completing his studies at the merchant marine academy didn't seem as important as finding a way to help his grandmother and assist her keep the family business thriving. It struck him as ironic, he was torn between destiny and desire.

As he weighed options and consequences, a strange feeling came over him. The hair on the back of his neck began to tingle, his focus became acute, and for just a moment, he had complete control over his life and his surroundings, and everything became perfectly clear in his mind.

It was, for Ian, one of the few times in a lifetime where all questions seem answered and there came a sense of calmness over mind, heart, and soul, almost god-like. He knew at that moment he'd remake himself and offer his services and commitment to his grandmother and the family dynasty.

Then reality descended on Ian and he began to question himself. *What about my family at home? I don't speak Dutch. I don't have any business background or education. I don't have any education. How could I possibly hope to survive in this world? What about the academy and Captain Horne on the 'American Spirit'?*

In Amsterdam, Madam van der Waterlaan anticipated Ian would be reconsidering his plans to return to sea and she was ready to open the door for him to become the next CEO of the company.

She'd already created a strong and loyal team to surround Ian while he learned the art and science of finance and business. The team would keep the company running smoothly, she would continue to make the strategic decisions, and groom Ian in the art of strategy.

She would remain out of the limelight, like she enjoyed, and her young and handsome grandson would be presented to the world as the next "ultra" tycoon of industry.

She thought as she gazed out the castle window, *It's a shame Johan's death was necessary for this to happen, but time is running out.* Only she and her doctor knew the reason why.

In the meantime, she reached for the phone and called the castle and asked for Ian. After a few moments, Ian picked up the phone. "Madam Grandmother? This is Ian."

"Yes dear … how are you and your mother? I'm sorry I've been away so much. I was hoping you'd join me here in Amsterdam."

"Yes grandmother, but I don't want to leave my mother alone." Ian politely said.

"Yes dear, I completely understand. I'll send Hans to look after your mother and you can join me here. I have much I want to share with you."

"Okay, Grandmother, I also wanted to tell you I want to help you anyway I can."

She smiled as she said, "Thank you dear, I'll have the car drive you down in the morning. Goodbye for now, my love," and she hung up the phone and turned to Hans.

"Hans, you'll return to the castle and take care of Susan. She must be happy and not distract Ian while I prepare him for his coming-out. She's pretty and I think you'll find this a pleasant assignment. Remember, keep her preoccupied and happy so she doesn't interfere."

Hans stood, clicked his heels, and bowed. "Yes, my lady. I'll leave at once." He turned and left the room.

With his back to his employer, he smiled and his face lit up as he prepared for the two hour drive back to the castle. He'd take his Porsche 911 instead of the company limo. He loved to drive the car and it would give him time to think.

Hans gathered a few clothes and some personal items and a 9mm Glock pistol and stuffed them into an orange athletic bag with his initials embroidered on the side. He looked around his room in the Amsterdam home, it served as a room, office, and sanctuary, if needed. He walked out the door and moved towards the garage and his car.

He could feel the excitement stirring inside him as he approached his Porsche. He stood for a moment in front of the closed door and then reached down and opened it. There she was ... his pride and joy. Hans had owned it for nearly three years and still every time he saw the car it took his breath away. It was a 911 with lowered racing suspension and a tail providing stability at high speeds, something he could rarely do in Holland but, across the border to Germany, on the Autobahns, he routinely drove his car in excess of one hundred and twenty miles per hour. It was a rather unique color, bright orange, and to the best of Han's memory, he'd never seen another that color in Europe.

It had been a deadly combination ... a handsome man in a head turning car, and though not a player like his good friend Ian van der Waterlaan had been, Hans had shared company with some of the best looking women in

Europe. Unlike his deceased friend, he was far more discreet.

Ian had cut a wide path and was constantly in the tabloids for his excesses, Hans was always by his side, but just out of the paparazzi view or interest and he liked it that way.

Hans brought the car to life with the key fob. The alarm chirped as it turned off and the engine roared to life. Hans could feel the adrenaline flow through his veins and his senses became more acute than usual. He opened the door and tossed his bag on the passenger seat, climbed into the running car and buckled in. He reached for the buckskin gloves waiting for him and he strategically placed an expensive pair of dark glasses over his eyes. A quick glance in the rear view mirror confirmed he looked good and was ready to go. The air cooled engine came up to temperature and the gauges confirmed the machine was ready for the sprint to the country. Hans put the car in gear and, man and machine, together in harmony, moved to the security perimeter and in a moment were on the congested streets of the ancient city.

He slowly made his way to the northern edge of the Dutch capital and pulled onto the highway heading northeast. The traffic reduced, the roads improved, and Hans began to relax and enjoy the experience of being one with the road.

Soon the highway was replaced with two lane country roads complete with sweeping turns and gentle hills. The city concrete gave way to open fields on either side of roads with little traffic. Hans liked this part of the trip best and he began to put his sports car through the paces as he sped closer to Susan.

He knew much more about Susan than she thought. He'd been the one who entered her home shortly after Ian met the madam. Hans carefully pawed through all of her drawers and the entire home. He'd studied her and Ian from afar and embarrassing close. He knew her clothes size, the colors she liked and even the type of bras and panties she wore. There had been no guess about size or colors when he stocked Ian and Susan's closets in Holland.

He'd discreetly observed Susan, Maria, and Ian as they went about their daily business and reported every detail back to his employer. Yes, it was dirty work, but he was well paid and liked it. He'd wire-tapped the phones and been through Maria's, Susan's, and Ian's bank accounts and learned much more. Pulling on a few details, he'd uncovered Susan's life in Tampa.

Lastly, he knew about Maria and John Gates and had pictures and video footage of their illicit liaisons. The madam was aware and Hans knew she'd use the information at the appropriate time to destroy Susan's trust in Maria and poison the relationship so she'd stay in Holland with her son and start over. Hans liked the idea and relished the possibilities.

Hans thought about all this and more as he drove his car skillfully and fast through the turns on the dark country roads. All this, he could never tell Susan. The van der Waterlaan family had been good to him and he was loyal to his employer and wouldn't hurt the lady who kept him preoccupied over the last few weeks.

He neared the turn onto the private road to the security gate and access to the van der Waterlaan castle off in the distance. He looked at the clock on the dash of the Porsche, *Great! It only took an hour and forty-two minutes.*

A new record! He slowed as he approached the security gate and one of the guards left the guard shack and walked over to the car. He saw Hans and motioned to the other man to open the gate. The gate opened and, as if to provide some entertainment for the security team, Hans chirped the tires and sped away towards the castle. Unimpressed, the guards closed the gate and returned to their shack.

Hans pulled his car into the back to a discreet garage where the house employees kept their cars. It bothered him his beautiful car had to share a garage with rather ordinary cars, but he had secured a private stall with ample room to avoid dents and unwanted scratches.

He parked, removed his gloves, and placed them in the glove box. He stopped the engine and climbed out with the bag in hand and moved forward to the opened compartment at the front of the car. He lifted the lid and removed a cover. The garage was dusty and he wanted to keep his car clean.

After closing the boot and locking and alarming the car, he covered it with the perfectly fitting cover. One more look over his shoulder and he walked out of the garage.

Susan's image pounded in his mind. He wanted her and his employer had given him cryptic orders, *she's pretty and I think you'll find this a pleasant assignment. Remember, keep her preoccupied and happy so she doesn't interfere.*

Chapter Fifteen
A Night of Freedom

Susan and Ian spent the day wondering what was happening. Ian's grandmother had called a few times and talked with them, but she was preoccupied with making the funeral arrangements for her brother. They had run of the large and historic castle and the plentiful grounds, but both felt as if they were prisoners in their own way.

Ian had nothing to do in preparation for his trip to Amsterdam in the morning. His clothes were waiting for him there.

Susan wondered if she should plan to return home. She was beginning to feel like a third wheel and was still unsure of how Maria was.

The butler came into the room where Susan basked in the sun reading a romance novel and sipping ice tea. He politely bowed and said, "Ms. van der Waterlaan, there is a Maria calling from the United States. Would you like to entertain the call?"

"Yes, please." Susan said as she sat up straight and gave him a broad grin. The butler returned with the wireless phone a moment later and then closed the doors behind him as he left.

"Hello, Maria?" Susan spoke into the phone.

101

"Hello, Susan, your parents dropped by and said you were worried about me. Is that true?"

"Well, yes … I haven't heard from you. I leave you voice messages and it seemed strange to me. Are you all right?"

"Yes, I have been busy at the pharmacy and there is a patient of mine who has me preoccupied."

Maria couldn't believe how the truth came from her somewhere deep inside – it was the perfect cover. It flashed across her mind, *this is like that movie I remember were the character hid her lies by telling the truth.*

Yes, the patient was John, and he had kept her preoccupied, but not like Susan would think. Instead it was by making passionate love to her as if there were no tomorrow, and for him, there really wasn't. He would be dead in another two months.

His wife had long given up on his frequent and long disappearances and unexplained moods. She thought he was privately taking care of his affairs with the accountants and attorneys. Never did she suspect her upstanding husband of having an affair with the town pharmacist.

Susan and Maria talked for twenty minutes. Most of the conversation was Susan talking about all she and Ian had seen and done. It was fine with Maria, for she really had nothing to tell. She certainly couldn't describe her frequent and desperate rendezvous' with John.

After twenty minutes, Maria politely told Susan she needed to go and they said good night. As Susan put down the phone, she felt better for the first time since her arrival. Then, without knocking, in walked Hans and her mind began to spin again.

"Good evening, Susan, I'll be staying here with you while Ian returns to Amsterdam. I hope that is okay with you?"

"Ummm, yes as a matter of fact. Do you think we could eat less formally tonight since the madam will not be with us? Ian and I would like to have pizza or burgers or something like that, okay?"

"Of course it is, my dear, I know a wonderful pizza parlor about twenty minutes from here. If you'd like, we can drive there and eat in the restaurant."

"Oh, yes, we would like to. Could we go soon, I'm starving?"

"Yes, you get your son and I'll bring the car around. Let's say about fifteen minutes out front?"

"Fifteen minutes it is," Susan said and nearly dropped her book and jumped to her feet like a school girl. She moved quickly through the door to find Ian and put on a little make-up for Hans.

Hans cancelled dinner to the glee of the kitchen staff called for Raul to bring around the car and notified security, they'd be dining out at the local pizza parlor. Security growled because spontaneous activities made it hard for them to ensure the safety of the van der Waterlaans. It wasn't the first nor would it be the last. Some of the old-timers remembered the challenges they faced with this young man's father. He used to sneak out or ditch his security details with regularity and it drove them nuts. "This young man is much easier, at least so far," the grey beards acknowledged.

Ian wore shorts, a T-shirt and sneakers. Susan was in a pretty sun dress and sandals as they anxiously counted the minutes at the front door. Raul brought the black limo around to the front and they both frowned. Hans came up to them in nicely tailored slacks, a bright shirt, and soft leather shoes.

He saw Ian and Susan were not thrilled about riding in the limousine. He smiled and said, "Just a moment, please," and he walked down to Raul and they spoke for a few seconds, Raul got back in the car and drove away. Hans returned up the stairs to Susan and Ian and complemented them on their clothing choices.

As they chatted, Raul reappeared in a four door Mercedes Benz. He parked it and got out of the car. Hans turned to Ian and Susan, "Is that better?"

"Oh, yes," Susan gushed. A security guard sat in the passenger seat, Raul got out as Hans said, "Raul, I'll drive, thank you." Raul smiled and stepped away from the car. They jumped in and Hans drove the car down the road to the security check-point and then down to the pizza parlor he'd promised.

It was a small restaurant and clearly catered to a young crowd. Ian's eyes lit up and he started to mingle. Hans and Susan found a table in the corner and climbed into the booth. The seats were old and covered in red plastic and the table was covered by an inexpensive red and white checkered table cloth.

The security guard stood in the corner, visible, but, at the same time invisible, to the patrons. After a few minutes a waitress came to the table, blushed and pulled slightly on her dress as she looked at Hans.

"What would you like to drink, Susan?" he asked in a kind and gentle voice.

"I'd like a light beer please." Susan said and Hans looked up at the waitress. A pitcher of Amstel Light, aus tu blieft."

The waitress smiled and turned away to retrieve the pitcher and two glasses. In the meantime, Ian was talking with the locals and often they'd tilt their heads back and roar with laughter.

Hans and Susan enjoyed their beers and passed the time in conversation. Susan said, "I heard from Maria and all seemed well." She didn't notice Hans bristle every time Maria's name was mentioned. Instead, she concentrated on his pleasant smile and gorgeous eyes.

Susan talked about home, Maria, her job, and raising Ian and Sarah, her daughter living in California. Hans was attentive, like he was hearing this for the first time. Finally, Ian returned to the table. "Can we order a pizza? I'm starved?"

"Sure, junger … what would you like?"

"Hans, I'd like to have a pepperoni and mushroom pizza and a Coke-a-Cola, please."

"As you wish junger, and for you, my lady?" He looked and smiled at Susan.

"That's fine, Hans," she said and smiled back. Ian returned to the crowd of young Dutchmen and the adults to their conversations. Susan asked Hans, "Tell me about you Hans."

"There is not much to tell, really, my mother was a Swedish woman who was in love with a prominent Dutchman. I guess you could say I was a lucky baby. I never knew my father but he provided money so I had a good education and my mother was cared for. I studied at Utrecht and majored in business."

He shifted in his seat and continued, "When I was eighteen, I met Ian at a night club and we became friends. I admired him for the way he was 'bullet-proof'. He did what he wanted and took what he wanted without remorse or conscience. It was only later I began to understand he was really a good and kind man inside the exterior shell he'd created to hide his pain and fear. I think you saw the same thing in him and he was beginning to respond to you. With your help he was exorcising the demons of his past."

I'm getting ahead of myself, he mused and leaned forward and said, "He and I grew to be good friends, through him, I was introduced to the family and soon I was part of the staff, and here I am today."

"Interesting, are you married or do you have a girlfriend?" she asked.

"No, I stay too busy supporting madam to have a steady relationship."

"Are you a playboy?" she asked.

"No, anything but ..." he responded with a glint in his eye.

"Oh," Susan sounded disappointed. Hans changed the subject.

"How about you ... are you in a serious relationship?" and Susan's eyes flashed and then softened.

"I was, but I am not so sure any longer."

"Then I guess we can spend time together without feeling guilty." Hans said and smiled as his eyes roved her face looking for clues.

The waitress cleared her throat to get their attention and held a large pizza in front of her. She set it down in the middle of the table and a moment later returned with plates and grated cheese.

"Would you like anything else?" she said. They shook their heads, *no*.

Ian saw the pizza arrive and bolted to the table and the three of them ate and giggled about being where they were relaxed, comfortable, and unrecognized. All the time, the security guard kept a vigilant lookout for trouble.

After dinner, they were tired and agreed to return to the castle for the evening. The small talk in the car appeared to annoy the security man while he focused outside the car and called back to the castle from time to time to check-in.

They pulled up to the security gate, were waved through with minimal delay and the car stopped in front of the house. They stood outside the car and then both leaned back into the car, "Thanks, Hans, we had a wonderful time tonight."

"Junger, Ms. Susan … you're welcome. Good night."

They closed the car doors, walked up the stairs towards the front door, and there she stood looking down at them. Susan and Ian stopped. Susan gushed with excitement and said, "Madam, welcome home. We had a wonderful dinner in town with Hans. It was nice. It is great to see you, what a wonderful surprise."

"Indeed," madam said looking slightly down her nose at them. "The funeral will be day after tomorrow. We'll talk about the program of events in the morning. I'm tired and will retire for the night. Ian, we'll return to Amsterdam in the morning after breakfast. Good night," she said and they responded in harmony, "Good night, madam."

The older woman turned and walked into the house. The other two stood still on the steps for several minutes until they knew the madam had retired to her suite for the night.

As they waited, Hans came up behind them. He hadn't seen the events a minute or so before, but he could tell in an instant.

"Oh, she must be back," said Hans, and he went on, "I must bid you good night and see to the needs of the madam. See you in the morning." The comfortable and informal Hans, they'd seen just moments before, was replaced with a stiff and proper gentleman. He slightly bowed and clicked his heels, bid them adieu, turned, and quickly left.

Ian and Susan looked at each other wondering, *what had just happened?*

"Are you ready to call it a night, mom?" Ian asked.

"Yes, dear, I think I am," her face didn't look sincere as she stared at the spot Hans had just left. The two walked up the stairs and entered their rooms. There would be no music this evening. Hans quietly entered the madam's office and provided her the details of the evening. She listened and was pleased with the report.

"Things are coming along nicely, Hans, thank you."

She poured him a drink, "Hans, sit with me for a few minutes and enjoy a drink." They sat across from each other and without a word sipped their Scotch and thought about the possibilities.

Chapter Sixteen
Coming in from the Cold

The next morning Ian prepared to escort his grandmother back to Amsterdam. He was dressed in a dark blue sport coat and the family tie. His gray flannel slacks were perfectly tailored and fit well. Susan was dressed more casually, anticipating a leisurely day with Hans doing, well, anything would be fine. Her mind was filled with endless possibilities.

The two of them entered the breakfast room and the madam was already seated sipping her coffee and reading the paper. She looked up at the two and nodded her head in approval at the way Ian had dressed and presented himself. Susan looked nice too, but she was not the matriarch's focus for the time being. Margareta thought, *Hans will keep you busy and out of the way, Susan.*

She smiled at Ian and said, "Ian, you look very nice, come and kiss your grandmother," she reached out for him as he approached and kissed her on the cheek.

She turned and looked at Susan, "Dear, you will be fine. Hans will stay with you and provide you everything you need and take you anywhere you'd like to go. Ian and I will only be a phone call away." She sipped her coffee and continued, "You'll join us tomorrow for Johan's funeral and then Hans will return with you here while Ian and I tend to the business. We'll be back here in four or five days."

"You're a beautiful woman, Susan. I'm so proud you are part of this family." She smiled as Susan approached her and kissed the madam on the cheek and then took a seat herself.

The madam and Ian took the limousine because the helicopter hadn't been replaced and were understandably skittish about flying so soon after the accident. Madam looked forward to the two hour drive back to the city with her grandson and she wanted it that way.

Satisfied all was prepared, madam stood and looked down at Ian and Susan still seated at the table, "Junger, it's time for us to go. I'll meet you out front in a few minutes." Her clear blues eyes looked at her grandson, and she shifted her focus to Susan, "Dear, enjoy and make yourself at home." Just then, as if on cue, Hans came around the corner.

He entered and the attention in the room was diverted and Susan was glad. For some reason the madam had a way of making her feel like she was the center of attention when she spoke to her. In all of Susan's years, only one other person had captured her attention and made her feel like she was the center of the world when he spoke to her. That person was Ian's father and the son of this powerful yet kind woman. Madam looked at her with gentle eyes, steeled with an iron will.

Hans bowed to the madam and Susan then addressed Ian, "Good morning, junger. Off to Amsterdam this morning, have fun. I'll escort your mother to the city tomorrow and meet you for the ceremonies." Hans smiled and seemed more like the man they'd eaten pizza with the night before than the very proper and rigid gentleman he'd been most of the time. He was dressed casually and Susan's eyes brightened as she smiled at him.

He stood there relaxed in tailored clothes and the light behind him outlined his frame. His hair was neatly groomed, but slightly mussed, giving him an athletic and active look that he pulled off naturally.

Hans held the chair for Susan as she stood from the breakfast table.

The madam was on the move to her office to collect the equipment and personal effects she'd take to the city.

Ian ran to his room to brush his teeth and grab his new cell phone. He was back in the foyer waiting for his grandmother before she came down the hall from her office. Hans and Susan walked slowly over to Ian.

It was a big day for all of them. Ian was off on a new adventure, like a kid leaving for school the first time. Madam was headed back to the city to bury her brother and start mentoring her grandson in earnest.

Hans was standing next to a beautiful woman he knew so much about and he'd only one task, keep her company and content.

Susan looked at her son with excitement and concern, as any mother would, when her child prepared to leave home to start an adventure of untold duration and danger. At the same time, she was irrevocably drawn to the handsome gentleman standing next to her.

Margareta walked to the group gathered at the entrance. She was followed by an assistant carrying a briefcase and a small personal bag. Madam van der Waterlaan was professionally dressed in a dark business suit, silk blouse, and high-heeled shoes. In one arm she carried her purse, and in the other, a silk sweater. She nodded to the group, and without a word, walked to the front stairs leading down to the limousine and Raul.

Raul waited by the passenger door of the car. Margareta walked erect and proud towards the car without assistance. She addressed Raul with a kind greeting and gave him her hand as he assisted her into the car. Once she was in the car, Raul closed the door. She lowered the window and looked back at her home. It was such an important part of her life and the place she'd always drawn strength from. She ached when she left, and now that she was fading quickly, it was all so much more acute.

Tears came to her eyes and she quickly rolled up the window. She hid her sentimentality and just how fragile she'd become.

Ian kissed his mother goodbye and shook Hans' hand, ran down the steps to the car. As Ian approached the car, Raul said, "Good morning, Herr van der Waterlaan. It's my pleasure to drive you this morning." Ian acknowledged the driver with a bright smile and entered the car. Ian was becoming accustomed to the security officer in the front seat. In addition, he noticed, for the first time, there was a black sedan in front and another behind the limousine. He wrote it off to the fact he was with his grandmother and she was a very important person.

The motorcade moved away from the castle. Ian looked over his shoulder at his mother and waved in vain through the dark windows. The security gate opened and the cars rolled through onto the country roads and maneuvered towards the city.

Ian's grandmother turned to him. "Junger, I have something I want to give you." She reached into her purse and produced a small gift wrapped in paper of the family colors.

"Thank you, grandmother." Ian said as he held the gift in his hand.

"Well, shouldn't you open it?" she asked.

He looked down at the gift and opened it carefully. Inside was a highly polished wooden box.

"Well, continue," she insisted and Ian opened the box to reveal a magnificent fountain pen. It was the finest writing instrument he'd ever seen or could have imagined. He looked at it almost afraid, to pick it up in his hand.

Madam said, "Ian, this is a special pen. In my family, when a member of the family enters the business he or she is given a fountain pen as recognition of their initiation into the trust. This pen is especially important, as it was the pen I had purchased years ago for your father when we thought he was returning to assume his role as the heir to the dynasty. It has yours and your father's name inscribed into it.

This pen signifies a covenant of trust and you must protect the family and the families' assets from those who would do us harm."

Ian listened to this in an almost surreal state as if hypnotized, "Yes, grandmother, I understand." The elderly woman smiled, she had exacted the first commitment for Ian to embrace and protect the family. *Enough drama for now*, she thought and leaned over and kissed Ian on the forehead. Raul discreetly watched the whole thing transpire in the rearview mirror as he piloted the limousine towards the city.

For now, the matriarch sat next to her heir and thought about the things and places she would navigate him through as she mentored him to assume command of the dynasty. It gave her strength and comfort to know she would be turning over the family business to such a worthy person.

She looked over at Ian and thought, *God, he looks and acts just like my son.* She smiled as he stared at the fountain pen. *The poor boy has no idea what is going on or what I'll introduce him to, nor does he have any idea what it'll do to his soul.*

She quickly averted her eyes, lest he see what she was thinking and be frightened away. After a few minutes, she said, "There is the matter about your enrollment at the ship school and your assignment to the ship coming to Rotterdam."

"What would you like to do?" she asked in a kind and gentle voice. What Ian didn't know, Captain Adriaan van der Meer was already prepared to discreetly engage Captain Horne of the *American Spirit* and the academy to drop Ian for "family reasons."

"Grandmother, to be honest, since Hanna dumped me, I've really been rethinking going back to the academy. I think I'd like to leave school and start over here if it's alright with you. I don't think I could face my friends or Hanna back at school again."

The grandmother smiled, a knowing smile, and she reassured him he was welcome to stay and start afresh. Behind those kind eyes was a lethal mind gloating over her cunning maneuver which had neatly ended Ian's desire to return to sea or the academy.

With that door closed, she'd be able to concentrate turning him into the next generation of van der Waterlaans. Her mind clicked as the pieces moved on her mental chessboard. She smiled discreetly and thought, *Ian you've 'come out of the cold' on your own -- well, almost ...*

Madam made a note to call Adriaan and have him start the process for Ian to be quietly disenrolled. It would be the last official record of 'Ian Blooker.' He'd be, from this day forward, remade into 'Ian van der Waterlaan' in the image of her beloved son.

Raul piloted the limousine through Amsterdam, bracketed by two security sedans. The madam looked out the tinted window, lost in deep thought as she considered the next step in the game to secure the future of her heir.

Chapter Seventeen
The Mentoring Begins

It wasn't until Raul brought the car to a stop in front of the security gate that Margareta came back from some place deep in the recesses of her mind. With a jolt she was back and alert. She transitioned from a woman thousands of miles away in thought, glassy eyed and still, to a fierce competitor with piercing eyes which cut like knives.

The car came to another stop in front of the house entrance. This time, the staff wasn't lined up on the steps. Raul opened the madam's door and assisted her to her feet. The security guard stood outside the car.

Slowly Margareta made her way to the steps with noticeable trouble. Ian ran up beside her and gently reached to her with his arm. She took it and made it up the remaining steps. She looked and smiled.

She appreciated the help, but most of all, the discretion with which he'd offered it. She thought, *He really is a gentleman.* This further invigorated her to thrust forward on her last and most important mission. She'd mentor, groom, and prepare Ian for the throne.

At the top of the stairs, she turned to Ian, "I'd like you to meet me in my office in fifteen minutes. There are some people I'd like you to meet. Now go and occupy yourself until then, junger," and she turned around and made her way towards her office.

Ian did as he was told and killed fifteen minutes by walking around the house, admiring the artwork and furniture. He felt the pen in his breast pocket and it reassured him knowing he had an article belonging to his father.

To the second, fifteen minutes later, Ian knocked on the office door and waited to be invited into the room. A few seconds later, the door opened and a gentleman in a dark suit motioned Ian forward. There were four other men and three women seated around the room. His grandmother was behind her desk. The seven strangers were slightly overweight and reeked of business elitism. Each had a briefcase and a serious face. Ian stiffened and shot a pleading look to his grandmother.

Margareta assessed Ian's distress and stood, "Ian dear, please come and sit here near me." Ian did as he was told and moved quickly, but with a sense of confidence, to a location next to his grandmother. Margareta watched and thought, *He is really a natural.* She announced, "Ladies and gentlemen, I'm proud and most pleased to introduce my grandson, Ian van der Waterlaan. Yes, there is an heir Johan and I have carefully kept from the world so he'd have the opportunity to grow up without the pressure and expectations which now as an adult, he's ready to assume."

She looked each person in the eyes and continued, "I have carefully selected each of you for your loyalty, competence, business acumen, and discretion. You'll be led by Herr de Reuter here to my left." She motioned to the elderly gentlemen beside her. "Your purpose is to groom, mentor, and help Ian assume the reins of the dynasty. Of course, I'll remain the final authority as long as I'm able. My challenge to you, get Ian to the point where he can function in the public eye as the CEO in six months and to have the understanding and knowledge to assume control eighteen months later. Your absolute discretion is demanded. Tomorrow will be my brother, Johan's, funeral. Ian will be introduced as the heir and Johan's replacement, and later in the day, there'll be a press release to make the announcement. Soon after, there'll be a run on speculation and people digging for information about Ian. Mr. de Reuter has already developed Ian's portfolio."

At that moment, de Reuter handed each person a folder. Madam continued, "Read the portfolio, destroy it or protect it. Only the people in this room are privileged with this information. Understood?"

"Yes, madam" was the unified response.

"Now take a few minutes to read over the folder while I walk with Ian. We'll return in twenty minutes." She stood from behind her desk and they stood. She looked at Ian and motioned for him to follow her. As she walked, he was a step behind. When they were beyond the door and it was closed, she looked at Ian and her eyes softened. "Sweetheart, I owe you an explanation. Walk with me to the parlor." She walked to the bar and poured herself a Scotch on the rocks and asked Ian if he'd like something to drink.

"Grandmother, I think I'd like a Scotch but do I have to go back into that room with you today?"

"Yes, dear, and a short Scotch will be good for you." She poured him a short glass with lots of ice. "Ian close the door, dear, and come sit here with me." She motioned to the same seats they'd used the first night they were together in Amsterdam.

She looked at the ceiling as he found his seat. She took a deep breath and began, "It'll all make sense if you listen and hold your tongue around others. You're the last hope of this family to continue our bloodline and keep control of the dynasty. It's a heavy burden and I regret you're saddled with it, but you are, and you have the lineage and the strength to succeed."

Ian paled and shifted in his seat.

"You're no longer a 'Blooker' and will not use that name again. You're a 'van der Waterlaan,' de Reuter has made all the necessary changes to your paperwork. Your history has been slightly modified to meet the expectations of the world audience for a van der Waterlaan. Part of your mentoring will be for you to become comfortable with the past we've manufactured for you. Study and learn it and never slip. For this, there is no going back."

"There are important reasons for this and many other things you'll be expected to do and become. You must trust me on this. You can only talk to me or de Reuter, no one else, not even your mother until she is read-in."

"Tomorrow will be your coming out. You'll be the center of attention in the business world and for many statesmen. It's most imperative you learn your lessons quickly and accurately for we can only keep you away from the press so long before they'll form their own opinion." She took a long pull from her glass. "As for the team in the other room, they are loyal and highly competent people I trust. You'll listen to their advice for the daily running of the company. Strategic decisions, I'll continue to make. But I'll discuss these with you so, one day, you'll be able to run the company. These people will have access to you via de Reuter. He will manage you in all regards until I'm comfortable you can fully assume control."

"Make no mistake, my son, your life has changed from this moment forward and there is no going back. Learn the new rules, understand the expectations, and remain vigilant of the dangers. They're real and lethal."

She threw back the remaining Scotch in her glass. Ian hadn't taken a sip as he listened to what some would consider a life sentence behind bars.

She sat there for a moment and watched Ian. She let it all sink in for another moment and she struggled to her feet, "Shall we rejoin them? We've a lot to talk about and, my dear, you have much to learn." She gently touched his hand with her frail fingers and her eyes softened as she whispered, "I'm sorry this is thrust upon you so abruptly. This has always been your destiny. I'll be here to guide and protect you as long as God is willing. I love you, my son."

"Thank you, grandmother." Ian thought, *this is the second time today she called me 'son' ... is it a careless mistake or something else?* For now he dropped the question and squared his shoulders and smiled at his grandmother.

In a strong and steady voice, he said, "Shall we?" He held out his arm and she took it as they proceeded back to the office.

In the twenty minutes, de Reuter had taken charge and had each member of the team sign a non-disclosure agreement. He had laid out the desired outcome and the madam's expectations. For their effort, she'd promised a two million euro bonus placed in an off-shore account for each. *Would it be enough?* She wondered.

Always careful, she had assigned a person to discreetly monitor and follow each member of the team. They reported back to her personally. These men were professionals and prepared to terminate their mark with extreme prejudice as required. An elite group of killers, they had a long history of clandestine work for the van der Waterlaan dynasty.

The meeting went well into the early evening. At 8pm madam stood up from behind her desk and said, "Enough for one night."

The men and woman closed their briefcases, shook hands, and made their way to their waiting cars. Ian excused himself and went directly to bed. Madam returned to the parlor, poured a tall Scotch and walked over to Monika her trusted piano and friend. Together they poured out nocturnes by Chopin. The music was light and full of life and optimism, reflecting the musicians' confidence coming out of the very productive meeting. *Everything is in place,* she thought as she played into the night.

As Margareta gently massaged the piano keyboard and pedals she thought, *Tomorrow, I'll bury my brother and then unveil to the world the van der Waterlaan heir.* She cried as she thought about her son.

Ian slept exhausted as everything she'd said rolled around in his brain, but the last sentence pounded like a migraine. *Make no mistake my son, your life has changed from this moment forward and there is no going back. Learn the new rules, understand the expectations, and remain vigilant of the dangers. They're real and lethal.*

Chapter Eighteen
The King is Dead -- Long Live the King

The next morning, the news media started long before sunrise with the announcement Johan van Winkle, the CEO of van der Waterlaan Transportation and Holding Corporation was being put to rest following an accident that tragically took his life. In the byline, there was acknowledgement that three other people had perished in the accident, but Johan was the focus of the media.

Madam was up early and hadn't bothered to dress. She sat in the breakfast room in her silk robe and slippers. She'd relax for a few hours and then prepare for the funeral, burial, and the bombshell she'd detonate at the appropriate time later in the afternoon.

She sat in the morning sun as it came through the windows and felt good this day. Today would put her one step closer to her goal. *The coffee was especially good this morning*, she thought, and she had a second and third cup.

She ordered a large breakfast of eggs and cheese and mindlessly ran her eyes over the morning paper. She was thousands of miles away from her body and the room she was seated in.

She was feeling comfortable and at peace with herself and looked up at the heavens and spoke privately to her God. She said softly, "Just a few more months and I'll be ready for you to take me. Please look after my dear

Hans Christen, Ian, and my family. Please ask Johan to forgive this ending, I miss him very much." Her private prayer over, she resumed sipping the coffee in front of her.

The butler came into the room and discreetly informed her Hans and Susan had left the castle and would arrive by nine o'clock that morning. She smiled and thought about the news. She had spent as much time considering a plan to keep Susan here and happy, to avoid any reluctance by Ian to stay, as she had planned how to maneuver him into position.

She could see there was an attraction between Hans and Susan, and as long as Hans kept his perspective and developed the relationship to her exact plan, it would be fine. There was no reason for her to worry about Hans, he was a determined and absolutely loyal solider. But he had never been asked to develop a relationship that at some point could cloud his judgment and possibly his loyalty. She'd have to watch closely. *God, I'd hate to lose Hans.*

Ian slept as long as he needed. He really didn't completely understand the implication or impact the day would have on him and the world. He woke and made his way down to his grandmother where she'd sat for nearly two hours reflecting. Ian came around the corner and his grandmother looked up and smiled.

She smiled at the next king of the business world and the beauty of it. He was innocent, pure, un-jaded, and unaware of the size and scope of his future.

Her face lit up as she saw him enter the room, "Good morning, my dear, did you sleep well? Your mother and Hans are enroute and should be here in another hour and a half."

"Are you ready for breakfast? We'll have a busy day and you'll need to eat." A maid entered the room with a glass of orange juice and toast. "Goede Morgan, Mein Herr van der Waterlaan"

Madam's eyes flashed at the maid and she said, "You will speak English when you're around my grandson and his mother, unless I say otherwise."

"Yes my lady," the maid bowed her head and ran out of the room.

Ian looked at his grandmother and in a respectful voice said, "Grandmother, with all respect, you were a little hard on the young lady. I'm in Holland, and I should learn to speak the language, shouldn't I?"

In a sharp voice she said, "Ian, I set standards and I expect them to be attained and maintained. She knew better." Her eyes still burned with intensity and then they gradually softened as she continued, "You'll learn, my son, if you're soft or non-committal with your staff or in business you'll be taken advantage of. Now let's talk about today."

She began to tell Ian about the events of the day, starting with the pre-funeral reception and so on. "You'll always be with either me or de Reuter at all times, Ian. We'll ensure you are introduced and the conversations are kept direct and to the point and any questions we don't want answered are avoided. This is very important because as soon as the world knows you exist, you'll become a target of opportunity for the media, business, and those who would try and exploit your youth and innocence. Hans will protect and escort your mother."

"Security is now a permanent part of your life. You'll always have a minimum of two security men detailed to you. Don't worry, you'll get used to it. Now we'll need to be ready to leave in about an hour, so please get ready. Herbert will lay out your clothes for the day. I love you, dear. Now eat your breakfast."

The recently chastised maid timidly brought Ian a plate of eggs, bacon and two pancakes. The maid set the plate down and bowed to the madam and quickly left the room without a word.

Ian ate his breakfast and excused himself to prepare for the day. Madam finished her coffee and then, with Herbert's help, she stood and made her way to her chambers where she prepared for the biggest day of her life.

***

Hans and Susan chose to travel discreetly in the Porsche without security. At this point no one knew who Susan was and Hans was just an employee. They got up early and after coffee and a piece of cheese and toast, they walked to the garage where Hans' pride and joy was waiting under a cover. He deactivated the car alarm and removed the cover with the flare of a bullfighter waving a red cloth before the angry bull.

The bright orange color filled her eyes and her imagination ran wild. *This handsome man, this beautiful car and I am living in Europe in a unique world where money is no object,* she swooned a little, then looked over at Hans. She could see his pride in the car and she complimented him on the beauty he'd just uncovered. He smiled. The ritual of romance and courting had moved to the next step for both of them.

Hans opened the door for Susan and she climbed into the road machine. Hans came around to the driver's side, opened the door, reached in, and pushed a button. The boot opened and he placed the cover inside and closed the lid. He climbed in next to Susan, reached for his gloves and glasses and fired up the engine. The car sprang to life and the engine purred with pure power and enthusiasm for the trip.

Hans looked over at Susan, reached across her lap with his arm and gently brushed her torso. He grabbed the seat belt and pulled it across her colored dress and securely locked it in place, "There now, you'll be safe," he said as he smiled. He looked forward as he thought, *Susan; you're the first woman to ever sit in this Porsche. Even this late in my life there are still firsts.*

Then his mind clicked back into business and he considered, *there are still things Susan has no idea abou. One was the nine millimeter Sig Sauer pistol secured under my seat, and the stiletto under the dash of this otherwise regular looking Porsche sports car. Oh, and I'm falling in love with you, Susan.*

He put the car in gear, started out of the garage, and headed to the security gate on the perimeter. The gate was opened and Hans and Susan hardly slowed down as they gathered speed on the country road. It was barely daylight and the road was in shadows from the forest.

The road was nearly desserted and Hans took the opportunity to put his car through the paces. Normally, Susan didn't like to go fast in a car and in any other situation she would have been nervous and uncomfortable.

With Hans at the wheel, she felt a sense of calm and excitement as the car powered through turn after turn. She enjoyed her time with him. *It's almost too good to be true*, she thought. Then Maria flashed across her mind and

126

Susan felt guilty being so comfortable with the man at her side.

Hans glanced at her and his eyebrows furrowed. "Are you alright, Susan?"

"Yes." she said, but her voice was as unconvincing as her body language. Susan sat there looking out the window wrestling with her feelings for Hans and her commitment to Maria. It was time for her and Ian to go home before she let herself do something with Hans she'd regret. She sat in the speeding orange sports car and tried to close the chapter, yet unwritten, or the romance that could never be between her and Hans.

Her mind tried to do the right thing, but her heart wouldn't let go. Hans was already in.

They stopped for a coffee and stoopwafels before getting onto the major road into Amsterdam. Hans called ahead to tell the staff they were on time and would arrive in thirty minutes. Hans held the door open for Susan who brushed against him and gently touched his hand. Their eyes connected for a long moment and without a word she knew the feeling was mutual. She sat in the car and Hans came around, climbed in, let out a long breath, and said, "Susan, forgive me, I must tell you I'm attracted to you and I know I really shouldn't be, but I can't help it. Please forgive me."

Susan took his hand into hers, "Hans, I feel the same way, but I have no right to, I am spoken for. Forgive me." They smiled and tears came to their eyes. Weaker people would have embraced and kissed passionately but their shared feelings were enough for now. Hans fired up his car and with the chirp of the tires he was speeding down the road to Amsterdam and the day ahead.

They rolled up to the security gate at the Amsterdam mansion and were quickly cleared and through the gate. Hans brought the car around to the front of the house and assisted Susan from the Porsche. "I'll park the car. Please go inside and you may want to start getting ready for a long day. I'll be there in a moment, Susan. I'll be your escort all day. Your son will be busy and the center of attention. Bye for now, and, thank you."

He smiled and winked at Susan. She smiled back with a broad smile from the heart. He drove around to the back and she climbed the stairs to her room. She was still torn between her heart and her conscience and resolved to reconcile it, but not today. *There was too much to do for now,* she thought to herself.

Susan made her way down the hall to her room when madam called her from behind. "Susan, welcome home, dear. I hope you and Hans had a good time together. He is a wonderful man and if I were to have had another son I'd have wanted him to be Hans. Don't you agree?"

"Yes, madam, he is a gentleman and very kind."

"Yes, dear and between us ladies, he's not hard to look at either? If you know what I mean." The madam said with a haughty smile.

"Yes, madam, he is very handsome."

"Dear, please get ready now. Herbert has placed a dress on your bed for you to wear. Hans will escort you and provide all the support and assistance you need. Ian will be with me most of the day. We must bury my brother in proper fashion and then prepare for the future."

"Ian and I will be leaving separately in a few minutes and you and Hans will join us at the church, dear."

"Yes madam," Susan said in a near trance as she kept playing back madam's words, *Yes, dear and between us ladies ... He's not hard to look at either! If you know, what I mean?*

Susan made her way to her room and dropped the clothes she was wearing on the floor and made her way to the bathroom. She needed to take a hot bath and think things over for a few minutes. She turned on the water and, in a moment, was lying in a hot bath.

In the room down the hall Ian was dressed in the suit Herbert had laid out for him. It fit, like all of his clothes, perfectly. He looked at himself in the mirror and thought," *Wow, I look good! I wish Hanna could see me now. Why did she break-off our relationship?"*

He brushed her memory away and walked out of his room with purpose and confidence. The report of his heels striking the marble floor gave notice he was on the move.

Madam was near the front door seated in a comfortable chair. She was wearing a beautiful, but somber, black gown with matching headdress. She had black gloves in one hand and her black purse in the other. Raul was outside waiting -- he'd remained overnight in Amsterdam in order to drive her on this difficult day and she was glad. Raul had always been her favorite driver.

Ian walked up to his grandmother and she gave him an approving smile. He smiled back and said like a true American, "Let's get it done, grandmother."

She smiled and with some effort rose from her seat and they walked arm in arm to the waiting limousine. Raul stood by the open door. He gently held her hand and eased her down into the seat as she slid her legs over the floor

129

board and her feet fell into the plush carpet within. She and Raul shared a second together as they discreetly looked at one another.

On the other side of the car, the security man held the door for Ian. With youth, flexibility, and strength Ian climbed into the car without slowing down. Because of the exposure and visibility, today there would be two security sedans and four police cars escorting the limousine to various locations. The motorcade moved out of the security gate and was picked up by the waiting police cars.

They moved to the Hans Klipter Funeral Home where a small pre-funeral reception and viewing of the closed casket was held. Five minutes later, the motorcade arrived and Margareta and Ian climbed out of the limousine. Hundreds of cameras were clicking away as the two were escorted up the stairs into the viewing room.

It was dark and quiet. They were the only ones in the room as madam made her way to the closed casket. She knelt beside it with Ian standing slightly behind her, his hands crossed before him.

She closed her eyes, put her hands together, and silently prayed for five minutes for forgiveness and absolution.

She prayed to her God and then she spoke silently to her brother, *Johan, forgive me for what I've done to you and the others in the helicopter. For too many reasons, you'd become an unmovable obstacle. I'd always hoped you would pass on naturally before me, but my time is short and I could no longer wait. Forgive me, brother, I'll see you in heaven soon.*

She opened her eyes, recomposed herself, and Ian stepped forward and assisted her to her feet. The two made their way back to the car out front of the home. By the time the limousine moved away from the funeral home, the casket was loaded into the hearse and headed to the Basilica of Saint Nicholas in the center of the oldest part of the city. The madam and Ian traveled slowly with police escort to the front of the cathedral while the casket was received in the side entrance and prepared for the precession.

The church was full to capacity and people poured out well into the streets as on-lookers waited for a glimpse of the rich and powerful people attending.

Madam van der Waterlaan and her grandson arrived and there was a hush over the crowd as they watched with fascination one of the most powerful women alive and an unknown young man who moved with purpose under heavy security escort up the stairs and into the church.

Cameras were rolling and reporters talking into their microphones as they speculated and filled the air with their own view of what they saw unfolding before them.

Madam was silent and somber. Ian kept his eyes down and walked behind his grandmother. They were escorted to the front of the church to reserved seats. Already seated were Hans and Susan.

Moments after the madam was seated, the service began. It was a high mass and there were eulogies from four prominent persons. Two were senior and powerful executives of international concerns and two were noble and landed members of the Dutch aristocracy. Each spoke in glowing terms of Johan and the caliber of a man he was. Honest, humble, trustworthy, companion and friend. *If the eulogies were only half true, he was an amazing human being and would be freely accepted by Saint Peter at the gates of heaven*, Ian thought.

Ian looked over to his mother and they shared a comforting look, then he looked over at the madam where she sat as if she were made of stone. Not seeing nor hearing.

The cardinal finished the mass and the casket was carried by the pallbearers from the church. The family and close friends were ushered out immediately behind and navigated into waiting cars by security and the funeral directors. The cars moved in mass to the Buitenveldert Cemetery in the northwestern part of the old city.

The cardinal made a few comments and madam's brother was laid to rest deep into the ancient soil of the old cemetery. The cardinal consoled Madam van der Waterlaan on her loss and she cried on his shoulder for a moment.

Though it was a private ceremony, the media had encroached as close as the security and police allowed. The growing focus of the media was the young man who was always at the side of Madam van der Waterlaan. Rumors were beginning to circulate and the media was beginning to make up their own news about the handsome stranger.

The family had reserved the Hilton Amsterdam banquet hall for the post funeral reception and meal. There would be over five hundred guests attending. As with everything van der Waterlaan, the madam had out done herself and the event was extravagant. The event was kept private from noon to 5pm.

The guests made their way to Madam van der Waterlaan to offer condolences and sorrow and they were introduced to Ian van der Waterlaan. Security had discreetly blocked all exits and installed a local jammer to disable everyone's personal cell phones and PDA(s). These were discreet people and they would not have run to the media, but she wouldn't take any chances.

At five in the afternoon there was a press conference arranged in the room next door. At the appropriate time the madam cleared her voice and walked with Ian to the podium and stood before her guests and friends.

"My dear friends, I've scheduled a press conference in the room next door. Anyone who'd like to attend is most welcome. You're welcome to stay here and enjoy the food and company as long as you'd like. Ian, my grandson, and I will excuse ourselves for a few minutes while we address the press. God bless each of you and thank you." The audience applauded and madam and Ian left the stage to walk to the room next door to address hundreds of curious and aggressive reporters looking for a scoop to shock the business world.

Security opened the door and the two walked through with a handful of curious guests following behind. Hans looked at Susan and said, "We should go and hear this." She smiled, he took her hand for the first time and they walked into the press conference.

Madam van der Waterlaan walked to the stage and looked at the audience of hungry reporters, steadied herself, and began, "Today we buried Johan van Winkle. He was my brother, my friend, and my family. You knew him as the CEO of van der Waterlaan Transportation and Holding Corporation and one of the most powerful and clever businessmen the world has ever known. I lost my brother and the world lost an important man of business and a driver of world economies."

"Many of you are wondering who will replace Johan at the helm of the van der Waterlaan dynasty and that, my friends, is the reason for this conference. To my left, is my only grandson, Ian van der Waterlaan." The room erupted with noise as the audience reacted to the news.

She continued, "Ian was raised quietly in the United States and is now ready to assume his rightful place at the head of the organization. There'll be more information over the next few weeks about the transition, however, for the meantime the organization remains well-lead, profitable and leaning forward. None of you should worry about the van der Waterlaan dynasty. It will continue to thrive."

"Thank you no questions at this time, thank you." The audience began to explode with questions directed at her and Ian. She looked at Ian and they walked silently off the stage and returned to the private party next door. Hans turned to Susan who stood still with her mouth open.

"Susan, hold my hand and let's get out of here before someone recognizes us." They moved quickly back into the private party where it was more calm.

There was a glass of champagne waiting for the madam and one for Ian. She toasted him privately. "The king is dead ... long live the king," and she began to mingle freely with her friends. Ian's protector, de Reuter, took the cue and rolled in next to Ian, remaining there the rest of the night.

Hans turned to Susan who was still in shock. "What do you think, Susan?" he said.

"Did you know this was going to happen?" Her eyes reddened with anger. "How long have you known ... you bastard?" She spat.

He said with his eyes downcast, "Yes, I knew and for a while."

She growled like a cornered tiger and slapped him across his face. With his training, he could have easily avoided the blow and killed her in seconds but he let her hand strike his face and held his temper. She turned to walk away and her eyes filled with tears. Hans was right behind her and grabbed her by the arm. She turned with fiery eyes and said, "Don't touch me."

"Susan, I need you to come with me and let me explain, in private." He looked sincere and hurt. She wanted to trust him.

She looked at him again and quietly shook her head and followed him as they slipped out of the Hilton and moved in the damp air through the streets of Amsterdam. The streets were quiet and it helped to calm them down. He led her to a cozy bar called Pieters' near the Dam Square a block from the Prizengracht. They found a private table in the corner and the waiter brought over two jonge jenever.

Han's threw his drink back and the waiter brought another. It was there he told Susan more than he'd been authorized to share. Uncharacteristically he poured his heart out to her and tears welled-up as his steel eyes softened. He was more vulnerable than he'd ever remembered before.

He started, "Susan let me explain. I'll tell you the whole story, but with it, I put my life in your hands. If any of this gets back to Madam van der Waterlaan, I'll be finished and I am afraid so will you. Can I trust you?" He held his hands out across the table and she put her warm hands into his.

"Yes, Hans, I guess we're in this together." He told her most of the truth. He didn't mention the fact he'd been in her home and touched her things and watched her, Maria, and Ian. Nor did he mention he'd driven Hanna away from Ian to rid him of the distraction. Oh, and there was the issue of Maria and John, he wanted to tell for selfish reasons, but didn't.

They sat in the corner and the waiter kept bringing the jonge jenever and Hans kept talking. Susan carefully watched his eyes to see if he was telling the truth and soon her anger subsided.

It was two in the morning when Hans and Susan returned to the home. Susan went straight to her room and the jenever put her to sleep. Hans parked his Porsche and entered the house. The madam waited in the parlor for their return. Hans entered the room, poured himself a tall drink, sat next to his employer, and looked into the fire. He told her of Susan's flare-up and most of what he had told her to get her back in the camp. It was the first time in his life he hadn't been completely honest with his employer. They spoke until the early hours of the morning and planned their next step.

Chapter Nineteen
Susan Betrayed

The next morning Ian and the madam were gone early to the offices in Rotterdam. It became a regular routine and Susan was finding herself feeling more and more isolated. She had forgiven Hans, but she had cooled down about him after the press conference.

Hans had to leave on a short business trip and was gone for two days. Other than that, he was there, and dedicated to keep her company and take her anywhere she wanted. Susan maintained a distant demeanor around him and she could see the hurt in his eyes.

It was during the second week Susan was walking in the garden with Hans. "It's time for me to go home. I have Maria, my family, and my job there. Ian is busy in his new world and I feel like a bird in a cage. I want to go home, please."

Hans' face fell and he let out a long sigh. "Susan you can have anything you want. I'll have the plane prepared to leave in the morning. I'll escort you and ensure you settle in. We'll need to tell madam and Ian of your plans this evening and make final preparations."

Susan felt more excited than she had in weeks and realized she'd been in Holland for nearly a month. With a light heart and a smile from ear to ear, she thought of

Maria and had an impulse to talk with her and tell her she was coming home.

In the last month, they'd spoken only four times and in every case it was Maria calling Holland after a half dozen messages from Susan. There was always an excuse about work or something which Susan accepted without question.

Susan went to her room for privacy and dialed the number to the house in Bristol. Like every other time, the phone rang until it was picked up by the answering machine.

"Maria, its Susan, sorry I missed you. I'll be coming home tomorrow. I'll get a ride from the airport. I miss you and can't wait to see you and hold you. I have so much to tell you, love you." she hung up the phone. *Where is Maria?* Susan wondered.

In the parlor, before their evening meal, Susan told madam and Ian she wanted to leave in the morning. Hans was there and had become a visible part of the private family unit since the press conference.

Madam van der Waterlaan sipped her Scotch, sitting close to the fire. It was late fall and the weather was getting colder and the days shorter.

Ian said, "Mom, I don't want you to leave, but I know I haven't been around much. It can't be much fun for you here alone." Ian shifted in his chair. "I hate to admit it, but I know you'll be happier back in New England with Maria."

"Thank you for understanding, Ian. My life is in Bristol and although this has been an amazing trip, it's time for me to go home."

Hans had already told Margareta to anticipate this several days before and discreetly called her earlier to prepare her for the news. He called the hanger to prep the plane and muster the crew for a trip to New England with a one night lay-over and the return the following morning.

Madam moved her eyes away from the fire; her face warmed, and looked at Susan as she stood there like a school girl asking permission to go to the dance. Madam's eyes were warm, soft, and caring.

She took her time and then in a sincere voice said, "Dear, I understand. You're always welcome to come back here anytime you want and stay as long as you want. Bring your family and they are most welcome too, especially, your daughter Sarah and her children, and, of course, your dear parents."

Madam clasped her hands together and continued, "Susan, the jet will be ready for you and will be at your disposal. I'd like Hans to escort you to ensure you get home and settled before he returns. Dear, the house won't be the same without the love and kindness you brought to us. Please come back often, I love you, Susan. I know why my Ian loved you so. You're all that is good and you have none of the ugliness which festers in most of the human species. Finally, thank you for supporting Ian as he fulfills his destiny at no small sacrifice to you, my dear. Remember you're a van der Waterlaan. You're a member of this dynasty and we'll protect you and your family."

Madam reached out to Susan. "Now come here and let me give you a kiss." Susan approached the old woman and leaned over and the madam lifted slightly out of her chair and kissed Susan on her cheek very close to her lips and then fell back into her seat.

The remaining minutes before the meal were spent in comfortable chatter about work and the things Ian had seen and been involved in. Susan moved over to the couch next to Hans and sat next to him. She gently put her free hand into his. It was her first public display of affection since they'd met a month ago on her front porch.

He smiled and gripped her hand. Madam and Ian had their backs to the two seated on the couch and the moment was only theirs. They sipped their drinks and took turns looking at each other and then towards the madam as she faced the fire and soaked up the heat from the roaring flames.

The butler entered the room and cleared his throat to announce his presence. It brought the four dreamers back to reality. He spoke in a dry and low voice, "Madam, dinner is ready to serve when you wish, my lady."

She looked over her shoulder at Herbert and responded, "Herbert we'll be there in a few minutes. Let me finish my drink."

"Very well, madam." He clicked his heels and spun around. Madam took another sip and then a long pull from her Scotch glass until the rocks on the bottom protested the absence of liquid. She set her glass down on the table and looked at her grandson. "Ian dear, help an old lady to her feet, please."

He responded instantly and gently helped her up. Hans and Susan let free their grasp of each other's hand before they were discovered and the four moved towards the dining room. It had become routine to expect and enjoy a full seven course meal. One serving better than the other … The four ate in relative silence. Following the dinner, Ian excused himself and retired to his room. Madam van der Waterlaan looked at Hans and Susan and invited them back to the parlor. The three of them walked together and were met by the young attendant behind the bar. She had a glass of Scotch ready for her employer and waited to fill the other orders.

"Madam, may I have a glass of your Scotch?" Susan asked

"Of course, dear, this is your home. It's all yours."

"I'd like a brandy." Hans said and in an instant they had their drinks in hand.

Madam raised her glass, "My dear, to family." She looked into Susan eyes and then continued, "Susan, soon it'll be you that'll be the center and soul of this clan, and it'll be wholly better for it. For you'll bring goodness, kindness, charity, and forgiveness to the family and help us return to the way we were before things became jaded by war, personal loss, and corruption. Unlike the severely pruned thing it has become, your love will nurture it and allow ... and allow it to become healthy and grow again. Ian is the future, but you'll ensure our long-term survival."

Susan gasped. She began to see she was part of the grand plan and had her purpose alongside her son. She smiled at the old lady and felt like the weight of the world had just been placed on her shoulders.

"Now, please sit and I'll play for you two," she made her way to, Monika, her piano. This would be the first time in a long time she'd allow someone to watch her play.

She addressed her piano as she always did with love and gently lifted the keyboard cover. Hans had assisted Susan into a comfortable chair by the fireplace where she would be warm and comfortable. He took another seat near her and settled in.

Madam van der Waterlaan chose her first piece carefully and when she connected with her piano keyboard, Beethoven's Fur Elise poured out of the instrument like a woman's voice full of joy and happiness, love, and gentleness. The music and the passion of love as Beethoven had felt was revealed to Susan. Then Margareta moved her focus to Franz Liszt and his Hungarian Rhapsodies and the passion filled the room in the form of music which took on the three dimensionality only possible through the hands of the most gifted musicians playing from the depths of their souls.

The attendant refilled their glasses and the music continued uninterrupted into the night. The pieces of the puzzle were coming together for Susan. The music embraced her like angels surrounding her with their soft wings. It was late before they retired to their rooms.

The evening had given Susan so much. She had forgiven Hans and her feelings for him had returned. She felt she'd connected at a spiritual level with Margareta and she was going home with the invitation to return anytime. Lastly, she knew there was a place for her in the van der Waterlaan dynasty. She slept well.

Hans tossed and turned in bed. He threw off the blankets and sat up with his head in his hands. "Damn it," he muttered. "I'm in love with a woman I can never have. Has the madam put me in this position to torture me?" He ran his fingers through his hair and sighed. Finally, he fell back into a restless sleep.

The old lady smiled to herself as she lay in bed waiting for slumber to come. She was close.

***

The next morning the four gathered around the breakfast table and enjoyed their last few minutes together. Susan and Hans readied to go to the airport and Ian and Margareta prepared for a busy agenda in the office. There was this merger with an Italian ship owner and shipyard operator named Nappolini.

They said their goodbyes and left in separate limousines.

Hans and Susan arrived at the private hanger where the same jet was waiting that had carried her and her son from America. The pilot, Fritz, and his new co-pilot, Bill, greeted them and helped them get settled into the aircraft. Hans received confirmation they'd been cleared by Dutch Customs and Immigration and the plane was cleared to enter the preflight pattern. Ingrid was there as their flight attendant. It was clear she was still grieving over her lost lover, Captain Hans Dieter, who had died only two weeks ago. She had the champagne and oysters ready for the couple as they sat and prepared for the long flight to New England.

In the front cabin there were only two additional passengers. They quietly sat in their seats. Dressed in dark suits with company ties and a strategic bulge in their jackets under their left arm, dark glasses resting on their noses, it was clear they were the security detail. The pilot fired up the engines and the bird came to life. Ingrid closed the door and the pilot let the engines idle for several minutes while he ensured the gauges confirmed all was correct. In the meantime, he and the co-pilot checked and rechecked everything. Fritz had lost his friend and longtime flying partner a few weeks ago and now he was especially cautious.

The jet was cleared by the traffic controller to move. Fritz released the brakes and the jet gathered speed as it moved down the runway to the holding area awaiting take off. On approach to the holding area, the jet was cleared for immediate takeoff. Fritz traveled through the holding area and pushed the throttles forward. The agile jet gathered speed quickly, rotated, and was in the air in seconds. Everything was working correctly and the plane was brought to altitude and settled onto the proper course for Rhode Island while everyone onboard did what they needed to be comfortable for the six hour flight.

Hans and Susan spoke for part of the trip. The rest of the time she napped and read quietly. She was trying to detach from the handsome man next to her, and yes, she had developed feelings for him. She prepared to re-engage with her longtime friend and lover who would be waiting for her in Bristol.

Susan struggled. It was especially hard as, the night before in the parlor listening to Margareta, she had found herself closer to Hans than ever.

They shared smiles and held each other's hands occasionally as they watched the time pass and Ingrid kept the wine and food coming.

Fritz called back to the cabin to report they would be descending and landing in a few minutes. Hans looked out the window and he could see the towns and cities below, *it must be around four o'clock, local time*, he thought.

A skilled pilot in his own right, Fritz aptly maneuvered the jet down and onto the runway with precision. His friend and mentor, Dieter, would have been proud.

Fritz maneuvered the grounded jet to the corporate terminal and received notice from the tower the guests had been cleared by Customs and Immigration and a limousine was waiting for them. Susan reached for her cell phone and tried to call Maria, and the phone just rang until the machine picked up. Susan hung up the phone. She called her parents and they picked up right away. "Hello." Her mother spoke into the phone.

"Hello, mom, I'm home. I'm at the airport and will be back in Bristol in an hour or so. I have tried to call Maria and I get no answer, is she okay?" Her mother stammered. "Let me give you to your father," and she handed the phone to Stanley.

"Um ... Susan, I think you better come here first before you go home."

"Why, what has happened to Maria? Is she okay?"

"Susan, your mother and I think you better come here first. When can we expect you?" he said in a deep and authoritative voice.

"Dad, Hans and I will be there in an hour at the most."

"Honey, who is Hans?" Stanley questioned.

"The gentlemen who picked us up in the limousine a month ago, you'll remember him."

"Oh yeah, the good looking guy. How is Ian?"

"Fine, dad, I have to go. See you in an hour." Susan hung up the phone and looked at Hans and said, "My parents insist we stop at their house first. They seem very upset about something."

Hans looked concerned and said, "Okay, we'll go there first."

The jet came to a stop and Ingrid had the door opened. Security was out on the tarmac and the limousine approached the now idle jet. Fritz came back to check on his passengers and assured Hans the plane would be fueled and ready for immediate departure by seven in the morning. Hans nodded.

Together, Susan and Hans moved to the waiting limousine and were parked in front of her parent's home thirty five minutes later. Susan didn't question how the driver knew exactly how to get there.

Susan and Hans got out of the car and he asked, "Would you like me to go with you or would you prefer I wait here?"

Without hesitation Susan said, "You're coming with me, Buster." She led him up the stairs to the front door. She knocked and then entered, "Mom, dad, Hans and I are here. Where are you?"

Her father's voice came from the living room, "In here, sweetheart." Susan and Hans moved through the small house and saw her mother had made tea and put out some cake on the coffee table. Susan ran to her mother and kissed her and then to her father and gave him a long hug and kissed him on the cheek.

Hans waited until Susan was done greeting her family and then stepped forward, bowed and clicked his heels. "Hans van der Molen, at your service." Stanley looked at him, reached out to shake his hand. Susan's mother just smiled at the handsome man her daughter had brought into the house.

146

Stanley spoke to Susan, "honey, what we have to tell you, you may want to keep private," as he looked over at Hans.

Susan responded, "No, Hans stays. Anything you want to tell me he can hear."

"As you wish ... "Stanley looked at his wife and said, "mother will you pour us some tea first?" Susan knew it was serious, her father only spoke of his wife in third person when it was really bad news, *mother?*

Stanley motioned to the couch and adjacent chairs for everyone to be seated. Susan's mother poured tea and cut a piece of cake for each person then joined her husband.

Stanley cleared his voice and said, "Well, where to begin?" He looked to his wife for moral support.

"Susan, we have known for nearly a month and most of the town did too. It seems Maria took up with John Gates on the day you and Ian left for Holland."

Susan gasped, "John Gates ... my boss?"

"Yes, dear, apparently he was very sick with cancer and some say that's why they entered into their sordid affair. Who really knows? The fact of the matter is two respectable and important people in this town took up, and I might add, not very discreetly. Someone even took videos of them having, well you know, in the hotel in Swansea and posted it on the Internet. The whole town knows."

Susan began to tremble.

Stanley's face was racked in pain as he said, "Gates destroyed his wife and his reputation and Maria was threatened with losing her practice, the pharmacy, and her license. Four days ago, Gates and Maria spent the night in your home and after a desperate night of, well you know what, they hung themselves in the master bedroom."

Susan was crying and Hans moved over to put his arm around her. She leaned into him and put her arms around him and continued to sob uncontrollably. Her parents looked at each other and waited for Susan to compose herself.

"The funerals were yesterday and kept discreet. The rug factory is closed and the workers are unemployed until a new owner is found."

"There's one final thing … They left a joint suicide note. They swore a pact to each other. They turned their back on God and swore their only love had been each other and all others in their lives were instruments of exploitation and nothing more." Stanley said with a confused look on his face, "I am not sure what that's supposed to mean. We're sorry to give you this news." He reached for his wife's hand and gently squeezed it.

Susan was no longer crying. She was angry Maria would have betrayed her and then killed herself and left such a mean-spirited note to crush her and John's wife. How could two people she loved and respected turn so bad?

They sat together for a few more minutes until Susan said, "I'm tired and need to go to the hotel. I'll be back in the morning when my head is clear." All four stood up and walked to the front door. Susan kissed her parents and thanked them for the news through her tear stained face. Hans shook Stanley's hand and kissed Ellen on the cheek.

Susan led the way back to the limousine and Hans followed quickly behind. They climbed into the limousine and Susan turned to Hans, "Take me to a hotel and make love to me!"

Hans nodded and the driver put the car in gear, he knew just where he was headed.

Chapter Twenty
The Morning After

The next morning, Susan woke in Hans' strong arms. The passionate evening they'd shared together was an explosion of lust, need, passion, and animal desire. The intensity of their union was a function of how long they had denied themselves.

The emotional news, although painful, released Susan, as if sprung from the cage gilded in morality and commitment, and she was free to love again.

In the morning light and after-glow of their physical and fulfilling lovemaking, they lay there. Hans had contacted the pilot and told him they needed to stay another day. He also reported the events to Margareta, assuring her he was confident Susan would return to Holland in a few days.

The sun poured into the hotel room and they embraced and made love again, ending in the synchronized explosions that left them dripping in sweat and physically depleted. What had started out as "revenge sex" had quickly become love with intensity few have known and many would kill for.

They got out of bed and prepared for the day. Breakfast was quick and without the ordeal Susan had become accustomed to in Holland.

The limousine driver held the door for this remarkable looking couple. They were in excellent clothing, groomed perfectly, and both movie star attractive. The locals took notice of the two as they climbed into the long black car holding hands and clearly in love with one another.

It was a short drive back to her parent's home. Stanley and Ellen were inside waiting for Susan and her gentleman friend. The four spoke for several hours and Hans seemed comfortable and relaxed in the presence of Susan's parents.

Around noon, Susan stood up and said, "I want to go to the house." Her mother and father tried to discourage it as the place was still the way Maria and John had left it and there were still obvious indications of the suicides.

She insisted and Hans followed quietly behind. He already knew what the room looked like for he had seen pictures the night of the suicides. Only he and Margareta had seen these photos and they were quickly destroyed. Another secret he hadn't divulged.

Susan opened the front door and walked through the house lost in memories, driven by a need to understand why Maria would have done this to herself. Maria's infidelity could have been forgiven and forgotten, but killing herself was a betrayal Susan couldn't get her head around. Yes, Susan could see how John would have been a fling, even a long-term romance, but nothing could justify killing herself.

"Why? Maria, why?" Susan kept saying as she walked from room to room. Hans and her parents followed behind her. Stanley and Ellen were holding hands, Ellen was notably shaken. Susan made her way through the kitchen, dirty dishes still in the sink. She instinctively began to wash them. The others watched as she went through the motions and then began to cry. Her mother jumped to her side, "Here, I'll finish," and took over in the sink.

Susan continued into the living room where she and Maria had spent so much time together and where Sarah and Ian had grown up. The room sang with memories and Susan absorbed everything through her tear filled eyes. Again, there were clear indications the lovers had used this room as it was in unusual disarray.

Susan made her way up the stairs to the bedrooms. She looked into Ian's room then Sarah's room and realized how much she missed her daughter. She opened the door to the bedroom she'd occupied for years. It was just the way she had left it. Lastly, she walked to the master bedroom door. Stanley cautioned, "Honey, don't go in there, please …"

Susan didn't listen, she pushed open the door, and there before them was where it all happened. The bed was a mess from the lover's passionate entanglements. The night stands were full of cigarette butts. Stanley said, "The police had removed the drug paraphernalia including a mirror, razor blade, cocaine, and weed." Across the overhead was a strong wooden beam connecting one end of the room to the other. Susan had often looked at the beam while she lay in bed with Maria. It was the beam Maria and John had affixed their suicide nooses to and kicked out the chairs they stood on.

According to the police, they had tied a shoe string around their wrists to ensure in death they were holding hands with one another. *Gruesome but romantic,* the local paper reported.

Susan stood there for a moment imagining how it happened and the distress they must have felt. "Why, Maria? Why?" Susan repeated as if she expected an answer from the grave.

After a long moment, Susan turned and walked out of the room. She moved down the stairs and out the front door with Hans a step behind.

They were alone for a moment while Stanley and Ellen were busy closing doors and taking their time coming down the stairs. Susan was trembling and her face was twisted in pain and anger. She looked deeply into Hans' eyes and said, "Burn the fucking place to the ground." She continued to stare into his eyes with such anger he was forced to look away.

It was the second time in two days Susan felt pure anger, no, hatred. The hatred became rage, and her rage had her feeling like she would lose control. As quickly as it had come upon her, it began to wane and soon she could feel herself regaining control. Her parents came out of the front door and rejoined them.

Susan looked at her parents, "Hans and I will be returning to Holland in the morning. I'll start a new life with Ian and try and bring Sarah there too. You're always welcome to come and stay as long as you'd like. I'll come back to visit you regularly, I promise."

Then she looked at her lover and said, "Hans, please take my parents back to the house and I'll walk over there and meet you. I need to be alone for a few minutes."

"As you wish, my lady." He said and bowed slightly from the waist and clicked his heels. Susan turned and walked away.

Hans escorted Stanley and Ellen to the car and after a short drive delivered them to their home. Stanley invited Hans in and they sat together on the porch sipping coffee and stared off into the distance, both lost in their own thoughts.

"I can't say I'm happy about Susan's decision to move to Europe," Stanley finally said. "It is just too far away. I don't know these people she'll be living with, and I barely know you."

Hans leaned toward Stanley. "Sir, rest assured, she'll be well-taken care of. I'll see to it myself."

Stanley raised an eyebrow. He appeared to be about to ask a question, then mumbled, "I suppose it's none of my business."

There was silence between them as their eyes drifted off in the distance. The men sat next to each other thousands of miles apart when Susan came around the corner and walked towards them. The men welcomed her and the rest of the day was filled with conversation and promises.

Susan and Hans left for Europe first thing the next morning.

Chapter Twenty-One
Sickness Drives the Timeline Forward

Susan and Hans returned to Holland. Raul was at the hanger waiting for their arrival and quickly had them on their way to the country where madam and Ian were waiting. Susan was exhausted and leaned against Hans' strong shoulder gently drifting off to sleep. Halfway through the drive, Susan's cell phone rang and she sleepily answered the phone. "Hello?"

"Susan, this is your father. The strangest thing happened a few hours ago. Your old home caught fire and it looks like it will burn to the ground. It's on all the news stations. They suspect a gas leak and a huge explosion literally removed the roof off the building. Thank God no one was hurt … I'm sorry to give you this bad news, honey."

"That's okay, dad, thanks. We're back in Holland and headed to the country home. I'm going back to sleep now. Good night, love you and mom," and she hung up the phone. Still half asleep she looked at Hans, "The house is burning to the ground."

"Imagine that!" Hans said and gave a devious smile.

"And of course, you had nothing to do with it, did you?" she said.

"No, I was on the plane with you, remember."

Another smile and she closed her eyes. The last few days had been hard on her. She was on an emotional rollercoaster and her body needed the downtime. She drifted off to sleep on her handsome lover's shoulder. They were back in Holland and she no longer had ties to America, Madam would be pleased.

Raul professionally maneuvered the car along the country roads with the bodyguard sitting quietly in the seat next to him. The roads were dark and wet from the rain a few hours before. Leaves were beginning to fall from the trees and a chill was in the air.

Susan snuggled in closer to the warmth Hans provided. She had noticed a change in the weather too and it had only been a few days.

The limousine pulled up to the compound security gate and was quickly through the check point. Another quarter mile and they'd be home. Hans gently nudged Susan.

"Honey, we'll be home in a moment or so. Wake up." She stirred and then stretched like a cat as she woke. Rubbing her eyes, she looked at Hans and said, "Hello, good looking. I guess we better back off on the display of affection for a while. I need to break it to Ian gently. Will the madam approve?"

"I'll discuss it with her in private, but I can't see why she wouldn't." he said.

"Okay," she said and stole a kiss just as the car pulled to a stop in front of the steps leading to the entrance. Raul opened the door for Hans and the bodyguard opened the door for Susan.

The house was exceptionally quiet as they ascended the stairs. When they entered the foyer and the butler approached quickly his face flustered and his voice trembled,

"Madam van der Waterlaan was rushed to the hospital in an ambulance an hour ago. Master Ian is with her. She was in the parlor and collapsed in front of the fire. She was unresponsive and we called the emergency rescue."

Hans instantly gave orders like a battlefield commander, "Herbert, please call Raul back. We'll leave at once for the hospital." Susan reached for Hans arm to steady herself and leaned into his shoulder for additional support.

They turned around and descended the stairs and waited for the black limousine to return. A moment later, the car came around the corner of the building. Raul was noticeably upset.

This time Hans grabbed the car door himself and opened it. Susan dove into the car and he followed. The car was moving at a high rate of speed as they drove through the open security gate.

Raul had them at the emergency entrance in fifteen minutes as they got ready to leave the car, Raul pleaded, "Please tell the madam I'm praying for her safety and health," he broke-out in tears. They nodded and bailed out of the back seat.

Susan and Hans entered the hospital and headed to the front desk. The nurse was talking with a van der Waterlaan security officer when they approached. He told her who they were and she turned and ushered them into

Margareta's room. Madam was lying unconscious, a number of tubes and machines connected to her.

Margareta was lying on her back under a thin blanket in a hospital gown, Susan thought, *this was the first time I've seen her not in control of everything around her. It was sad to see even the powerful succumb to nature.*

Ian was in the corner when he saw his mother and Hans come through the door. He rose and ran to his mother. He was a man, but for this moment he was his mother's little boy and he hugged her and cried. Susan held him and cried too.

After a few moments, Ian composed himself and looked at Hans and shook his hand. Hans on one side of Susan and Ian on the other, they leaned against one another for support They looked at the matriarch of the van der Waterlaan dynasty lying there at death's door and their hearts ached.

The doctor came in the room looked up from a clipboard in his hands and addressed them. "Hello, I am Doctor Schmitt. I'm Margareta's physician. I'm afraid her stomach sarcoma has progressed more quickly than we'd hoped and is now lymphomas."

Ian said, "Doctor Schmitt, can you tell us in layman's terms what is going on?"

"Why yes, of course," the doctor blushed. "Your grandmother has been battling stomach cancer for over a year. We've tried to manage it and were doing well until … well, now. The type of cancer known as sarcomas involves the connective tissue of the stomach like fat, muscles, and the vascular infrastructure. It has now spread into her lymphatic system, and, well, there is nothing we can do."

He took a breath and removed his glasses and said, She'll recover from this bout, but will be weak. She may have several months left at best. I'm sorry, now if you'll excuse me, I'll tend to her."

The three of them considered the doctor's words carefully as they spent the night in the waiting room. In the morning they awoke to the sounds of madam giving the attending nurse a tongue lashing for something she didn't like.

They came running in from the waiting room and she saw them coming through the door. "Well now, there you are. Welcome back, dear. I missed you," she said as she addressed Susan. "Ian, give your grandmother a kiss," she lightheartedly said and Ian leaned over and kissed her on the cheek. "Hans, you look well. Are you keeping my daughter-in-law out of trouble?"

"Yes, madam," he smiled and looked away.

Margareta was sitting up in her bed and looked remarkably better than the night before. She had color in her cheeks and her eyes were dark blue and focused. They could see the madam was back -- at least for a while.

It would be another day and a few more tests before she'd be released. She would come home to the castle where she'd live out her days as she demanded.

Her arrival back to the house was a rather fancy affair. Raul drove her home with the utmost care and proudly held the door for her. He leaned into the car to help her up to her feet. She stood in the sunny morning light looking up from the driveway to the staff proudly lining the stairs and clapping and smiling at her. She was still weak, but she responded with the confidence of an actress on the red carpet. The staff's energy and excitement gave her the strength to stand tall and move with the grace they'd seen for years. Madam van der Waterlaan was home.

Later in the evening, she requested Ian, Susan, and Hans join her in the parlor for a drink before dinner. The attendant behind the bar prepared their drinks and left the room. She closed the door behind her. The madam was seated in her chair in front of the fireplace. She looked at the others and lifted her glass, "To your health, and to the family. May it continue forever."

The four raised their glasses and in unison said, "To the family, may it continue forever ... Cheers!"

Margareta then asked everyone to sit and they did as they were told. She cleared her throat and spoke in a low and raspy voice.

"You may already know, I'll be dead in months, six at the most. The damn cancer is consuming my stomach. This doesn't leave me much time to turn over the business to you, Ian, and Susan, the reputation and human side of the dynasty to you. Hans, you'll have a major role in running the dynasty as I leave this earth. I know I can trust all of you and you'll do the right thing to correct all the wrong I'm responsible for."

She stared at the ceiling and spoke, "My last request is for each of you to be honest, firm, compassionate, and do good with the wealth and power I'll bestow upon you. Keep the family name alive and respected for all times. For this, I implore each of you. Do not cry or fret about me. I'll be in good hands. I love each of you more than you can imagine." Madam's eyes welled up with tears as she finished.

The room was silent while each person considered the role and responsibilities she had, in just a handful of words, levied.

Chapter Twenty-Two
Ian is a Quick Study

The next morning, Ian's ramped-up education commenced. The team of selected members of the company he'd met two weeks before in his grandmother's office were ready to start in earnest. Ian was read into the corporation, its earnings, major assets, and business plan. He was briefed on the projections and key vendors and customers.

The shipping briefing was the most interesting and his ears perked up when he was told about the steamship fleet owned and operated by the van der Waterlaan Transportation Corporation. There were even pictures of several of the newest ships provided in the briefing.

He was briefed on the planned merger of the Nappolini fleet and holdings and he noted to himself he'd watch it closely.

The briefings were nonstop and continued into the night. Food and drinks were brought into the office. Over the long hours, the members shed their coats and ties and the women removed their shoes. Ian was strong and able to keep focused and asked remarkably well-informed questions. The whole time his grandmother sat in her chair and listened approvingly. It was nine in the evening when they broke for the night with a promise to reconvene at eight the next morning.

Margareta was exhausted but remained focused and occasionally asked questions or even corrected the briefer. The whole time de Reuter watched and orchestrated the meeting.

After the staff left, de Reuter waited behind and spoke with the madam for a few minutes. He listened and shook his head then bowed and left the room. He was smiling, as if pleased, with the day's events.

Hours before, Susan and Hans had eaten alone on the balcony. They shared a bottle of wine and small talk. Susan looked at him. "How did the house burn?"

"I don't know, and you shouldn't worry." He said with a wink and she changed the subject. She had figured it out a long time ago that he knew much more than he was letting on. Regardless, she was hoping he'd slip into her room later.

They enjoyed the time together and watched the lights of Amsterdam burn throughout the city. As it cooled off, they retired to the parlor and waited for madam and Ian to arrive.

The tired pair shuffled in shortly after nine, exhausted from the day of briefings.

Ian's head pounded as he entered the parlor. He was relieved to see his mother and Hans together and his mother so unusually happy and relaxed. He walked over to her and kissed her on the cheek, greeting her and then shook Hans' hand. Margareta walked, or more correctly, shuffled to her favorite chair and nearly fell into it.

The attendant brought her a Scotch on the rocks. She sipped the liquor as the attendant addressed Ian, "Your pleasure, sir? Ian looked at the pretty young girl and wondered *what it would be like to* … and then ordered,

"Scotch on the rocks for me too, please." It was poured and served and Ian walked over to a seat next to his grandmother. "Are you content with how the day went, grandmother?"

"Yes, dear, you are a quick study. Another few days and we'll start to travel to our companies and clients. Susan, I hope you and Hans will come with us. It'll be a whirlwind tour of the world, I'm afraid. Are you up for it?" She looked over her shoulder at Susan who by now was beginning to sit a little too close to Hans for there not to be anything going on. Margareta smiled a little and didn't say a thing.

Susan eyes lit-up, "Yes, madam, I would love to accompany you and Ian and of course Hans," and without thinking, reached over and squeezed Hans' hand.

The four of them sipped their drinks and talked a little, but they were all tired and soon Susan and Ian retired to their rooms.

Hans stayed behind with the madam. "Well, Hans, it looks like she has taken you off the market." The old woman looked at him and smiled. "You best get up to her room and keep her warm, if you know what I mean," and she winked. Then with a wave of her hand, she said, "Now go, and good night!"

"Good night, madam," and he sprang from his chair and was gone, bounding up the stairs to his lover's arms seconds later. Susan lay in bed and hoped he'd visit.

The next two days were the same grueling routine. Briefing followed by briefings ran nonstop well into the night. It was exhausting, but Ian learned quickly. After four consecutive days, the madam announced, "Ian, it's time, tomorrow we will leave on our trip."

In the parlor that evening, Margareta laid out the itinerary for them, "We'll start with Saudi Arabia, then Beijing, Hong Kong, San Francisco, New York, Italy, and then home. We'll be gone for two weeks. Plan accordingly."

She motioned to the attendant who brought over a large shopping bag and the elderly woman leaned over and looked carefully into the bag and pulled out a wrapped package and turned to Susan. "Here you go, my dear, something for the trip." She handed the gift to Susan.

"May I open it, madam?" she asked

"Of course, dear, please do."

Susan opened the gift like a girl on Christmas morning. As the contents were revealed, Susan gasped with excitement. It was a Louis Vuitton travel bag and matching purse. Susan's eye filled with tears. "Thank you, they're beautiful. I've never owned anything from Louis Vuitton before, thank you."

"Look inside the purse, dear," Margareta said excitedly and Susan did as she was told. There were two more gifts inside. "Madam, you shouldn't have." As she pulled the wrapped gifts out and opened the first one, she found a stunning bracelet made of gold and studded with diamonds and sapphires. Susan put it on her wrist and beamed. "Thank you, it's beautiful ... no ... stunning."

Margareta said, "After the unfortunate fire, we'll have to start your jewelry collection over again. Let this be a start. Now open the best," Susan reached for the last gift and opened it. It was a matching Vuitton wallet for her new purse. "Open it." The older woman said and Susan did. Susan stood still and stared at the full purse. It had a dozen credit cards, an ID, and thousands of Euros. Her eyes bulged.

"You'll need money and credit cards for the trip, dear. Spend as much money as you want and buy whatever you desire. I love you, dear." The madam said with excitement in her voice.

"Thank you, madam. Your gifts are too generous, I love you." Susan said with tears of joy streaming down her face. The two ladies shared something special and the older woman remembered what it was like to have someone to sincerely care for and love.

Margareta looked into the bag again and reached in. She struggled to pull the next gift out of the bag because it was heavy for the old woman, but she managed.

"Ian, this gift is for you." she said and Ian approached the seated woman. Susan had sat down next to Hans, tears still running down her face. Ian took the gift and opened it. He seemed startled and his mouth turned downward. There were three books inside: Carl von Clausewitz -- *On War*, Sun Tzu -- *Art of War* and Mao -- *On Protracted War.*

He looked at the titles and then to his grandmother, "Are we going to start a war?"

"No dear, but these are important books you need to read and reread and understand thoroughly. Business can be likened to war and some of the best lessons for you to understand are in these books. You'll have a lot of time to read on the plane over the next two weeks and I'll help you."

She gave a theatrical look of surprise and said, "Don't look at me like that, yes, a woman can read and understand the theories of war and business." She smiled and everyone laughed. She looked deeply into Ian's eyes, "We'll stop in Maranello, Italy on the way home so you can pick out a new Ferrari." Then she turned to Hans, and studied him for a moment.

She looked at the attendant in the corner trying to be inconspicuous and ordered a fresh round of drinks. When the drinks were delivered, the madam looked at Trish, "That will be all, Trish. Please close the door and I do not want to be disturbed."

"Yes, my lady." Trish said and the heavy door shut behind her seconds later. The four were alone.

Madam van der Waterlaan looked back into Hans' face, her eyes teared and her voice trembled, "Hans, sit here by me." She motioned to the chair beside her. Susan and Ian sat behind them on the couch. Madam took a moment and the whole time looked at Hans. She stiffened herself with a long pull from her Scotch, cleared her throat, and raised her glass. "Here's to health and the family -- van der Waterlaan."

Then she reached out and put her hand on Hans'. It was the first time she had touched him.

Her eyes were soft and caring, "Hans, its time you knew the truth."

Chapter Twenty-Three
Hans van der Molen

Hans' mind was firing on all cylinders. His keen survival instincts were in overdrive and he tried desperately to stay one step ahead of the madam. It was a useless endeavor for he had never been able in the past and he was getting scared. He had no idea what was coming.

He was a strong, trained, and disciplined killer who'd made his life out of having the upper hand. He had been void of emotion with the exception of the pleasure he'd found driving his Porsche and now falling in love with Susan. He wondered, *had my distraction over Susan caused me to let down my guard?* He wondered and almost regretted he'd allowed himself to fall in love. It was too late.

For the first time in his life he was on the defensive without weapons or cover. He swallowed hard and prepared to meet his fate, whatever it was.

The madam seemed to know what ran through his mind and let him process the moment before she began. In fact, by the sly grin on her face, it appeared she rather enjoyed the last few moments she alone would know the secret she'd kept to herself for forty-five years. She took her time before beginning her story.

"There is much of your family history you know nothing about and it's time for me to share it with you. I want Susan and Ian to hear the story. I think when I've finished, you'll understand why." She took another sip of her Scotch and stared into the ice rocks for a moment.

"Your father was my first born son. It was during the war in the castle. It was a cold winter night when the Nazis had occupied the castle and mother, Johan, and I were evicted to the servant's quarters. I was only fourteen at the time. My mother and brother were in the field working to gather firewood and I was in the house practicing the piano when he came in the door. He was a Nazi SS officer and he was drunk. His eyes were cold and piercing blue. He had blond hair and a chiseled face that offered no expression and he looked like a devil. He came for one thing and wasted no time in pulling me from the piano."

Margareta's eyes were full of tears. "He pushed me down on the couch and raped me twice in rapid succession. He left moments before my mother and brother returned.

I was crumpled, clothes torn, violated, in pain, and emotionally devastated. I'll spare the detail, but your father would come from that violent act."

Hans looked confused, angry, embarrassed, and for the first time disoriented. His hands were wringing, eyes downcast and perspiration beading on his brow. After a long moment he looked up into the madam's face and she continued, "Your father was discreetly born nine months later and no one knew I was pregnant or I'd been raped."

"I was moved to the convent and the baby was placed in the orphanage at birth. I returned to the castle several weeks later and no one outside of my brother and mother knew. My mother was still a wealthy and landed woman and had connections to the Dutch Resistance."

169

"They took great pleasure in orchestrating the Nazi rapist's long, painful, and humiliating death." She looked off into the distance as if she was reliving the whole thing once again.

"After the war, I met Ian's grandfather and we fell in love and married. He would never know about your father or the fact I'd been raped. I was his virginal bride on our wedding night. He's the only man I've loved or made love too."

She stopped for a moment to gather her thoughts, took another sip of her Scotch, and finished it. She looked at Ian, "Love, will you pour me another drink? Thank you, dear." She braced herself and continued.

She moved in her chair as if uncomfortable, picked up her glass and struggled to her feet and walked over to the fire place, placed her drink on the massive hearth and warmed her hands by the fire.

With her back to the others she wiped a tear from her eyes then reached for her glass, took a sip and returned to her seat, cleared her throat and said, "Shortly after I was married, curiosity got the better of me and I began to make discreet inquiries about the boy who was brought up in the orphanage attached to St Mary's Convent."

She took a sip of Scotch and looked deeply into the fire, "Over the years I was able to find your father. He'd been adopted by a couple living in Lieden. I took great pleasure, from a safe distance, watching him develop into a man.

"Unfortunately, he carried the genes of his father and was dark, cold, and at eighteen he got involved with your mother, a Swedish girl by the name of Anna Swenson, and you were conceived. Your father left her pregnant and joined the French Foreign Legion and you and your mother never saw or heard from him again. The secret benefactor who provided assistance to you and your mother was not her rich lover but me through a Swiss bank account."

Hans watched her as she spoke, his heart doing backflips and his shoulders twitched.

"Your father went to Indochina and came back a calculating and cold man who'd become callus to killing and torture." The emotion of her words caused her to tremble. She steadied herself and Ian handed her another drink. She lifted the glass to her lips and took a sip, thought for a moment and continued,

"Shortly after your father returned from Indochina, my husband, Hans Christen, was murdered. After his death, I wanted to reach out to your father, but was afraid of what he'd become and I feared for Ian's life and safety."

Susan reached for Hans' hand and lifted it to her, placing it on her lap in a show of support and sympathy. Hans looked over and then looked back at his grandmother as she continued her riveting story.

"Your father became an enforcer of sorts. He worked for a number of people as muscle or influence, if you will. I was told he was void of conscience and good at the work. Finally, he was killed while working for a Hong Kong shipping company Y.G. Yang. He was found shot dead in the owner's office. The owner was dead too." The three reeled as they visualized the scene in their minds. Ian flinched.

"Now to you," another sip of Scotch and she looked up into Hans' face, "I've kept a close eye on you from the day you were born. It was no coincidence you met my son Ian. I, well sort of, arranged your meeting and hoped you'd become friends because you were related. Of course, neither of you knew it. No one knew, except me. I arranged for you to come and work for me so I could keep a closer eye on you." Another sip and it was clear the madam was getting tired, but committed to finishing her story. She caught her breath and continued. Everyone in the room was on the edge of their chairs as she spoke.

"You have much of your father's cold and calculating manners and are a skilled killer like him. But there is a softer side of you I've seen for years. It gave me hope it would come to the surface and I could then embrace you and recognize you as a van der Waterlaan. I always knew it was there, but with Susan in your life it's clear the goodness in your soul far outweighs the darkness passed down by the Nazi pig."

Isn't it ironic, the son of a son born out of wartime violence would be in love with the woman who loved my son and gave me a grandson? In a few weeks, the van der Waterlaan tree developed two new branches and now has the possibility of growing and surviving."

Hans' mind was drowning in so many thoughts and questions, he could barely breath. He squeezed Susan's hand hard. Her face twitched in discomfort.

The madam said, "Hans … you are a van der Waterlaan. You're no longer an employee, you're family. You and Susan have my blessing to see each other and display your affection for each other publicly, albeit discreetly. Remember, you are van der Waterlaans and we have a reputation. I also want you to come into the business side of the family and become one of Ian's mentors and protect him as he grows and matures in this dog eat dog industry." She paused for a moment and then took Hans's hand in hers, "Hans, I have one final request ... will you accept the name van der Waterlaan?"

He was stunned and off-balance. He looked at the madam, then Ian and Susan, and then back at his grandmother and said, "Yes, madam."

"Wonderful and I'd like it if you address me as grandmother and Susan ... I'd request you address me as mom."

"Now I have a gift for you, Hans." She reached into the bag one more time and pulled out a gift and handed it to him and leaned over and kissed him on the cheek. He opened the gift and it was several papers. With a wave of her hand she said, "Lawyer's stuff, please sign them. They're your official name change and it'll seal your past records. The lawyers will perform their magic and you'll have always been a van der Waterlaan like Ian here and Susan who was married and didn't know it until she arrived in Holland. Lawyers can do anything for the right price."

"Hans, please arrange to have your things moved from the staff quarters to a suite where we live. I'd expect the one next to Susan would work out fine?" She smiled at Hans and Susan and they smiled back.

With that, the air lifted and the conversation was light and comfortable. Hans signed the papers and handed them back to Margareta and kissed her on the cheek.

"Thank you for all your kindness from the beginning. I never knew my guardian angel was right next to me all the time." Hans began to weep with joy and Susan rushed to his side and put her arm around him.

Before they knew it the clock was striking twelve times.

"Best get to bed, we have a long day tomorrow." Madam said and they kissed and hugged each other good night.

They were now a family of four. Margareta walked by herself down the dark hallway. She was spent, but smiled as she thought, *Checkmate ... I've won!*

Chapter Twenty-Four
Formidable to the End

Fritz and Bill had checked, rechecked, and triple checked everything in the van der Waterlaan corporate jet. They'd worked up the navigation plans and recalculated the transits carefully. Several of the intended legs over the next two weeks would put them short of fuel reserve so they carefully plotted their intended course noting diverts they'd take in an emergency.

Fritz was an excellent pilot. Unlike the flamboyant Dieter, the famous fighter pilot, Fritz had been trained in the commercial sector where risk was minimized or eliminated altogether. He was a cautious man by nature and the recent accident that killed his friend still weighted heavy on his mind.

After a long day, he and Bill were satisfied the bird was ready to fly. Ingrid had spent the day preparing the cabin and accepting the provisions and luggage for the trip. She, too, was tired at the end of the day. The three knew tomorrow would be an early "show time". The family would arrive around 7am.

Fritz got home in time to tuck his young children into their beds. He enjoyed the opportunity to do little things and took every opportunity to be home with his adoring wife and kids. After he finished with the children, he entered the kitchen where his wife Pamela was

175

preparing a bite for them to eat. She offered him a glass of wine and he declined, "Honey, I have a long flight in the morning. Thank you though."

They sat and ate together with a candle between them. They had been married nine years and still took every opportunity to spend time together and keep the romance alive.

Fritz leaned in and said, "Honey, we'll be gone around two weeks. We'll be flying around the world and stopping in the Middle East, Asia, the United States, and then back here to Europe with a short stop in Italy. I'll call you and the kids every chance I get."

"Be careful," she said and then stood up to clear the dishes. "Help me with the dishes so we can move to the bedroom. If you are going to be gone two weeks, we have a lot of loving to do tonight." She smiled with a sexy, almost sultry, look. He jumped to his feet to help. He knew, theirs would be a night to remember.

The next morning Fritz arrived at the hanger early and once again went over his check list when Bill and Ingrid arrived together. Apparently Ingrid was over the death of Dieter and had moved on. It was clear to Fritz she and Bill had a 'just-got-laid' look in their eyes and he hoped for their sake it would be kept discreet. He knew the madam wouldn't approve and would require changes.

The three of them continued to prepare the plane when the limousine pulled into the hanger. The family climbed out of the car and walked to the plane. Fritz grabbed his cap and ran to meet Madam van der Waterlaan.

He stood straight and said, "Good morning, madam. The jet is ready for immediate departure and it looks like we have a nice day to fly."

"Yes, Fritz … Let's get to it," and she continued up the stairs to the cabin. Ian, Susan and Hans were right behind her. Their luggage had arrived the night before and already in the belly of the plane.

Fritz returned to the cockpit where he joined Bill and they started the final check before turning over the engines. Soon the passengers could hear the jet roar to life as Ingrid secured the fuselage door and poured champagne for the family. She immediately noticed the difference in the people she'd served a month before. First off, it was obvious Susan and Hans had become a couple.

Damn, she thought. *He'd have been fun to bed for a while.* And the young man, Ian, was more confident and already more mature. He was no longer a timid, albeit, polite boy, he was a handsome, confident man. The word, she'd heard, was he was the new Johan and therefore would become a very rich and powerful player. *I wonder if he'd take me,* she thought as she poured the champagne into the glasses resting on the table.

Her mind was running wild with a fantasy of Ian and her in the jet at thirty thousand feet. She had an insatiable sexual appetite and she knew she needed to be careful. If not kept in check, it would destroy her life.

Fritz watched the gauges settle-in and moved the jet from the hanger to the pre-departure holding area. The corporate jet was cleared immediately and he pushed the throttles to max thrust. In seconds the jet jumped into the air and flew with the confidence of an eagle.

For Fritz it was routine, his training, experience, and preparation took over and the corporate jet headed down the first leg of the journey. Next stop Turkey for fuel and then Riyadh.

The flight to Istanbul was a quick trip. During the entire transit, Ian was in class. Three of his mentors and trusted guides came from the crew spaces and sat around the table with madam, Ian, and Hans and they briefed, taught, and mentored the young man. Madam sat and watched approvingly and engaged occasionally.

Ian was strong, smart, and was able to absorb and remember the material which bombarded him. The meeting stopped briefly during the descent, and resumed shortly after takeoff.

The second half of the trip Ian's education focused on the van der Waterlaan interests in the Middle East and the people he'd be meeting in a few more hours. The security chief came into the room to brief the security situation in Saudi Arabia as it concerned the madam and Ian. He assessed the threat was low, but he had added additional security for the visit.

They'd be staying at one of the royal prince's estates, which would make things easier. It would also make it more comfortable for Margareta, Susan, and the other women on the trip.

There would be no need for the modesty precautions expected of Muslim women in Ali Benamini's home. He was a western educated man who liked the western ways better than those of his country and opened his home to western visitors regularly.

The jet landed in Riyadh and the passengers were whisked away by four black armored SUVs. The motorcade made a high speed run to the prince's sprawling estate outside of the city.

The security team was always relieved when the detail was without incident. The prince and his handlers were waiting at the steps to greet their guests.

Ali was a distant relative of the royal family and for all intent a black sheep kept at arm's length by his powerful relatives. Regardless, he was shrewd and clever in business and had become a wealthy man through the transportation and handling of oil.

He owned and operated a fleet of off-shore ships and had long-standing arrangements and lucrative charter agreements with ship owners like the Nappolini family and of course the van der Waterlaan shipping interests. Over the last twenty years, he'd managed to control over six percent of the export oil leaving Saudi ports.

He was an important client and longtime family friend. He and Johan had been very close and he respected and, quite honestly, was intimidated and even afraid of Margareta. At one point in history, he could have destroyed the van der Waterlaans, but now it was the other way around.

He would be gracious and welcome the new CEO and show him around the company and entertain lavishly while he looked for clues to the future. Would young Ian be as formidable as his grandmother and her brother or would Ali have an opportunity to out maneuver him?

We'll see, he thought as he watched the guests climb out of the SUVs. Ali approached Margareta and shook her hand and welcomed her to his home. The guests were escorted to their rooms and given time to relax and change before their meal. The host had an elaborate feast prepared for his guests.

The first day Margareta did all of the talking and Ian listened carefully.

Hans and Susan spent the rest of the day sitting by the large pool. The staffers were in an air conditioned conference room working lower level agreements for their principles. As the day came to an end and the sun withdrew, the temperature dropped and the guests sat outside around an open pit as the fire raged within the ornate rock circle. So far the trip was working out well. The principles had worked out a transportation plan for the next four years with options mutually beneficial for both parties.

It became clear to Ali and Ian that Margareta had the Nappolini family in her crosshairs. Ali could care less as long as he wasn't a target and could fill the need for ships the demise of the Nappolini fleet would create.

Ian, on the other hand, wondered why. He was by no means an experienced business man nor did he understand the details, but something about the conversation left him full of questions and doubts about the course his grandmother was charting.

He couldn't say for sure, but it sounded like a petty and poorly laid-out plan. He would need to talk with her privately about the decision to drive the Nappolini fleet from the seas.

The next morning, the guests were treated to a tour of Riyadh and Susan and Hans were encouraged to go shopping while Ali took Margareta and Ian to several minor clients and politically influential men. This was a must to operate a successful business in Saudi Arabia.

Promises were made, well-wishes exchanged, and the van der Waterlaan tribute to these men was discreetly deposited into their bank accounts. It was only business and Ian was seeing it firsthand.

The guests returned to Ali's home for a lavish meal and a good night's rest before the long flight to Beijing.

The next morning, after a large breakfast, the host bid his guests goodbye. As they departed company, Ali gave each one a gift of gold in the resemblance of the family seal. He kissed each on both cheeks and said, "May Allah be with you."

As the SUVs drove back to the airport he commented to his aide, "I like the young Ian. I think we'll be able to do a good business with him in the future. He's an honest and honorable man like my friend Johan was." He turned and climbed the marble staircase and entered the house to get out of the morning heat.

***

Fritz had the jet loaded and ready to depart when the SUVs arrived. The passengers moved hastily between the air conditioned cars and the plane to avoid the scalding temperature.

A few moments later the jet was moving down the runway and Fritz had the plane in the air and pointed in the direction of Beijing.

Before the aircraft had climbed to attitude, Ian was surrounded by his mentors and his grandmother, and class resumed. This time the focus was the lucrative shipping opportunities China had to offer.

Susan was seated in the corner and Ingrid kept her content with wine and an endless array of snacks. Susan was glad she had good books to occupy her time. She looked over at the table where Ian, Hans, and Margareta were focused and busy in endless meetings preparing for the visits they'd make in the Chinese capital.

She wondered if making all that money was really worth the pain. She nodded her head and returned to her book, burying herself in a romantic fantasy.

Soon Fritz called back to the owner's cabin, they were descending and would be on the ground in fifteen minutes. That was the cue for the meeting to end and none too soon. Susan was beginning to feel like a neglected rich girl with everything but company. She caught Hans' eye, Margareta noticed too.

"You better pay attention to that pretty lady over there." She pointed towards Susan. "She needs your time more than we do, Hans," and she smiled as did Ian.

Hans nodded and walked over to Susan, leaned over, kissed her softly on the cheek, and sat down next to her and said, "You heard it. I've been officially directed to focus on you and I hope you're ready." He smiled with a devilish glint in his eyes and the room erupted in laughter.

The plane bounced slightly as it touched the runway and ran smoothly until Fritz veered it off onto a side road leading to the private hanger where the plane would be bedded down for the night.

As was customary anywhere the van der Waterlaan jet would travel, Customs and Immigration were pre-arranged and drivers and security were waiting for the jet.

Beijing was no exception. Chinese soldiers lined the perimeter of the hanger. Ian noticed and leaned over to his grandmother. "Is this normal for soldiers to be here?"

She responded without looking at him, "Ian, the Chinese are very careful and so should we."

Ian thought about it for a moment and realized he didn't understand. He decided he'd be quiet, observe, learn, as he remembered one of the things Grandpa Stanley had drilled into his head as a kid, *you'll learn more by using your ears than by using your mouth.*

The plane stopped in the hanger and Ingrid flung open the door and the ladder deployed just as the engines began to spin down and their whine faded away.

There was some commotion on the hanger floor as several high ranking Chinese officers approached the ladder prepared to meet the guests.

Margareta stood strong and alert. She was impeccably dressed and groomed and moved with the grace and elegance of a woman thirty years younger as she made her way to the door. She smiled like she was greeting her fans, then descended the stairs to the waiting generals.

Margareta shook their hands and kissed each one on the cheek and in turn they blushed like school boys. She was the master of manipulation.

She moved to the waiting car and climbed in. Ian was directly behind her, shook each of the officer's hands, and they welcomed him, addressing him as Mr. van der Waterlaan. He smiled and made a nice comment about being happy to visit their wonderful country, and the excellent security they had provided.

He had learned his lessons and was a natural at working the crowd. Ian joined her in the limousine, the door closed, and they were driven away to the Crown Plaza downtown. Hans and Susan were ushered into a second limousine and they too were whisked away to the hotel.

Behind the limousines followed a large well-appointed bus to transport the rest of the travelers to their hotel. Fritz, Bill, and Ingrid remained with the plane to conduct inventories, safety checks and make arrangements for fuel and maintenance, etc. They'd join the rest of the travelers later in the evening when they finished preparing the jet for the next leg to Hong Kong.

The madam and Ian were escorted to their rooms to relax for a few hours before they were expected to attend a cocktail party with members of the government and captains of the booming manufacturing industry.

"Drinks and high intrigue," Margareta had warned Ian. "Mind your tongue, they'll try and get you to commit in a roundabout way. They're very clever. Herr de Reuter will be at your side the entire night."

"Yes, grandmother, I'll be on my guard," Ian promised as they walked in arm in arm. The older woman stole the moment when she entered, and the room became quiet while some of the guests admired and others envied the classy and elegant elderly woman who carried herself with the grace of a young actress and the confidence of a prize fighter. Soon the room erupted with voices and clinking glasses.

Margareta was a formidable woman and the guests knew and respected her. The young man on her arm was another story. He was still an 'unknown." There was already a concerted effort to gather intelligence on him and they would make it their business to learn all they could. Tonight, however, was for drinks, small talk, and plotting.

Margareta moved off by herself to allow the games to begin and the room slanted with a migration of guests moving towards her. Ian and de Reuter moved slowly over to another part of the room and the curious guests made their way to him, introduced themselves as they tried to figure out who the new CEO of such a powerful company was.   They'd all known and respected Johan and here was his grandnephew. *Would he be a kind and fair man or an unscrupulous business man consumed by money and power?* They wondered.

Mr. de Reuter watched, prepared to step in at a hint of trouble, but remained aside and satisfied Ian was doing very well. The crowd liked him. He skillfully avoided probing questions and worked the crowd with the smoothness of an actor or politician. Mr. de Reuter discreetly smiled. He would report on Ian's performance to his employer later in the evening. He knew she'd be pleased.

In another part of the hotel, Hans and Susan enjoyed a light meal and a glass of wine together. It was obvious to the others in the restaurant they were in love.

They sat a little too close and couldn't take their eyes off each other. They held hands under the table and leaned in for a gentle kiss with regularity. As the bottle of wine came to an end, she invited him up to her room and he accepted. In moments, they undressed each other and fell onto the bed where they would remain entwined until the morning. Hans had given up any hope of restraint, he was so far out of control he wondered what would happen if this didn't work out. He'd be lost, for he could never be the man he used to be and he could never love like this again.

The next morning, the four met in the madam's suite for breakfast and coffee. Susan and Hans would spend the day downtown shopping and seeing the sights. Ian and Margareta would spend the morning with government officials and the afternoon with four of the major manufacturers and exporters.

Ian and his grandmother made the short trip to the government office building and met with the minor ministers and then the next meeting was with the Minister of Industry and Economic Growth. He was an ardent communist, obese, and covered in sweat. His clothes were crudely made and fit poorly. He was a simple man and a carryover from the time of Mao and other hard line communists. The minister was more interested in protecting the Chinese shipping industry than cost effective shipping options.

Margareta noted his lack of vision and mentioned it later that afternoon. His days would be numbered and he was thirty years behind the times and an obstruction to business interests and those of the blossoming government interest in commerce and hard currency.

The afternoon was far more productive for business. The men Ian and Margareta met were like-minded and interested in moving their growing volume of products to their international consumers cost effectively.

They told Margareta and Ian, "Yes, the American and European markets will continue to grow, but at a measured rate and the infrastructure is in place to meet the demand. We want to be positioned to take advantage of the potential massive growth in the South American and the North African markets. In the next five to seven years, these will become big markets for our products."

That was a strategy all parties could get behind and soon there was a concept their respective staffs would mold into a transportation plan. In several hours, all parties agreed on the concept and over a Scotch agreed to allow the staffers to work out the details and they'd gather again in the near future to make the agreement formal.

Margareta raised her glass and toasted, "Gentlemen, it's a pleasure doing business with you. Thank God, pesky communism is becoming a thing of the past." They had another drink and their business was done.

The men gathered their briefcases and were off to their wives or mistresses. Margareta and Ian returned to the hotel.

Once again Margareta had demonstrated she was a formidable and worthy opponent in business.

For the second time, she'd maneuvered herself in front of Nappolini and by her actions had excluded him and his company from providing service when there was plenty to go around for both. *Why?* Ian asked himself.

The next day they flew into Hong Kong. Fritz always hated the airport because it required pilots to fly an "S" pattern over Victoria Island and make a sharp turn on final descent. To make matters worse, a strong cross wind was predicted. He'd be glad when they were safely on the ground.

His training and thorough preparation kicked-in and coupled with his excellent pilot skills ensured he perfectly executed the maneuver and his passengers never had an inkling of his concern.

During the trip from Beijing Margareta mentioned, "Hong Kong will be a one night stop to see the offices of our shipping company. It was once owned and operated by a man called Y.G. Yang who was found dead in his office in the mid-seventies. The van der Waterlaan interests quietly purchased the entire company to break into the Chinese export market. With ships operated out of

Hong Kong and staff and many crew members being Chinese, we were carrying Chinese goods long before anyone else."

She looked at Ian and said, "It was the best business decision I'd ever made and put the family at the top of the pile of shipping companies."

"Why did you choose this company?" Ian asked

"It was in extremis after the owner was killed and I saw opportunity." What she wasn't saying was she had intended to destroy Y.G. Yang from the moment she'd learned her son had died on a ship owned and operated by him and her illegitimate son was murdered in his office.

She turned to Susan and said, "Hong Kong is one of the premier shopping experiences," and gave Susan a few store names. "Let them know you're my daughter-in-law and they'll take good care of you." She became serious and looked deeply into Hans' eyes and said, "Hans, I'll need you to be with Ian and I."

"Yes, madam," Hans responded and stood a little taller.

The days were beginning to run together for the travelers and in each city the same things occurred. Limousines met the family and whisked them to a nice place where they would freshen up and it was off to an evening of entertainment followed the next morning by a series of business meetings.

This time they were visiting their own company, not customers, clients or government representatives. Margareta was the undisputed boss and everyone was on egg shells. They arranged for the family to stay at the Four Seasons Hotel looking right over the harbor. Margareta had a favorite room and it was reserved for her.

The evening gala was spectacular and the hotel provided a large room exquisitely decorated. Members of the Hong Kong shipping elite mingled for another evening of small talk, drinks, and Ian honed his skills as a communicator, engaging, but noncommittal at the same time.

As the evening wore on, Hans and Susan slipped out and Ian was getting tired. He excused himself and went out to the street to see the city for a few minutes. He stood across from the Star Ferry Terminal. He remembered stories from school about the ferry between Kowloon and Hong Kong and he was there.

He was standing outside the hotel in his Armani tuxedo and patent leather shoes and looked more like an international spy than he could have imagined.

It was then the impossible happened.

He heard the voice which had haunted his dreams for months. "Ian, Ian is that you, Ian?" He heard the voice, at first it didn't register. Impossible, was it, could it be … Hanna? He turned around just in time to face her as she ran into him and put her arms around him.

"Oh, Ian, it's you. I can't believe it. God, I missed you." Ian held her for a moment and it felt good. Then he gently pushed her away. "Hanna, what are you doing here?"

"I am on my last ship, I fly back to California tomorrow and then a couple of days later it's back to the academy. How about you?"

"Why did you dump me? I really loved you." His eyes began to tear.

She cried, "I didn't want too. I was told I needed to because you couldn't have any distractions, it was the only right thing to do for you."

"What? Who told you that?"

"Ian, I don't know, I guess it was someone from the family who wanted you to be focused on whatever. That was then and this is now. Why are you here in Hong Kong?"

"I am here on business with my grandmother and my mother. We are looking at her Far East Shipping Company."

Hanna's face became animated as she said, "Oh yeah, I heard you left the academy and are taking over the family business and you're using the family name. Forgive me, Ian van der Waterlaan," and she bowed deeply from the waist. He was embarrassed and she laughed. He realized he still loved her and she had never stopped loving him.

She looked at her watch and said, "I need to catch the last ferry back to Kowloon so I must say goodbye. I loved you Ian and I still do, and will probably forever. Take care and call me if you'd like." She kissed him and ran down the hill to the ferry terminal with tears streaming down her cheeks.

He watched her and in a whisper said, "I love you too, Hanna, and I always will." He turned, braced himself, and made his way back to the party to mingle with the guests in the banquet room.

From the shadows out of sight de Reuter had observed the chance rendezvous and knew exactly who the young lady was. It had been him who had convinced her to end her relationship. He remembered how she pleaded that she loved him and would never hurt him. It took his best persuasive skills to finally convince her it was best for Ian to end it. Now this -- *What are the odds?* He wondered and returned to the party to watch over Ian.

Later that evening, after the madam had retired to her room, there was a discreet knock. She opened the door and in walked de Reuter with his report. She accepted the report without a word. He left and she made her way to her bed. She was exhausted and her stomach burned with pain from the cancer eating away at her flesh.

The next morning, the four gathered in madam's suite for breakfast and to discuss the day's events. Susan would be escorted by de Reuter and Hans would be with Ian and Margareta. They'd leave for the company headquarters for a nine o'clock meeting. Hans and Susan left early and prepared for the day. Ian lingered a moment longer until he was alone with his grandmother. "Grandmother, I bumped into Hanna last night in front of the hotel. When I asked her why she dumped me, she said she was told to by someone from the family. Is that true?"

The woman's eyes flashed with anger. "I only want the best for you, and you and Hanna were in two different worlds. It was unfair for both of you to try and maintain a relationship so far away. Later, when your lives settle down, maybe you'll find you're right for each other.

"There is no time for distractions now, Ian. Do you understand me?"

"Yes, grandmother."

"Good then we'll never speak of this again." Ian turned and left the room. He knew his grandmother was right. He couldn't be distracted and Hanna was a major distraction.

He knew he must trust his grandmother's judgment. His head said she was right, but seeing Hanna last night made his heart ache all over again. He made his way to his room and prepared for the day in Hong Kong.

As he thought of Hong Kong, something hit him like a ton of bricks … the story Margareta had told the night before they started the trip. Hans' father was killed in the room with the owner. His mind began to twist around as he stripped and entered the bathroom. He shaved, showered, and dressed in a light, but well-tailored silk suit with the family tie and fine Italian shoes.

He looked at the books his grandmother had given him, Clausewitz, Sun Tzu and Mao and said to the books, "It's only a lot of reading if you do it!" and he walked out of the room to meet Hans and the madam in the lobby.

It was a typical day in Hong Kong. The sun was bright, the air muggy and hot. In just the time it took for the short walk from the hotel lobby out to the waiting car, their clothes were soaked and their foreheads beaded in sweat.

The three of them climbed into the dark Rolls Royce. It was a late model car and still had the new car smell. There were two security men detailed to the assignment. One in the front seat and the other was sitting in the cabin facing to the rear. Ian climbed in next to the man in a silk poorly made suit with a sub-machine gun across his lap. He was large and was struggling in the humidity.

Ian thought, *He's not from here, uncomfortable and probably dangerous because he's miserable. He must be new. I've never seen him before and he's not wearing the family tie like all the security men in his grandmother's employment did.* Ian looked over his shoulder at the security man in the front seat and immediately sensed a problem. The man in the front seat was also not from the family security team nor was the driver. Ian was new to this life, but knew whenever they didn't have family security, they were briefed beforehand and the security officers were brought in and introduced to them.

Hans had already assessed the situation and had discreetly reached for his concealed Glock 9mm. Hans coiled like a snake ready to strike. He looked at Ian as if trying to get his attention. Ian knew in a second what he needed to do.

As the driver turned the car around the corner, Ian threw himself against the mountain of a man with the gun next to him. Ian used all of his strength and caught the man off-guard, he'd been focused on Hans as the threat.

The gun fell off his lap onto the floor and Hans sprang like a cat and had the man on the floor boards. He handcuffed him and put tape over his mouth before disarming him. By the time the car was on the straight away the man was sitting erect with his back to the driver and his buddy in the front seat.

Hans whispered into his ear, "Make a move or a sound and you're dead." The man's eyes were wild with fear and confusion and he complied. From the front seat, all looked fine in the cabin and the driver continued to the pre-agreed location.

Hans whispered in the madam's ear a code word and she became alert and Ian could see the resolve in her eyes. She pushed the button of the intercom and called the driver. "Driver, stop the car, I need to use the restroom immediately. This damn Chinese food is going right through me."

They could see the confusion in the front of the limousine as the driver looked over at the man in the front beside him. The thug looked over his shoulder and saw his friend still sitting there and nodded to the driver to stop at the hotel on the right. The driver responded to madam, "Yes ma'am, just another minute please."

By this time, Margareta and Hans knew the driver was not taking them to the shipping headquarters, but to another location. They were in the process of being either kidnapped or possibly being taken somewhere to be disposed of. The driver was now off-balance and his driving became erratic. The man in the front seat called into his walkie-talkie to someone to let them know about the diversion. He became agitated.

Margareta saw this and added to the confusion by pushing the intercom button, "Damn it, make if fast or I'll soil your damn Rolls. Stop the car, NOW!" she yelled at the driver. That must put him over the edge, because he stopped the car on the side of the road. Hans was the first out of the car, Margareta second with Ian right behind her.

Ian grabbed her arm and nearly carried her into the building off the street and made for the back door. As they made their escape, Hans was ready for the second thug as he got out of the car. In a violent lightning fast series of strategic strikes to the man's throat and upper chest, he was left unconscious and slumped back into the seat. The driver's eyes were the size of silver dollars as he watched. Hans leaned into the car with his pistol drawn. "Give me the keys." The driver stopped the car and handed over the keys.

"Who hired you?" Hans asked with the pistol barrel pressed against the driver's forehead. The man was shaking and urinated all over his seat and started to cry.

"I don't know! I was just told to drive these two men and follow directions." Hans looked into his eyes and studied his face for a moment and realized he was telling the truth. The man next to him could not speak and may never regain consciousness again so he looked back at the man in the back seat. Hans climbed back in to the cabin as the car sat along the side of a busy Hong Kong street. He pulled off the tape on the man's face and asked with the pistol barrel against the man's forehead. "Who do you work for?

"Fuck you, Dutchman," said the man in an eastern European accent. Hans pulled the pistol back and with a sharp thrust he struck the man across his face. The pistol handle tore open his face from the bridge of his nose down to his jaw. His nose was broken and leaned over on the side in an unnatural position and bled profusely. Hans put the gun back against the man's forehead and repeated the question.

"I don't know, it was just a job," he said. Hans reached behind the man and snapped his neck. He was dead from the neck up, but his heart kept pumping blood that poured from the gash on his face. Hans closed the door to the cabin. The new Rolls Royce was full of blood and urine. Hans looked back into the front of the car at the driver, wondering what he should do with this man who could identify him. The decision became easy when the driver fumbled with a gun he had produced from somewhere under the seat.

As the gun came into sight, Hans instinctively responded and had three rounds in the man's face before the gun was above the man's lap.

A gun had been discharged, and, instantly, the car became the focus of the people on the street. Hans knew he needed to disappear fast and fade into the scenery. He took one last look into the car for items that belonged to Ian or his employer. Satisfied there was nothing, he did what he was excellent at, he disappeared.

An hour later, the three of them met back at the hotel. This time, the family security team was visible and on high alert. Mr. de Reuter was busy making inquiries into the people behind this attempt. Madam was still a little shaken, but resolved to continue as if nothing had happened. Ian was still high on an adrenaline rush. He'd been instrumental in saving his grandmother from the would-be abductors.

Margareta turned to him, "Ian you have the heart of a warrior. You performed well today. Thank you, my dear." Ian smiled and walked over to her and kissed her on her cheek as she sat in a comfortable chair. She held a glass of Scotch in her shaking hand. Ian noticed she'd gotten old and frail in the last few hours.

She looked over to Hans. "Hans, my dear friend, I'm glad you were there for Ian and me today. Thank you, now please bring Susan back here immediately. I fear for her safety."

"Oh shit." Ian said. He hadn't even considered the fact his mother was in the city shopping and completely unaware of what had happened. She may be in danger.

Hans spoke to Margareta, "Madam, I made that call right after the incident. She and Herr de Reuter are in a safe house and I'll retrieve them within the hour."

Madam smiled. "Hans, I should have figured. You're in love with her. I should have known you'd have ensured she was safe. Good for you, my dear. Now go get your lady and we'll leave as soon as you retrieve her. I for one have had enough of Hong Kong and high intrigue."

Fritz had the plane prepared and special security teams ensured nothing had been done to the plane. The provisions were checked and cleared. Within minutes of Hans retrieving Susan, they were back at the hotel and the four reunited in the madam's suite.

Susan ran to Ian and kissed him. "Thank God, you're all right. Madam, are you all right?"

"Yes dear, I've been in closer calls before, but Ian and Hans protected me."

"Ian?" Susan said and looked back at her son.

"Mom, we need to get to the airport now. We'll tell you the details on the plane."

The four of them with armed family escorts made their way to the lobby and directly to another car. This time, her security was in the car after carefully checking it for hidden dangers. In addition, there were cars in front and behind the limousine with additional security. Herr de Reuter had made arrangements for the other members of the staff to be transported to the plane awaiting the family's arrival.

It was barely visible to the family, but there was a military style evacuation plan in place with, to the minute, coordinated movements for the safe and expeditious departure of the family from the hostile environment.

As the limousine pulled into the hanger, Fritz had the jet running and straining at the reins to fly away. Without ceremony, the family boarded, the traveling security men boarded, and Ingrid had the door secured as the plane began to make its way to the departure location. The plane was cleared for immediate departure and Fritz had the plane in the air a moment later. Everyone let out a sigh of relief as the jet climbed to altitude and left Chinese airspace. Ingrid opened a bottle of champagne and served the family.

Margareta looked at Ingrid and said, "Open several bottles for the staff and security too. They deserve to celebrate. Please bring me a Scotch on the rocks." Ingrid tended to the Scotch first then delivered the champagne to the staff and a celebration ensued in the forward cabin compliments of Madam van der Waterlaan.

The plane flew quickly towards Hawaii for fuel and then to San Francisco. The fatigue of the long trip and the endless meetings were enough to try the strongest, but the emotional strain the attempt on her and Ian's life was more than even she could handle. As the plane flew steadily towards the west, she consumed three Scotches in succession and then retired to her private room for the remainder of the trip.

Susan and Hans curled up together on the oversized couch and fell asleep in each other's arms. Ian picked up Clausewitz and began to read,

"Kind-hearted people might of course think there was some ingenious way to disarm, or defeat an enemy without too much bloodshed, and might imagine this is the true goal of the art of war. Pleasant as it sounds, it is a fallacy and must be exposed; war is such a dangerous

business that the mistakes which come from kindness are the very worst... "

Clausewitz offered his first warning and it rang in Ian's ears. Ian continued to read the great theorist of war, keeping his grandmother's words in his mind, *these are important readings you'll need to read and reread to really understand the theory. Business can be likened to war and some of the best lessons for you to understand are in these books. You'll have a lot of time to read on the plane over the next two weeks. I'll help you ...*

Ingrid quietly watched Ian as he studied and concentrated on the book. Occasionally, she would ask if he'd like anything. He'd set the book on his lap and look into her face. She'd blush as she gazed back at him and they'd share an intimate glance, "No thank you, Ingrid, but thank you very much."

It was a long trip to San Francisco and Ian read the entire way when he was not in the briefing his grandmother had arranged for him.

On arrival, the family was transported to the Hyatt Regency, Embarcadero overlooking the San Francisco Bay. The family was getting tired of the constant travel and chose to get a good sleep. Susan and Hans now openly slept in the same room, "why the pretenses?" Ian had commented and they all laughed. "Hans, if you marry my mother will you be my father or my cousin?" With that, the three of them laughed again.

The next morning, the four gathered in madam's suite and ate together. Ian and madam would take a car up the hill to Market Street and visit the van der Waterlaan U.S. Shipping Company Headquarters. Susan and Hans would spend the day shopping and visiting the sites around the Fisherman's Wharf and Pier Thirty-Nine.

Ian was prepared for the meeting and his grandmother encouraged him to engage and participate freely in the discussions. She could see de Reuter was correct. Ian was a natural at business and had the confidence and instincts necessary to succeed. As she watched him confidently ascend to the center of focus at the meetings, she thought to herself, *He's nearly ready. I can prepare myself to leave with confidence. The dynasty is in good hands.* She smiled approvingly at her grandson.

Ian made a strong and positive impression on the board members and senior staff he was introduced to and later they would talk among themselves, "The new CEO is a kind and honest man of superior intellect just like his grand uncle, Johan."

Later in the evening, the four gathered together for a drink. Susan and Hans had an interesting day and Susan had purchased a few things. Hans was relaxed and happy by her side and the sight of the two made Ian smile.

Margareta complimented Ian on his performance at the office today and he blushed.

The thought of Hanna crossed his mind and he realized she lived near San Francisco. All of a sudden, he had an uncontrollable urge to talk with her. He bid his family good night and made his way back to his room, with Hanna on his mind.

He fumbled through his personal items and found his address book and turned to "H" and there was her number under Horton, Hanna. He quickly dialed the number and listened to it ring.

"Hello?" on the other end

"Hello, my name is Ian van der Waterlaan, may I speak with Hanna please?" he asked

"Just a minute," a young male voice said. "Hey, 'Handy', some guy is on the phone for you ... some guy named Ian van der something or another."

"Hello, Ian?"

"Hi, Hanna, I'm here in San Francisco and wanted to call, and say, hello."

The conversation continued well into the night. Ian told her about what happened from the time he and his mother had boarded the corporate jet two months ago. He told her about the trip and the places that he was visiting. He told her about Hong Kong with excitement and she listened and gasped.

In turn she told him about her sea year and the places she had visited and then she right out of the blue asked, "Have you got a new girlfriend, Ian?"

"No, Hanna. I'm still in love with you, silly."

"Good. I still love you too," she said. They noticed it was after one in the morning and they reluctantly said good night. As Ian put the phone down, he asked himself, *Will I ever see her again?*

The next morning, the family returned to the airport. Fritz, Bill, and Ingrid had worked much of the night to prepare the jet for the next leg of the journey, New York City, and they'd be there for several days. It was madam's favorite city and she went there for the theater and shopping. She loved the energy and the passion she only found in New York.

On the trip across the US there were no briefings. Madam spent most of the trip in the cabin reading and retired to her bedroom for a nap. Susan and Hans sat on the couch and read magazines and dozed off from time to time. Ian enjoyed the time to himself and he continued to read.

Ian focused on Sun Tzu and he read,

"For to win one hundred victories in one hundred battles is not the acme of skill. To subdue the enemy without fighting is the acme of skill..."

Sun Tzu lectured from the grave. Ian set the book on his lap and looked up. He noticed Ingrid was sitting in the corner looking his way. "Ingrid, may I have a glass of ice tea please?"

"Yes, Mr. van der Waterlaan, right away." She jumped to her feet and proceeded to the bar. Ian thought back to the Sun Tzu passage and realized, little by little, he was beginning to understand there were practical applications for the theories of war. He set the book on the table as Ingrid brought him his tea.

Ian saw she was bored and invited her to sit with him and talk for a while. She raised an eyebrow at first and she was only the help, but she accepted and sat across from him and they spoke freely for over an hour.

Chapter Twenty-Five
New York City

The plane landed at Kennedy International Airport and the family was met by two limousines which rushed them to the Intercontinental, New York on Times Square. It was the most spectacular location, lavishly appointed and the perfect place for the family to relax a little and enjoyed New York City. Located on West 44th Street, it was in the center of the theater district and the epicenter of madam's interest.

As the limousine moved through the city, Susan and Ian could see a transformation come over Margareta. Since the close call in Hong Kong, she'd noticeably aged and become frail and somewhat withdrawn. Now in New York she was as alive as she'd ever been.

They noticed the color had returned to her cheeks and she sat tall in the seat and looked at the sights she so dearly loved and adored. Her voice regained the confidence and strength they'd come to expect from her. In short, she'd risen like the Phoenix from the ashes. Mother and son glanced at each other and smiled as they shared the excitement of seeing the wonderful and complex woman reenergized.

The limousine stopped in front of the hotel and security exited the cars first to secure the perimeter and the aide moved to the front desk to retrieve the room keys. Ian was the first out of the car, then Susan, Hans, and Margareta emerged.

Madam came out of the car like royalty, more regal and spectacular than Ian could imagine. She was almost angel-like in her movement and her acknowledgement of the people stopping to see the important and internationally recognized woman. She was the matriarch of a dynasty and controlled fortunes. "These are the rich and famous," someone said in the gathering masses. Margareta smiled and addressed strangers as she walked towards the hotel lobby.

Security tried in vain to manage the crowd as they were drawn towards her like moths to an open flame. Behind her were Ian followed several steps behind him, his mother and Hans. Clearly the focus of the crowd was on Margareta and she responded with the energy and grace of a much younger woman.

Ian watched her and thought, *Grandmother, you're the most amazing person in the world. Your grace and class are unmatched.* Inside he yelled, *you go, Grandma ... you rock!!!* He smiled as he watched her enter the lobby while security blocked the entrance to allow separation between the crowd and the family. Ian looked over his shoulder as the security staff held the people back. The crowd seemed to follow the madam like mindless zombies.

Margareta turned to the family members in the elevator moving quickly to the penthouse floor. "We'll meet in my suite at six for a drink then we'll leave for dinner and the theater. This evening will be a black tie affair and your clothes will be waiting for you. If you need anything just call the concierge. After tonight, you'll be free to play for the next few days."

"Yes, madam," they said as the elevator came to a halt and the doors opened. Hans, with Susan on his arm, bowed to the madam. "Good day, madam. You too, young man," Hans turned to Ian and smiled. Hans clicked his heels. Ian bowed and clicked his heels, mirroring Hans' sign of respect, and smiled back.

Hans and Susan left for their room and Ian lingered a moment and respectfully said, "Grandmother, you're a remarkable woman. I've never seen a person with the strength, class, and grace you possess. I'm very proud to have had the privilege of knowing you and sharing time with you. It's really all that matters to me. Thank you for everything you've done for my mother. She's a good woman who has been hurt too many times. I love you very much."

Tears came to her eyes. She said, "Ian, my love ... I love you and your mother very much, and for that matter, I love Hans too. He is a good man and will take care of your mother for the rest of their lives, that I am sure. Now I'd like to rest before the theater this evening. See you at six, my dear." She disappeared behind the door and was gone.

Ian found his room and dropped onto the bed and began to think about Hanna and their conversation the other night. *Was she the one for me or will there be others?* He asked himself, but he already knew the answer.

At six they came out of their rooms dressed in appropriate attire and moved to the end of the hall where the madam was billeted. The door was open and they entered. Margareta was sitting in front of a baby grand Steinway piano sipping her Scotch. They entered and she smiled, glanced at her drink and said, "I couldn't wait," and smiled.

The bartender quickly had drinks poured to order for the other family members and they sat around the piano. Madam focused on the keyboard and then reached for the keys, and with her eyes closed, she and the Steinway selflessly filled the room with Mozart's D Minor Concerto. Not a word was spoken, everyone was overwhelmed with the beauty and depth of the music surrounding them. Margareta was a musician, no, an artist of music who was without equal. Another dimension of this incredible woman became apparent to her family.

She played for thirty minutes and her audience was transfixed with the emotion and beauty Margareta, projected through the Steinway. Susan's eyes were full of tears with awe and love for the woman who had done so much for her and her son. Hans gently squeezed Susan's hand.

Margareta completed the piece and, as her fingers lifted from the keyboard, her eyes opened and she became aware of her surroundings again. For the last thirty minutes, she'd been in another world communicating with angels. She looked at her family and could see they were still in awe and she smiled knowing she still had the talent to entertain.

Margareta took another sip of her Scotch and felt the burning in her stomach. The doctor had told her to stop drinking, because it would only aggravate the cancer and cause her pain. "To hell with that advice, Schmitt," she told her physician. "Drinking Scotch is one of only a few pleasures I still enjoy." The pain in her belly reminded her, the doctor was right.

She rose from the piano and said, "It's time to go. We have reservations at my favorite Italian restaurant in town." She nodded to de Rueter who called for the limousine out front. One more sip of Scotch, and the gentle burn it generated, and she set down the glass and picked up her shawl and moved to the door, the family in tow.

The madam was in a long, black evening gown, perfectly tailored. She was adorned with diamonds and gold. The accessories she wore were subtle, tasteful, and wickedly expensive. Susan was in an equally nice dress properly accessorized with expensive jewelry.

The limousine waited and the driver held the door for the family. The curious passersby stopped to watch these beautiful and expensively dressed people move like royalty to the waiting long, black car. The media had already gotten word there was an ultra-wealthy family staying at the Intercontinental and they couldn't get the family name from the hotel staff. Reporters and the paparazzi were closing in, they smelled a story. But for now, the family was still below the New York radar. The car rolled up to DeCarsenzo's, a small and exclusive Italian restaurant, just off of Broadway and a short block from the theater. The owner rushed through the front door to greet Margareta. She'd been coming to this restaurant for years and he and she had become close friends.

He'd arranged for the special table in the back to provide her and her family some privacy while they dined.

Family bodyguards were first out of the car. Several stayed with the car and the other two went into the restaurant and returned a moment later. The door was opened and the family exited the vehicle and made their way to the owner who greeted them.

Margareta held out her hand and Mario DeCarzenzo took her hand and kissed it. She leaned in and kissed him on the cheek and whispered in his ear, "Mario, sorry about the security, we were almost killed in Hong Kong last week by assassins. Nothing personal ..."

Mario's eyes grew worried and he leaned back and looked at the madam. "My God, it won't happen in my restaurant. I only have very important and connected clients."

"I know, now let's get off the street. Tell me what's going on in New York, my dear Mario." Margareta took his arm and steered him through the door and navigated them back to the table she knew well, talking the whole way. Mario was putty in her fingers. No sooner were they seated and a fleet of waiters surrounded them in a flash and the table was adorned with fresh bread. A moment later the bartender delivered Grey Goose martinis with blue cheese stuffed olives, madam's favorite drink in New York.

Mario personally presented the menus and went into excessive detail about the specials for the evening. The waiter stood over his shoulder as if he were a soldier on the parade field focused off in the distance until the guests were ready to order. Then he was focused like a bird of prey on the movement in the grassy field below.

With the meals and wine ordered, the family took up their martinis. This time it was Ian who proposed a toast, "I'd like to acknowledge the wonderful lady sitting by my side. She's a formidable warrior, a gentle lady, one of unmatched grace, sophistication, and a woman who has a gift of creating music coming directly from the angels themselves. She is this and so much more. Here's to you, madam grandmother. Thank you from the bottom of my heart for all you have done for all of us." As he said the last words, he moved his glass in a gentle circle around the table to include Hans and Susan.

They all raised their glasses and said in unison, "Prost" and took a sip, careful not to spill on the table cloth.

Not to be out done, madam kept her glass in the air. "I love each one of you. Thank you for being part of my life. The last few months have been some of the best and most memorable times of my life, because you have been there sharing it with me. God bless."

They shared small talk and the madam gave a short summary of the play they'd see after dinner. Then the meal began to arrive. The same fleet of waiters surrounded the table with a number of plates full of food and began to set them down on the table under Mario's careful supervision. Satisfied it was correct, he released the waiters and lingered to ensure Margareta was satisfied.

"Thank you, Mario, this looks wonderful, my friend," Mario smiled and disappeared into the crowd to give the family privacy. Margareta said, "I'd like us to hold hands and say grace together." They complied and she bowed her head. "Bless us, O Lord, and these, Thy gifts, which we are about to receive from Thy bounty. Through Christ, our Lord … Amen." Then she continued, "Please take care of my Hans, Ian, and Johan who are in your kingdom. Thank you for the gift of knowing my grandson and his lovely mother, and for Hans. Thank you for giving me the wisdom and courage to acknowledge his birthright and embrace him as my own. The family is strong and stable and will now survive and thrive. My work on earth is nearly done and I'll be ready to present myself to you, dear

God soon. Amen." Everyone made the Sign of the Cross before and after the prayer.

There was a chill in the air after. It would be a few minutes before the conversation resumed, but it did and dinner was a pleasant experience.

Mario came over and thanked the family for dining with him as they readied to leave. He walked Margareta to the door, wished her the best, and asked her to return again soon. She assured him she would, knowing she wouldn't, and kissed his cheek.

It was a short walk to the theater and the family was seated in the front row. The orchestra conductor noticed madam and came running over. They were professional acquaintances and had performed together years ago. He introduced himself then excused himself to Ian and Susan and spoke to Margareta in Dutch for several minutes and then in English asked, "Margareta, would you grace us with a short performance before the show? Possibly you would perform a classical piece on the piano? I can arrange it in a few minutes. It would be good for these simple people to hear and enjoy real music as only you have the gift to perform," and he bowed deeply.

Normally, she would have declined, however, after a few seconds she agreed. The old gentleman was ecstatic, kissed her hand, and turned and literally ran down to the orchestra pit. He gave some orders and soon a concert grand piano was being wheeled onto the stage. It was a magnificent instrument.

Margareta looked to her family seated to the left of her. "Forgive this old woman's vanity and desire to perform one last time. I have missed performing on stage for all these years. It has always been in my blood.

Performing was always my passion and desire, but when my Hans Christen was taken from me, I was driven away by destiny. Ian, you have released me from that burden and I'm now free to perform as long as the good Lord will allow."

As she finished, tears gathered in their eyes. The orchestra conductor walked out on stage to get the attention of the audience. The show wouldn't start for fifteen minutes and they were moving slowly to their seats and conversing with friends and other guests. After a few seconds, the room became silent and the conductor continued,

"Ladies and gentlemen, I'm so very pleased to announce we have a special guest and good friend of mine in attendance tonight. She's an incredible woman, who, those of you in the business world know as Madam van der Waterlaan, the owner and chairman of the largest privately owned shipping company in the world. Her business holdings extend far beyond that, as well, and I think I may have already said too much."

There were gasps throughout the theater. The conductor paused until everyone settled down. "But the reason I'm standing here is to introduce Madam van der Waterlaan, my friend and most accomplished classical pianist I've ever known. She is one of a small number of true musicians and performers who can give a soul and wings to the music she performs. She hasn't performed in public since the tragic loss of her husband, her son and brother. Tonight she's graciously agreed to play for us."

"Ladies and Gentlemen it is my sincere pleasure to invite, my friend, Margareta, to the stage." The crowd clapped enthusiastically and the conductor, with an open hand and theatrical stage presence, pointed to Margareta; still in her seat.

She leaned on Ian, "Help me up, dear."

As she stood, the crowd's enthusiasm mounted. The old woman was young again and she waved to the crowd and they responded with their applause. Ian walked with her and ensured she climbed the stairs with the grace and sophistication she deserved. Ian walked her to the conductor on center stage. The audience still offered their encouragement. Margareta kissed the conductor on the cheek. "What would you like to hear, my friend?"

He whispered back, "Franz Liszt's Liebestraum if you remember it."

Margareta looked at him. "Liszt's Liebestraum … it is" She walked to the piano, sat and admired the beautiful instrument for a moment.

The conductor spoke to the audience, "Ladies and gentlemen, Madam van der Waterlaan has agreed to play a piece from Franz Liszt. It was the first piece I heard her play after the war in Europe. Ladies and Gentlemen, Liszt's Liebestraum, 'A Dream of Love' … Margareta van der Waterlaan." and the crowd erupted with enthusiasm and curiosity at the old woman sitting before a behemoth instrument.

Margareta reached for the keyboard and as she connected to the instrument the sound filled the theater. The audience young and old stilled, and if breathing weren't a reflex, they would have stopped. Everyone was silent as she created music with incredible depth and soul. It wasn't just music, it was a gift from God himself.

The music began slowly and soulfully and transitioned to a powerful flood and ebb of emotion, and the audience could feel the impulse of love and the helplessness of being lost in a dream from the sound she produced. People wiped tears from their eyes as she continued to play.

Soon the actors came out from behind the curtain to listen to the woman perform as a perfect medium between the angels in heaven and the mere mortals lucky enough to be in her presence. She continued until the piece was finished. It was a flawless performance that left the audience stunned and mesmerized for a moment. She gradually opened her eyes, leaving behind the world she'd entered during the performance.

The conductor had remained on stage, off in the wings. He was crying uncontrollably. She had the gift he and most musicians would kill for and never came close to achieving and she had it naturally. It was sad, she had squandered it all these years and kept it from the world, but for the few that she'd played for in private.

All at once, the audience came out of their trance and they went wild with applause and stood to reinforce their extreme pleasure with the Margareta's performance. Ian returned to the stage and stood beside her and helped her to her feet. She smiled and thanked the audience.

For a moment she relived her youth and her dream. As the lights blinded her and the audience encouraged her, she thought, *this is heaven, Lord, I am ready. Thank you for this one last opportunity.*

After minutes of uncontrolled applause, she left the stage with Ian at her side and returned to her seat.

The play started a few minutes late as a result of the prolonged applause, but no one cared. The play was excellent, but days later the audience would remember the piece by Liszt and the gracious woman who performed it so perfectly and vaguely remember the play, characters, or plot.

After the play ended, the family was ushered to the rear of the theater to a private exit where their car was waiting. Hans was relieved to be safe. From the moment Margareta agreed to perform until they were in the car, he had transformed from family and Susan's love to bodyguard and his eyes and senses were in overdrive to protect his grandmother.

The next morning, the four gathered in the madam's suite for breakfast and coffee. They were all a little spent from the day before and sat at the table and sipped their coffee and tea. Herr de Rueter came into the room carrying several newspapers and handed them to the madam and whispered, "The headlines, madam …"

She opened the Daily News' column "Who Knew?" and read the article. It was a story about who knew this "wealthier than God" woman could play the piano with such incredible skill and went on. She set the paper down and said,

"Blasphemy … more money than God … my dear," then she picked up the New York Times. "Madam van der Waterlaan Provides a Surprise Performance at the Gershwin Theatre." She read that article and set the paper down. "Now that is more of a measured account of the evening. Thank you, Herr de Reuter," and she continued to sip her coffee. Then she looked over to Susan.

"Dear, I'd like to spend the day with you. Let's go to the spa and then we can shop for the remainder of the day. Just us girls." She looked over at Hans and Ian as if to say, *don't even!*

They read the look and smiled. Ian chimed in, "Grandmother, I'd like to go back to the academy for a few hours, please."

"Dear, you do that. Take Hans with you and you boys have fun -- but not too much fun." The four laughed and Ian's thoughts locked on Hanna. He was so close to her he needed to see her again.

Chapter Twenty-Six
Time Together

Margareta and Susan made their way down to the lobby with two of the security detail escorting them. The limousine was waiting and delivered them to the Great Jones Spa, ten blocks away. They were met at the door as the staff was expecting them and had everything prepared.

The ladies started in the sauna and it allowed them to talk privately. Margareta turned to Susan, "Tell me more about you, my dear. I want to know everything."

"I am not very interesting and I think I've told you all that's worth telling."

Margareta looked over, "Dear, let me get one thing out of the way between us. I took special care to ensure there is no record or possibility of anything from your past surfacing ever. Only you and I know our secret. I want you to tell me every detail about my son and your time together. You have read his letters and know he was in love with you and you were the one who had given him the strength to re-engage in the life you and your son are now living. I'll always love you for that and for bringing my grandson into this world. Now please tell me everything you can about my Ian."

So Susan told the whole story about her and how she found herself pregnant with Sarah and alone. How and where she met Ian and how their relationship developed.

She told of the torment and trouble Ian carried in his soul and how she tried to help by being a good listener and never judging him. He was good with Sarah, and at some point, Susan had fallen in love with him, but couldn't tell him. She was afraid it would have scared him away. Susan told about the last time they were together and the ship, the *Amore Islander,* and how much he loved it and the men aboard. It was his family, but Sarah and Susan had become part of his family too.

Then Susan cried as she thought about Ian and the painful way he must have died as the ship sank.

Margareta put her arm around her. The sauna was hot and moist and very relaxing. "Susan, what do you know about Ian's death?"

Susan replied through her tears, "All I know is he died on the ship when it sank."

Margareta kissed Susan on the forehead and continued, "I swore at the moment I was told he was dead, I'd get revenge. The men responsible would pay. It was the passion that consumed my life until I found you and Ian. Thank you for teaching me to love and forgive again. I've been angry and bitter for so long. Thank you and I love you, dear. Keep love and charity and honesty part of the family code of honor."

Just then, the spa assistant came in and politely informed them the hot tub was ready and escorted the two women to the showers and then the private room with a steaming hot tub. They both moved into the tub carefully as their bodies acclimated to the temperature. Margareta continued, "Susan, Tell me about you and Hans …"

Susan started, "Madam…"

Margareta interrupted, "Dear, call me mother, mom, or if you prefer, Margareta, please I insist."
"Yes, mom and thank you," and with that Susan spoke honestly and candidly with her mom like she'd confide in a close friend or her mother back in Rhode Island. It felt good.

Margareta was a good listener and the two grew closer by the minute. When Susan finished, Margareta told her about her husband and how they were together as a couple and her memories of Ian as a child.

By the end of the day, the two women were as close as any two people and there was a tighter relationship they had created through trust and the commonness of shared experiences. Susan had a new best friend she could confide in.

Shopping was a whirlwind experience as Susan watched Margareta walk through the various stores, pull things from the racks for herself and Susan, and hand them to an attendant. Soon Susan was doing the same thing. Her sensibilities and concern for the price tags soon vanished. Together they spent thousands of dollars in several hours of shopping and had the packages sent to the hotel.

Margareta turned to Susan and she looked tired, she took a moment and said, "Dear, I'm exhausted, let's return to the hotel and relax. I could use a Scotch. Let's relax and wait for the boys to return."

Susan smiled, "Me too, I'm beat. Thank you for a wonderful day … mom."

Back in the lobby the security team moved the ladies to the madam's penthouse where security was much easier.

There was still no word on the person or organization responsible for the kidnapping or assassination attempt in Hong Kong, so security remained extra vigilant.

Chapter Twenty-Seven
Return to the Academy

About the same time the ladies had made their way to the spa, Ian and Hans left by car for Long Island. The limousine made its way slowly in the eastbound traffic towards the island. Hans was thinking about what he was going to see and what role he should take. He remembered his activities to check the legitimacy of Ian's birthright by hacking into the academy files. He knew more about Ian than even Ian did, and for that matter, Hans knew much more about Susan than she thought. He knew more about Maria and that Maria's and John's suicides were not quite what they seemed. Only he and one other man knew the story and the other man was dead.

Would Hans be the excited and supportive cousin (maybe future step father) or his bodyguard? How much if anything should he divulge to Ian? He looked out the window and realized his life had gotten so much more complicated and at the same time so much less complicated since he had fallen for this kid's mother. Oh, the announcement, Hans was part of the family had thrown him for a loop, too. Hans wondered how the day would unfold.

Ian, on the other side of the limousine, was looking out the window remembering all the good times he and his classmates had enjoyed in New York City, Queens, and the towns surrounding the academy. It took nearly an hour before the limousine pulled up to the academy gate.

Mr. de Reuter had called ahead and the administration had cleared the limousine and its occupants to enter the gate. The driver stopped outside of the barracks and the two men exited the vehicle. The driver and car disappeared and Hans and Ian looked at each other. Ian said, "Ready, Cuz?"

"Ja, junger, show me around."

Ian took Hans around the school and told him about the history and the experiences he had while attending. Ian kept bumping into his classmates who'd just returned from their sea years and they were excited to see him.

"Why are you in civilian clothes, Ian?" they would ask as the regimental year had resumed the day before and midshipmen were in uniform. Few midshipmen heard Ian had voluntarily disenrolled for 'family reasons'. He must have explained that to forty of the friends and classmates he met.

Hans watched and realized Ian had really loved being part of the regiment of midshipmen and had his heart set on the life of a merchant officer. Hans knew he was in large part responsible for stealing the dream away from his cousin and felt the pain of guilt and remorse as he watched.

They continued the tour of the academy. Ian walked Hans down to the mariner's chapel and they admired the beautiful structure adorned with a large gold dome overhead. Then it was down to the waterfront where Ian told Hans about his time with the sailing team and how he used to spend every afternoon down there sailing and training for collegiate regattas.

221

Hans watched his young friend and saw firsthand the emotion and passion he had for the place and the life it would have prepared him to pursue. Hans felt regret in the pit of his stomach and he tried not to show it.

Several hours after they'd arrived Ian and Hans had completed their tour and were preparing to walk over to where the car was parked. Just then, Midshipman Hanna Horton, Second Class came out of the administration building and nearly knocked Ian over.

Startled, she dropped her books, looked at Ian, and forgot where she was and kissed him. "Ian, I was just thinking about you. Tell me you're coming back. God, I love you so much, I don't know if I can make it here without you." Then she looked over at Hans. "I remember you from the night we met Ian's grandmother. You were there."

"Yes, I was, Hanna," Hans responded. He was trained to be very observant and he had quickly assessed Hanna and Ian were very much in love with one another and guilt reared its ugly head again. He was involved in the decision to severe their relationship too. Hans realized, in the case of his cousin, he'd been responsible for taking the things he loved away so he would do what was expected. While he was in his own thoughts, Ian and Hanna were chatting away.

Ian said, "No, I will not be coming back to the academy. I must return to Holland and learn all I can so I can help my grandmother with the business. That seems to be my destiny. I am good with it. Will you come and spend time with me?"

"Of course I will, when I can, but we're just starting class and I'll be busy until summer. I'll come see

222

you then," she said. "I'm late for class and I have to run. I love you, Ian, and I always will." She kissed him long and passionately and knew that she would probably get demerits for the 'public display of affection' but she didn't care. She'd do the restriction time with a smile on her face.

"I love you, Hanna, and I'll call you. I'll visit you as often as I can. I love you."

As they parted, Hans realized he needed to do what he could to bring these two young lovers together, not keep them apart. He decided to make it a personal goal of his and he knew a good co-conspirator, his Susan.

Hans and Ian stopped for a sandwich at the Deli on the Green at Ian's request. He used to love the Italian hoagies and wanted one for old-time sake. Hans joined him, and with sandwiches in hand, they crossed the street and ate their lunch in the park on a bench.

Ian told Hans this was one of the simple pleasures he used to enjoy when he was granted liberty from school. Hans listened and began to realize how special this young man really was. He had willingly left his life and everything that defined him, to step into a foreign world with danger and intrigue he was ill equipped to cope with. In remarkable time he'd prepared himself to ascend to one of the most powerful yet dangerous positions in the world and he did it without fear, but with modesty and humility. He was honest, kind, intelligent and had none of the arrogance or recklessness of his father. He was the right choice. Hans smiled at the young man who had captured his respect and admiration.

After they finished their lunch, they returned to the city to reunite with the ladies.

The next day they would travel to Rome and a visit with Nappolini. He was her number one competitor and longtime rival. Ian knew the next leg of the trip would make Hong Kong pale by comparison.

He'd stay close to Hans.

Chapter Twenty-Eight
Rome

The next morning the family gathered for an early cup of coffee and toast because they'd eat on the flight to Rome. The plane was fueled and serviced the day before and the crew had everything in place for the family's arrival. The limousines pulled up shortly after eight and the family and staff boarded.

The pilot met the family at the brow and welcomed them aboard as the co-pilot readied the cockpit. Fritz returned to his seat moments later and the final preps were completed. As soon as the fuselage door was secured, the pilot lit off the engines and the aircraft came to life. The lights inside the fuselage burned bright, the air conditioning system kicked in, and the plane began to move towards the desired temperature. Ingrid ensured the family was secure and ready for departure and served mimosas.

Cleared for departure from the corporate runway, Fritz brought the plane around, pointed it down the runway, and pushed the throttles forward. The thoroughbred leapt from the ground with the strength of a bird of prey and quickly climbed into the sky. Fritz pointed it in an easterly direction and settled in for the six hour flight.

As the jet reached cruising attitude and the family finished their mimosas, Ingrid served breakfast and poured more wine for her clients. She liked her new boss. When she catered to Ian, her eyes sparkled and her cheeks turned rosy.

The vacation was over and now it was back to business. The staff entered the cabin and continued briefing and mentoring Ian. The purpose of the trip to Rome was to meet the owner of the Nappolini Shipping Company. It was a family owned business that had become a major provider of bulk cargo tonnage, and it had been for years in direct competition with the van der Waterlaan fleet. In the past there was always enough cargo for these two giants. It was the little guys they ruthlessly squeezed.

Ian was a good student and quickly absorbed the information. This time madam did not sit at the table, she chose to sit away in a recliner and read a book, comfortably nodding off from time to time. Hans sat at the table and offered constructive comments, but watched Ian as he gathered the information and put it in a logical order for his personal use.

They worked diligently on strategy to buy-out the Nappolini fleet. If it couldn't be done up front, the maneuvering had already been done to close his market and force the sale. If that didn't work, a hostile takeover would be put into play. One way or another, the company would be struck from the roles. This made no sense to Ian as he listened to his coaches. Finally, he asked if he could have a few minutes alone with his grandmother.

The staff nodded, gathered their folders and left the owner's cabin.

Ian approached his grandmother and sat next to her. "Grandmother, please explain why we are destroying one of the finest shipping companies and one of the finest men in the industry. There seems to be plenty of cargo for both of us to carry without getting in each other's way."

She looked over at Ian, "It is time for me to tell you the whole story. Hans, you and Susan need to listen too. Susan, you know more than Ian."

Madam reached for Ian's hand and said, "When your father died, I had a discreet investigation done and it turned out there were criminal activities directly responsible for the *Amore Islander's* loss. I vowed I'd make the men responsible pay dearly. I've spent the last twenty years doing just that. Nappolini designed and built the ship and therefore, in my mind, contributed to his death."

Ian spoke softly, "Yes, grandmother, but he had sold the ship ten years before. It was not his negligence or greed that caused the accident. From what I learned in school, Nappolini was a visionary and designed excellent ships. *The New World Order*, the original name of the *Amore Islander*, was a state of the art ship for her time. She was built to higher safety standards and offered better living conditions than any other ship of its time. I respectfully think you're unfairly holding Nappolini responsible for something he had no control over. Moreover I think an alliance with Nappolini would better position us against recession and allow the two partners to fill the China expansion projections we heard about in Beijing."

Margareta was silent a moment and scratched her chin. "Ian, you're wise beyond your years. I see you've been reading your Clausewitz and Sun Tzu. We'll talk to Nappolini with an open mind and see where it takes us. Okay?"

"Thank you, grandmother, for allowing me to discuss this openly with you. Thank you for telling me the truth about my father. Will you take me his grave when we get home? Now that I know more about him it would mean so much to see where his memories are buried."

"Yes, dear, I think your briefings are over. Let's relax for the remainder of the flight." She smiled and touched his hand.

Hans and Susan watched the exchange and were taken by how well Ian had approached and prevailed on her to rethink something born of revenge. Hans leaned over and whispered into Susan's ear, "Your son is very special, he is one to watch." She looked back and smiled and gently kissed his lips.

Four hours later, the jet transitioned from flight to rolling down the airport runway outside Rome at a hundred and sixty knots. The pilot brought the plane to the corporate terminal. There were no hangers to park the jet inside, so Fritz parked in the assigned location. A black sedan arrived and security disembarked and arranged for the family to be taken to the InterContinental De La Ville Hotel.

The location was selected to place Susan near the Via Condotti shopping district and Ian and Margareta minutes away from the Nappolini offices.

The family chose to eat in, so they had a fine Italian meal sent to the madam's suite where they served themselves and relaxed. Susan especially appreciated an evening without extras hanging around to serve them. She still found it uncomfortable having all the help around all the time. After dinner, Margareta walked to the bar and poured herself a drink and took orders from the others.

It was the first time in many years she had served someone else. She hummed a tune as she mixed their cocktails. They realized how special the moment was and each sat there silently and watched until Margareta returned and sat with them.

The four enjoyed their drinks as Margareta moved to the piano and played for an hour or so. The music was light and playful. Susan and Hans were the first to call it a night and left hand in hand. Shortly after, Ian kissed his grandmother good night, and slipped out the door. Margareta sat at the piano, her stomach burned and she was afraid to move until the pain subsided. *It won't be long,* she thought as she shuffled her way to the bedroom.

Ten was the agreed time for the meeting of two of the most powerful and recognized ship owners in the world. Margareta and Ian arrived right on time and were met at the car by a representative of Angelo Nappolini. The young man named Mario Nardi escorted them through security to the executive elevator.

The building was well-maintained and showed the owner's pride and commitment to keeping things he owned nice. Both Ian and Margareta noticed how the employees seemed happy and productive. It was clear they liked their work and respected their employer.

The elevator took them right to the top floor. The door opened and Ian saw a large expansive greeting area with tasteful furniture and elaborate artwork. Adorning the walls were high grade pictures of ships from the fleet. Each looked well-maintained and modern. An attractive young lady came out from behind her desk with a bright smile and escorted them to the conference room to the left. As she led Ian and Margareta to the room, she said, "Mr. Nappolini will be with you in just a moment. He sends his warm regards and regrets for the slight delay. May I pour you coffee or tea?"

"Coffee would be fine," Margareta said as she sat.

"That would be fine, thank you." Ian said

The receptionist returned with the coffee just as the door opened and a handsome, older gentleman entered the room. It was Angelo Nappolini. He was impeccably dressed and was still in good shape for a man in his eighties. He walked over to Margareta and shook her hand and kissed her lightly on the cheek. "Margareta, it's so nice to see you again and welcome. I look forward to our conversation … and this must be Ian van der Waterlaan." He walked over to Ian and shook his hand. Angelo had a strong and powerful hand shake which reinforced his character and confidence.

"I see you have coffee, good. Maria, one for me too please, thank you," he said to the young lady. She smiled and returned with a coffee just the way he liked it. Angelo sat, focused on Margareta's face and said, "Now what would you like to talk about?"

Margareta took a moment and then cleared her throat. "Angelo, tell me about one of your ships, *The New World Order*."

Angelo looked confused for a moment then he regained his composure, "That is a rather odd request, never-the-less. It was a new concept a young architect developed on paper and I liked it. It was built in Japan to safety standards that greatly exceeded the minimums of the time. It had large living quarters and was an experiment to see if having families on the ship would improve the quality of the officers and crew we would attract. It was fitted with a self-discharging conveyor system. At the time it was state of the art. She was big too. I think she was around seventy thousand tons. For her time, she was a monster. Today, not so much. We operated her for five years or so and sold her. I think that was in the late sixties. From there I lost track of the ship. Why?"

Margareta took a deep breath, "My son, and Ian's father, was killed on that ship. It was called the *Amore Islander* in nineteen seventy-nine when it broke in half in a Pacific storm."

Angelo stirred,

"Margareta, I'm so sorry to hear that. I didn't know." She looked at him and said,

"What do you know about the accident?" He thought for a moment.

"We're old friends, this is all I know." With that he started his story,

"In the mid to late seventies, the North Koreans were trying to get high grade iron ore from mines around the world. The free world wouldn't allow these shipments so a black market was established. I was discreetly approached by the North Koreans to move their cargo and I quickly declined. I am surprised you weren't too?" He looked at Margareta.

"We declined too." She said. He nodded and continued,

"I guess Y.G. Yang, a disreputable man, from Hong Kong took the work. As my people have surmised, ships were grossly overloaded in the Peruvian port of San

Metalous. It was an ideal port for those crooks because there were no agents or authorities to oversee the loading and the government reps on site were easily bribed. These overloaded ships crossed the Pacific along an untraveled route so no ships would see them. They stopped at a deserted island, off-loaded part of their cargo onto a North Korean freighter, and resumed their voyage to the steel mills in Japan with the remaining cargo aboard. The delay for the secret off-load was written off as weather delays covered in the charter party."

He sipped his coffee and gazed out of the window and said, "We think Y.G. Yang made millions of dollars doing this. The *Amore Islander* was poorly commanded and wound up in the jaws of a typhoon. In her over laden condition it's a miracle she remained in one piece for as long as she did. I'm not surprised she broke in two. I was told she was fifty percent overloaded at the time."

Margareta scowled and shook her head, "What a disgrace," she said

Angelo continued, "Y.G.Yang had over insured the ship and was still able to convince the underwriter it was an "Act of God" that took the ship. Fate has a way of catching up and he didn't live long enough to enjoy the money. He had a dispute in his office and he and another man of shady background were found dead in the owner's office of apparent gunshot wounds. I think they killed each other in a dispute. Then you rolled in and bought the company before the blood was washed out of the carpet."

"That's all I know," he finished, and took another sip of his now cool coffee.

Margareta looked at him and knew he had told her the truth and he was a good and honest man. She took a deep breath. "Thank you, Angelo, I'll be honest with you. I had made it my business to ruin everyone who was directly or indirectly responsible for my son's death. Yes, I took Y.G. Yang and others for that very reason. It was the reason I came here today. I planned to put you out of business one way or another, because in my mind, I held you accountable because you built the ship. It was my grandson here who convinced me I needed to come here with an open mind and hear you out and he was right. I have no issue with you, my friend, and thank you for filling in the rest of the story for us. I want to offer you an alliance to protect us from the impacts of the forthcoming recession and position us for Chinese market growth projections in North Africa and Latin America. I think it's time we combine our resources instead of competing." She looked over at Ian and smiled. He nodded and grinned back at her.

"I'd like you to meet the new Owner and Chairman of the Board of van der Waterlaan Transportation and Holding Corporation, my grandson, Ian. He'll be your partner. Treat him with the respect you have always given my brother and me. He is much smarter than I ever was," she smiled and laughed.

All of a sudden the color drained from her face and she looked frail. She said in a weak and trembling voice, "Angelo, I'll leave you two to discuss the details. I'm feeling a little ill and would like to return to the hotel." Her stomach burned and it was all she could do to not buckle over. She sat for another minute until the pain subsided.

The two gentlemen stood and helped her to her feet and escorted her to the car waiting below. As she got into the limousine she spoke to Ian, "Continue with Angelo," then she addressed Angelo, "You're a good man and I have always respected you as a man of honor and virtue. God bless you, Angelo."

The limousine door closed and she was driven back to the hotel. Angelo had tears in his eyes as he watched her move into the Rome traffic. After a moment he wiped his eyes and they returned to the office to craft a strategy.

Later that evening, Ian returned to the hotel to find his grandmother in her room and very weak. The doctor was concerned she had a bleeding ulcer. He sat with his grandmother and told her about the progress he and Angelo had made on the alliance. She smiled and softly spoke, "Ian, tomorrow we'll go to Maranello so you can pick out your new Ferrari."

"Grandmother, that can wait, I don't need a car right now. We need to get you home so Dr. Schmitt can help you. We need to fly home as soon as you can move. We'll look at Ferraris another time."

She reached out and held his hand, "You're a good man, Ian. I'm so proud of you, my son," Margareta said as she leaned back on her pillow and fell into a shallow sleep.

The doctor said she would be able to move in the morning if nothing changed, but she needed to relax when she got home. Ian thanked the doctor and led him to the door.

Ian, Hans, and Susan all embraced each other. They knew the end was near for the matriarch.

Chapter Twenty-Nine
The Madam Dies

The family brought the madam home from Italy as soon as she was able to move and made her as comfortable as they could in her home in the country. She insisted, she wanted to spend her remaining days in her castle surrounded by the country she loved so dearly. Dr. Schmitt did all he could for her to minimize her pain and prolong her life without putting her in a coma. She insisted she'd die with dignity and pride. Ian tended to her every wish and spent many hours with her. She took every opportunity to impart as much information as she could before her time ran out and he sat patiently listening.

It was clear she was a fighter and, up to the end, she'd been a formidable business person and a remarkable strategist. The more Ian learned about the company, the more he realized she was the one behind the remarkable growth and financial success. Carefully hidden behind her husband and then her brother, she was the brains and the one responsible. He thought, *and to think that for so many years her motives were fueled by revenge for her son.*

As the matriarch faded away in her suite, Ian tended to the affairs of the company. His team of coaches and trusted mentors still provided the bulk of the recommendations and he respected nearly all of the advice he was given, but there would come a time soon he would free himself of his mentors and run the company the way he knew in his heart it should be run.

Susan spent the days with Margareta. She was her nurse and confidant, her friend and companion. The two women had grown close during the trip and especially during their day together at the spa and shopping. She was glad to be with Margareta as she faced the end and heartsick at the thought of losing such a wonderful woman.

Hans focused himself with the business and stayed close to Ian, providing advice and protection. Hans would also find ample time to sit with his grandmother. He'd always respected and feared her, but he had seen a softer side of her and he'd grown to love her too. They spent many hours talking together about the days and events they'd shared, the good and the not so good. But over all, they were good and they agreed she had a good and fulfilling life and would be remembered world-wide. Margareta blushed a little.

As the evening came, madam asked for her Scotch on the rocks, and though the doctor had forbid it, no one was going to deny the woman the only pleasure she still enjoyed. The family gathered around her bed in chairs and Susan sat on the bed next to her. Madam finished her drink and asked for another. Ian got up and poured her another and handed the glass filled with the amber liquid and transparent rocks of ice. Margareta smiled and cleared her throat then with her eyes focused like a bird of prey she said, "Hans, I want you to take Ian and Susan to my Ian's grave so they can visit it. I promised Ian. I want you to see that Ian goes to Italy and buys whatever Ferrari he wants. He is the Chairman of the van der Waterlaan dynasty and he must have an appropriate car. You need one for yourself, too. The company will buy it for you. I want you to promise me you'll protect Ian and Susan and remain as loyal to them as you have always been to me. And lastly, I hope you and Susan will commit and marry each other. Every time I see you two together, I remember how in love and happy I was and I hope you'll share the same happiness together. I love you, Hans."

She took another sip and focused on Susan's face, "Susan, dear, you are lovely, I have come to love and admire you. You're all that's good in the world. You're honest, charitable, loving, and forgiving. You're the center of gravity of this family and with your love and compassion, it will grow, stay healthy, and respected. I want you to bring your daughter and grandchildren here and give them everything they need. They're family and I regret I'll miss the opportunity to know them in this life. Please tell them about their great grandmother and hopefully you'll have kind things to say about me when I'm gone. I love you as a daughter and a friend. I wish we had more time together. Love Hans – always. He's a good man who you can trust and depend on, and be there for Ian, guide him in the matters of the heart. I love you, dear. God bless you for coming into my life. I'll miss you dearly." She was fading but continued … another sip of her Scotch. Susan bowed her head and wiped her eyes.

"Ian … my Ian … the angels brought you to me. This is now all yours. Manage it wisely and lead with compassion, strength, and honor. You've learned every lesson well and you're ready to take the throne of the family dynasty. I need to tell you one thing before I sleep. It was me who arranged for your girl Hanna to drop out of the picture. I was afraid if I didn't, you wouldn't have been focused on the task of replacing me. It was me who drove her away. She loves you more than you could possibly imagine. I need you to know I'm sorry for interfering in your personal affairs and I hope you'll find it in your heart to forgive me. I hope, with this information, you'll reengage with her and I wish you both the very best together, if it's what you young people want. You have my blessing and strong encouragement," she weakly smiled and was fading fast.

Susan said, "Mom, stop now, you've said enough. It's time to close your eyes and rest. I'll stay here with you," as she finished, the madam's eyes closed, she gasped briefly, opened her unfocused eyes for several more seconds and gently shut them for the last time. The madam of the van der Waterlaan family left this earth as she'd wanted, with dignity and pride.

As her soul left her body, she was met by her husband, her son, and her brother, who had long ago forgiven her for his violent death. The four of them made their way to heaven, the family reunited in peace.

The news of Margareta's death became front page international news. The media carried the story for over a week. The press was kind in their memories of the matriarch and she was remembered as a kind and philanthropic woman who loved to help charities and the under privileged world-wide. Ian, Hans, and Susan and a little well-placed money ensured the story was as they wanted her remembered. She was laid to rest in a family cemetery behind the castle where her body would always be part of the country she so dearly loved.

It was the end of a dynasty … The Queen is dead … Long live the King …

Chapter Thirty
Ian Ascends to the Throne

With the loss of his grandmother, Ian completely immersed himself in the business. He found he had a knack for the art and science of business and he read and reread Clausewitz, Sun Tzu, and Mao finding lessons his grandmother promised were there to be harvested by the patient and studious reader.

Shortly after his grandmother's death, Ian had statues of Margareta and Johan created and added them to the park where Ian and Hanna Horton had first become aware of the van der Waterlaan family. He thought about Hanna, *it seemed like decades ago this adventure all started in the park in the financial district of Rotterdam.*

Ian strengthened his company's relationship with Nappolini and he became close friends with Angelo and his nephew, Michael. Like Ian, Michael was groomed to run his family's company. They called each other routinely and met for holidays from time to time but they were both very busy men with tremendous demands on their time and little opportunity for relaxation – but still they tried to meet when they could.

Ian appointed Hans as the CEO and he ran the company with consistency and meticulous oversight, which gave Ian time to look at the strategic picture. Together they made a great team both in the board room and at home as relatives and friends.

Sarah finally had enough. Susan took the corporate jet and flew to California to bring Sarah and the children to Holland. Susan was thrilled to have her family all under the same roof.

Sarah accepted Ian's invitation to remain with them and raise her children in the van der Waterlaan home with all the privileges and opportunities he insisted they were entitled too.

It wasn't long after Sarah came to live with the family that she shared the stories of abuse and manipulation at the hands of her sadistic now ex-husband. The next day Hans had an emergency meeting with clients in Mexico. Coincidentally, several days after Hans returned from his trip, the Los Angeles police called Sarah. It seemed her ex-husband was found in his home hanging from the rafters in his garage. Apparent suicide, the officer told her. "The body was full of welts, cuts, and bruises which were determined to be self-inflicted. Most notably, was the self-mutilation of his genitals," the cop said, "That guy was into some pretty kinky stuff. He was really messed up. You're lucky you got out of there when you did." Sarah hung up the phone relieved he would never be part of hers or her kid's lives again.

Susan stood next to Hans as Sarah was on the phone and she knew instinctively what the call was all about. She gently reached down and took Hans' hand in hers and squeezed it. Without looking over, he gently squeezed it back. Susan would never know for sure nor would she ask, but then again she knew. Hans would always protect her and her family. He'd been given the sacred task by the madam on her death bed.

As the madam wanted, the business thrived under the control and leadership of Ian and Hans, and the family grew and the home was filled with love, happiness, and warmth. Sarah and her children became the darlings with the staff, especially Raul, who loved to take them for rides in the country. Security remained in place, but the threats to the family subsided to the point they were able to move more freely.

Sarah learned to play Margareta's pianos and her daughter, Morgan, became interested as well and soon the two became skilled musicians. Morgan wanted to follow great grandmother Margareta and she studied classical music and dreamed of becoming a professional classical pianist. Sarah enjoyed more contemporary music and loved to play for the family in the evenings. It was a happy time and so it would continue.

Ian often thought about Hanna and hoped someday their paths would cross again. Though he had endless opportunities to date rich and beautiful woman, he was only interested in the one he couldn't have. His first and only love was Hanna Horton.

Six months after Margareta passed away, Susan reminded Hans and Ian there was something they had promised the madam they hadn't done. They looked up from their drinks, both were staring into the raging fire in the parlor lost in their own thoughts. Sarah was playing the piano quietly and the kids were in the other room.

"What's that, dear?" Hans said.

"Really, you boys don't recall? Let me give you two a hint … Ferrari!"

"Quite frankly I had forgotten," they both said

"Well I think you two should have a boy's weekend out. Take the jet to Maralleno tomorrow and pick out a couple of pretty cars. Enjoy the weekend together and have fun. God knows, you both deserve it. I'll stay here with Sarah and the kids. Have fun!"

Hans and Ian looked at each other and nodded and smiled.

The next day, the ladies of Italy were buzzing with excitement when they found out two very handsome and wickedly wealthy bachelors had flown into Milan and were enroute to shop for Ferraris. The men walked through the assembly line and spent hours with the salesmen looking at a variety of cars. They even drove several of them around the local track.

In the end, they both agreed on the Enzo. Hans ordered his in yellow with black interior and Ian ordered his in red with tan interior. They'd be delivered to the castle in a month. Hans stroked a check for 2.2 million US dollars payable from the van der Waterlaan family account.

The guys found a local bistro and soaked up the sun on their faces and drank Chianti. Hans turned to Ian, "Do you want to stay for the weekend?"

"Honestly, I'd rather be home with the family." Ian said.

"Me too ... Let's fly home now, what do you say?"

"Let's go," Ian said and he called for the check while Hans called for the car and then the pilot to spin up the jet.

Within the hour, the jet was in the air headed north to Amsterdam.

Ingrid had made the men a Scotch on the rocks and they sat together in the cabin. Hans turned to Ian, "Ian, I intend to ask your mother to marry me. I have never felt so strongly about anything in my life." Hans reached into his pocket and produced an extravagant engagement ring he'd been carrying in his pocket. He handed it to Ian to examine. Ian looked at the ring and then back at Hans,

"Well, Hans … it's about time you made my mother an honest woman! Gee, cousin, does this mean I'll need to start calling you dad?"

"No, Hans will do." They laughed and the two stood, shook hands, and embraced. Ingrid reached behind the counter and produced a bottle of champagne and removed the foil. "Gentlemen, it sounds like you've got something to celebrate," and a loud "pop" announced the cork had left the bottle.

Ian looked at Ingrid, "Please bring three glasses, one for yourself." The whole time the jet moved quickly into the evening European sky. It was as if the metal bird knew the way back to its barn at Schiphol. Hans called Susan as the limousine moved out of the hanger.

"Honey, Ian and I missed you, Sarah, and the girls. We'll be home in a few hours."

Susan let out a squeal of delight, "I love you, Hans, hurry home."

It was around eight in the evening when the family gathered in the parlor and Hans knew this was the time. Ian knew what was coming and he had pre-staged champagne in the cooler behind the bar and told Trish to be ready.

Before the usual drinks were poured the family settled in to the comfortable chairs and visited. Hans picked up a crystal glass and struck it with a silver knife.

Clink, Clink, "Please, may I have everyone's attention?" Ian squirmed like a kid with a big secret. The room grew quiet and everyone looked at Hans. He continued as he walked over and stood in front of Susan, "Susan, I love you with all my heart. I have since I first met you and I could never imagine my life without you." He dropped to one knee at her feet and produced the ring he'd shown Ian a few hours before. "Susan van der Waterlaan, would you marry me and be my wife for eternity?" Everyone was silent as they waited for her response. She began to cry and her face flushed red. Her hands wiped the tears from her eyes and finally she blurted out, "Yes ... oh my God, Yes!"

Hans stood and put the ring on her finger and kissed her. The family clapped and shouted with excitement and Trish popped the corks and poured the finest bottles of champagne the cellar could produce. It was a remarkable evening and the couple's happiness was fairy tale perfect.

A month later, there was a small Catholic wedding held at the castle. Susan had flown to Rhode Island to bring her parents back for the wedding. She was a magnificent bride and her father was as proud as any father could be of his daughter. Ellen cried though the whole ceremony. The reception was small and included immediate family and close friends.

The wedding couple left that evening for their honeymoon and were gone a month. The trip included a round the world flight stopping where ever the newlyweds desired. Such a gift came compliments of the Chairman and Owner of the van der Waterlaan dynasty. It was the least he could do for his mother and his new father.

In the shadows, a number of people continued to hold their personal grudges against the 'perfect' van der Waterlaan family. Could this change of events provide an opportunity to get even? They wrung their hands and considered the possibilities.

Chapter Thirty-One
Love Returns

It had been four years since the madam had passed away and Ian had developed into a respected and powerful leader of business in his own right. In the tennis clubs and on the golf courses around the world, he was the topic of discussion and in every comparison he had superseded both Johan and Margareta. He possessed the compassion and honesty of Johan and the strategic mind of his grandmother, but his moral compass kept his maneuvering fair and transparent. Anyone who would try and deal with him unethically would feel the power and finality of his resolve. Though Hans didn't get his hands dirty any longer, he kept a few "dogs of war" on the payroll and wasn't adverse to using them without Ian's knowledge.

The list seemed endless of eligible young ladies who paraded before Ian hoping to catch his eye but all were in vain.

Ian focused on his immediate family and the business. Many in the industry compared Ian with his good friend Angelo Nappolini, a man who had spent his life focused on his family and the family business.

Angelo never found time to marry and have a family of his own but had found happiness with his sisters and their families. He was now eighty-six and beginning to fail. One afternoon he called Ian. "Ian, its Angelo, my doctors have given me two weeks. It appears I have the same cancer your grandmother had. Isn't it ironic? Look after my nephew Michael and the business. He's a good boy. I'm afraid, nowhere as smart as you are. May I give you one piece of advice, young man? Find yourself a nice girl and start a family. I regret I never did … Well with that … I'll say goodbye, my young friend." Angelo hung up and Ian sat there with the phone in his hand for a moment and thought about the call.

Of course, Angelo was right. Hanna was gone and it had been six years since he had considered dating. He set the phone down and decided to discuss it with his family over dinner. The intercom rang and his secretary announced the arrival of yet another naval architecture firm representative marketing another new concept in ship design. Ian told her he'd meet the gentleman in the conference room in a few minutes.

The middle-aged gentleman was escorted into the large conference room overlooking the Rotterdam harbor. The man was graying and his eyes were no longer as strong as they once were. He worked for Nappolini. Years ago he'd been invited to the Nappolini Shipping offices in Rome shortly after he'd finished his studies and Angelo introduced him to the woman who later became his wife, Angelina.

Ian entered the conference room and walked over to the gentleman and confidently said, "Ian van der Waterlaan" and he extended his hand. The other gentleman extended his and they shook hands.

"Alex Sparos, sir, I was sent here by Angelo Nappolini. I'm his senior naval architect and I have a ship concept he wanted me to share with you." Alex began to roll out a drawing of a vessel unlike anything Ian had ever seen or imagined.

"You say you were sent here by Angelo?"

"Yes, he told me you're the only one in the industry these days who would have the vision and the courage to build this ship," Alex said matter-of-factly.

"Let's take a look," Ian said and they opened the large drawings on the conference table. The vessel was nearly twelve hundred feet long and one hundred and sixty feet in beam. It was a catamaran design that provided a very large deck for cargo to be stored.

Alex cleared his throat and began and Ian could hear the excitement in his voice as he spoke, "The hull design provides the hydrodynamic characteristics to allow the vessel to transit at forty two knots for nearly half the fuel one of your containerships consumes. The size of the vessel allows it to carry four times the cargo current container ships carry and its size and configuration make it able to safely transit up to forty foot seas and hundred mile winds with absolute safety. In addition, the ship is nearly completely automated and would only require a crew of twenty. Sir, I present you a ship that offers the very best fuel consumption rate per ton of cargo carried, a ship that is nearly unsinkable and can be operated with a minimal crew."

Ian looked up at the architect and asked, "Where could a ship with such beam be built?" Ian asked.

"I've designed it so it can be built in sections and assembled in the water."

"What about when the ship needs routine and emergency repairs? There are no shipyards able to support a ship that size." Ian leaned back in his chair.

"The ship is designed so it can be easily disassembled for these activities and then reassembled when it is ready to resume cargo operations. It can't go through the Panama Canal because its length but in the next ten years the canal locks will be large enough for these ships."

Ian was getting excited and they talked about the concept ship for another hour and then another hour after that. At the end of the day, Ian and Alex sat in Ian's office and had a drink together. Ian liked the concept and he liked and trusted the man who sat across from him. Angelo trusted him and Ian could see why.

Ian asked, "What other concept ships have you designed?" Alex ran the list down in his head.

"My first concept was a self-discharging bulk carrier ship. I had lived and worked on a French ship as a guest of the captain and his wife. They became my second parents and I saw how well the ship worked with wives sailing with their husbands. It was one of the major themes I adopted in the design."

"It was large for its time and used a new idea of conveyor belts to discharge cargo. It was designed to self-discharge seventy thousand tons in thirty-six hours. Mr. Nappolini hired me on the spot and had the ship built in Japan. I was even sent there to help build the ship as his representative and I've been with him ever since."

"What was the name of the ship, Alex?"

"Mr. Nappolini named it *The New World Order*. Why?" Ian accidently spilled his drink and turned white. "Sir, are you okay?" Alex asked and slowly Ian regained control.

"Yes, Alex, it was years after it was built and had been calved from the Nappolini fleet when my father sailed on the then *Amore Islander.* It sank in a storm, and he was killed."

"Oh my God, I am sorry," Alex said, rubbing his temples.

Ian said, "I know what happened and it had nothing to do with the design or the way it was built which caused its back to break. The people responsible have been identified and punished. The case is closed, please continue. I'd like to hear about the other ships you've designed," and Alex continued. By the end of the evening, Ian knew he would build the ship and Alex was a genius in the art of ship design. Alex was Angelo Nappolini's gift.

Ian called his mother and told her that it was late and he was tired and would spend the night at the Rotterdam apartment. The family had come to Amsterdam to make it convenient for Hans and Ian to come home at night. "Son, you really should come to Amsterdam. There is a surprise waiting for you and trust me you'll want to come home. Silly, don't you remember it's your birthday tonight?"

"Okay, mom, I'll get home as soon as I can." He hung up the phone and pushed the intercom to talk with the driver. "Raul, change of plans. Please take me to the Amsterdam house."

"Yes, sir, right away," Raul responded and had the car pointed in the right direction a second later. Ian dozed in the back during the hour trip to the van der Waterlaan city home. Raul parked the car in front of the entrance and opened the door. Hans met Ian at the foot of the steps.

"Hello, Pop." Ian said.

Hans grinned and in an almost giddy voice said, "Get ready for the surprise of your life. Follow me!"

They walked into the house and Ian handed his coat to the butler and followed Hans to the parlor. As Ian walked in the door, the light came on and there was a surprise party complete with banners and streamers and the room was full of family and close friends. In the center of the room he saw her. It was Hanna.

She was in a pretty dress and she was more beautiful than he remembered. Ian just stared and the noise around him faded away. Hans stood next to him and struck him on the back and said, "Well, don't just stand there, go get the girl. She came here all the way from California to be here for you. Now go!"

Ian did as he was told. He felt the same way for her now as he had six years ago. He walked up to her, took her into his arms and kissed her. The audience clapped and the corks popped as more champagne flowed. Ian had forgotten he was tired, and for now he wasn't worried she would leave in the morning. She was here and it was his birthday.

Hans had his arm around his wife and Sarah stood beside them. All three smiled for they knew Ian was now complete with his love at his side.

The desire to touch one another again made them blush and their palms began to get moist. The family around them giggled as the two slipped out the door.

Chapter Thirty-Two
The Motor Vessel Margareta van der Waterlaan

The next morning Ian brought Hanna to the office with him, showed her around the building, and introduced her to members of his staff. She was impressed with his office and the people around him -- but not too impressed.

Ian had called for another round of meetings with Alex and invited Hanna to join in. The three of them discussed the concept ship further. Hanna looked over the plans, and now as a licensed marine engineer, she said she liked the vessel from an engineering perspective, it looked straight-forward and reasonably easy to operate and maintain. She was especially vocal about the ease with which the ship could be converted into two or three pieces for dry docking.

Ian continued to consider the ship as a replacement for three or four ships currently in the transpacific trade to free the older ships for the growing Chinese manufacturing markets in Latin America and Northern Africa. Ian would be able to move tonnage into the trade routes as the demand continued to rise.

It was a good solution and could keep van der Waterlaan at the apex of the transportation industry. Today the discussion was about the building projection and cost estimates for the leviathan.

The conversation continued through the lunch hour. Ian had food delivered to the conference room and they were just about to enjoy their meal when his secretary came in and whispered into Ian's ear.

"Oh no!" Ian said. "Find out what you can for me please." She nodded and quickly left the room. Ian turned to Alex, "Angelo died this morning. I know he was a good man and you respected him tremendously. I understand if you want to return to Italy immediately. We'll continue after we pay our respects to the Nappolini family."

Alex was flushed and notably upset, "Thank you, Mr. van der Waterlaan. I'd like to return to Rome at once."

"Fine, let me send you by our corporate jet, it'll get you there more quickly."

"You'd do that ... that for me?" Alex arched an eyebrow.

"Of course, we've just begun a long and prosperous relationship. I'll see you at the wake and funeral. Ciao." Ian had his secretary call the car and another call to prepare the jet for immediate departure.

In addition to being the right thing to do it gave Ian a few days to discuss the ship and the idea of working it into the transpacific route with Hans and other senior people he trusted. Alex gathered his drawings and asked if he could leave them with Ian. "Of course, I was hoping you would so I could consider them further and discuss them with my senior advisors."

After Alex was on his way home, Ian fell heavily into the chair next to Hanna. "I think I've had enough for one day, how about you?"

She smiled and shook her head. "Let's blow this Popsicle stand," she said. *Some Popsicle stand!* She was in one of the most lavishly furnished conference rooms in all of Europe with three hundred and sixty degrees of floor to ceiling windows on the forty-fifth floor. The entire city and harbor of Rotterdam were visible. Ian smiled and they left for the day. He hailed a cab and they headed to Murphy's for a beer and reminisce about their first time in Rotterdam together. Then, Ian had an idea.

"Follow me, I want to show you something." He threw money down on the table to cover the drinks. He took her hand and led her to the park where they'd discovered the statue of his grandfather. Hanna noticed this time there were three statues. Two looked new and as tastefully done as the original. As Ian led her closer, she recognized the lady in bronze standing to the left of the center statue. "It's your grandmother, Ian!"

"Yes, and the other is her brother Johan. You never met him. It's too bad, for he was a wonderful man, too," Ian said.

"Did you do this?" She asked

"Well ... Yes, sort of ..." and he blushed. She moved closer to him and kissed him gently.

"There, I have wanted to do that since I arrived. I hope you don't mind." He kissed her back softly at first and soon he had her in his Rotterdam apartment and they were making love with the energy waiting for six years had unleashed.

After their bodies exploded in erotic pleasure, they were both exhausted. Hanna was tucked in his arm as they lay beside each other. Ian turned onto his side and looked into her eyes. "Will you stay with me?" She propped herself up on her elbow and kissed him.

"Ian, I'm not ready to be part of this life yet. I must finish what I'm doing first. Then, if you still want me, I'll give myself to you for the rest of my life. Try and understand."

He kissed her. It would be early evening before they left the apartment to return home to the family. Ian understood how she felt but it tore at his heart nonetheless.

That evening, Ian began to discuss the concept ship Alex had brought him the day before. Hans quickly became as enthusiastic with the idea as Ian and assured him the company was in the financial position to build the ship outright and forgo financing charges if Ian was sure it was what he wanted to do. They agreed and shared a drink before dinner.

The girls were in the other room. Sarah and her mother were doing everything they could to convince Hanna to stay with Ian.

Several days later, the entire family and Hanna boarded the corporate jet and flew to Italy for the wake and funeral for Angelo Nappolini. It was a large and traditional Catholic ceremony, attended by a host of powerful international figures representing both businesses and governments.

As they left the funeral, Ian and Hans received a text message at the same time … *Your Ferrari arrived at the castle.*

Neither man seemed excited. The emotion of burying a friend, ally, and sometimes competitor left them both drained.

The trip back to Amsterdam was quiet. The kids and women dozed.

Sarah had met Michael Nappolini that afternoon and she began to wonder if maybe her future may have a man in it again. She'd been hurt, still she wanted the touch and companionship of a man. As she dozed, Michael was on her mind. She decided the possibilities were endless as she nodded off again.

It was a few days later when Alex Sparos returned to Rotterdam. Hans had confirmed the drawings and the probability of success with his engineering staff and had his own estimate of the cost to build the ship. The money was set aside and he and Ian were ready to commit to the venture. When Alex entered Ian's office, Hans was standing there. Alex had never met Hans before and was taken off balance. Ian saw this and reassured, "Alex, it's okay, this is Hans. He is married to my mother and is the CEO. We work very closely together."

"Oh ... well ... okay."

"Alex, please have a seat. Hans and I have a proposition for you -- we want to build your ship. We are prepared to start immediately, but we want you to work for us at least for the construction and sea trials. What do you think?"

"Well, I have a job with the Nappolini Company, sirs."

"I understand and I spoke with Michael Nappolini this morning and he really doesn't want to lose you, but agreed, if you agree, to have you temporarily assigned to my company until the ship is done. Oh, and we'll be happy to move your family here to be near you if you'd like or fly you home routinely, your choice. What do you say? You'll be our project lead and report only to Hans and myself regarding ship construction."

Messrs van der Waterlaan, I would love to. When can I start?" and so it began.

Within a month the Hakodate Shipyard in Japan was under contract and the massive steel order began. As designed by Alex, the ship was built in sections and assembled in the drydock. The two pontoons and deck were connected while it was afloat. The modular design allowed the construction to be accelerated and the ship was ready for her sea trial twelve months after work had commenced. The shipping world was on the edge of their seats as they watched the construction and listened to the projections and design features of the 'state of the art' ship.

Sea trials went smoothly considering it was a radical new ship design and concept. In less than a month, the ship was certified and accepted by the owner. The *M/V Margareta van der Waterlaan* was ready to enter the transpacific trade just in time to relieve the three ships Ian moved into the China/Latin America and China/North Africa trades. The world watched the first eastbound trip as the ship carried a record ten thousand containers, over twice what the largest conventional container ship could carry at the time. The ship set a transit record of thirty-four knots. Sparos and van der Waterlaan had turned the container world on its head.

The *M/V Margareta van der Waterlaan,* like its namesake, had changed the world of shipping and marine transportation forever. The gamble Hans and Ian had made paid off in spades and they commissioned the building of four more of these ships under the careful and methodical supervision of Alex Sparos.

The year was 2012 and Hanna had been away for two years. Ian was just about to give up on his love when she called him from the Amsterdam airport.

"Ian, its Hanna, I'm here in Amsterdam and I'm ready to make a commitment and live in your world if you'll still have me." *Silence...*

"Ian, are you there?"

Ian just sat there. It had been nearly eight years since he left the academy and the last time he saw her was when she dropped in for his birthday.

He said, "Hanna, you're welcome to come to the house and stay with us. We'll expect you for dinner. Sorry I have to go now, see you tonight." He hung up the phone and dialed Hans "Hans, can I see you in my office? Thanks."

Ian and Hans discussed Hanna's reappearance and what Ian should do. He was one of the most powerful men in the world and not someone who could be simply jerked around by a woman. Or could he? He wanted to see her and still loved her, so they agreed he'd see how it went and if she ran again he'd end it and move on.

That evening Hans and Ian shared a ride to the house. Ian had a plan.

Chapter Thirty-Three
Desire and Destiny

Hanna met Ian and Hans at the door. Standing behind her was Ian's mother and sister. It was clear from their smiles they were glad Hanna had come back and were watching to see how Ian would react. By now Ian and Hanna were both twenty-seven and had experienced the world. She had just finished her first and last trip as the Chief Engineer on an American containership. Her goal achieved, she'd come back to Ian as soon as she could. She didn't call often or tell him what she was doing because she wanted to accomplish her goal on her own and knew Ian could have made a phone call or two. She was proud and determined to do it on her own and she had. She stood before Ian with a piece of paper in her hands and gave it to him.

"Ian, if you will have me, you can keep this. I won't need it any longer." He looked at it and it became clear why she had been so distant and it all made sense now. He read the license out loud, "Hanna Horton, Chief Engineer; Any Horsepower Motor and Steam."

His eyes filled with tears. If he'd finished school he would have had a Masters license; Unlimited Tonnage Any Ocean, but his desire had been overtaken by destiny. He was proud of Hanna for sticking to her guns and finishing what she had set out to do. He rushed into her arms held her tight and said, "Congratulations. Welcome home. I hope I can convince you to stay indefinitely this time." They embraced again and the family moved in around them and they all embraced each other.

Ian and Hanna spent months traveling together and catching up. Their passion and love was still as strong as ever. They became inseparable and would be seen holding hands or walking arm in arm. Finally, after they had been together for months, Ian proposed to her one evening in the parlor in front of his family. She accepted on the condition they fly to California and he propose again in front of her family.

He agreed but made her promise she'd give the same answer in front of her parents and the room erupted.

They flew to California and drove out to Hanna's parents' home in Point Reyes. It was a rustic home, rather large with lots of windows, looking out over the Pacific Ocean. Hanna's parents were a nice couple and knew a lot about Ian through Hanna. Her parents both told Ian she really loved him and he was the only one she ever talked about from the time they met nearly eight years before. Her father told Ian, "She just had to get that damned chief's license before she could allow herself to do something about the way she felt about you." Together the men sat in the backyard, and sipped a local beer from the bottles, and looked out over the Pacific Ocean.

That evening before dinner, Ian proposed to Hanna again in front of her parents and she accepted again. The wedding was held two months later in the California Redwoods. It was elegant, but a modest affair to satisfy the California Marin County sense of modesty, yet with the expectation of old European money for elegances and perfection. It was a credit to the couple they pulled it off and both families and their respective sensibilities were satisfied.

The honeymoon was an extended stay at the Hilton on Waikiki beach in Hawaii. Then it was time for Ian to return to the helm of the company. Hans ran the company from the day Hanna had come back into Ian's life and, although he proved an excellent manager and leader, he lacked that special insight only a gifted few have. Clausewitz called it genius or Coup d'oeil which allows gifted elites the strategic perspective to navigate the shoal waters of war and, properly applied, it worked for business, too. This was the talent Ian possessed with a razor sharp keenness.

Ian's mother had established herself as a visible member of the community and was sought after for charity functions as a speaker and benefactor. She sponsored several homes for battered and abused women within the Netherlands and created a number of family trusts to provide tuition and assistance for gifted students from underprivileged families. She'd become all that Margareta had envisioned. Hanna joined in and the two van der Waterlaan women became world renowned for their philanthropic work. Ian and Hans had noticed their wives' passionate efforts to do good for the community had reflected positively on the dynasty's bottom line, too. It gave them something they could stay focused on and feel good about.

Sarah and Michael Nappolini gradually started to date. Slowly at first, but over time their relationship grew into something special. It took three years before they were married and by that time, her two children were speaking and studying in Dutch and chose to stay in Holland when Sarah moved to Rome to be with her new husband.

The time continued to fly and the family fleet had grown with the addition of three new "family ships". They were named after *Hans Christen van der Waterlaan, Johan van Winkle* and *Susan van der Waterlaan*. Ian promised his sister, Sarah, the fifth ship would bear her name. These ships had made the conventional ship design obsolete and the rest of the industry would lag behind for years before the dynasty had any appreciable competition. It was 2014 and Ian was on top of the world. What more could he want?

He knew.

Chapter Thirty- Four
Sailing off Together

Ian had an unfulfilled dream which started years ago on the waters of the Narragansett Bay. It started as a passing fancy, grew into an idea and further matured into a desire. He wanted to travel the oceans, pit himself against nature and try and connect with his father. As a young boy, Ian found a way to do it by sailing the boat he and his grandfather had built together and later by enrolling at the merchant marine academy where he was focused on sailing and assuming command of his own ship, like Captain Horne on the *American Spirit.* During his time underway, he'd further refined his dream. Now it included Hanna Horton-van der Waterlaan.

Then in a series of uncanny events, his destiny and his sense of honor and commitment to the family prevailed and his life changed. He was no longer striving to command a ship, but he was the most powerful man in the maritime industry and owned hundreds of ships and employed hundreds of captains. He had stepped forward to accept his destiny and had been successful. Now he decided to do something he had always wanted to do. He still had the dream and it was time for him to act on it.

He discussed his plan privately with Hans and they discussed how the company would be handled during Ian's extended absence. Hans was more than up to the task and he encouraged Ian to pursue his goal. They even went as far as to visit several Dutch boat builders to discuss the type and size of yacht necessary for the pending adventure. After hours of discussion and consideration, it seemed like a one hundred and fifty foot conventional trawler hull with twin slow speed diesels and twelve staterooms with ample entertaining space, a pool, and room for all the toys including jet skis and a sailboat.

Next Ian approached his wife and asked her if she missed going to sea and she thought for a moment, "Yes, Ian, I do … why?" and it was then he excitedly told her of his plan and he wanted to take a year or two and sail around the world with her. He wanted to share the experience with her like he had dreamt about when they were on the *American Spirit*. She smiled and agreed, "With one provision ..."

"Okay," he responded.

"I want to select the machinery and the hull layout. Your catamaran ships are ugly!" and they laughed.

"Yes, but they make a lot of money for the family, you must admit." He responded light heartedly and they laughed again. It was during the evening gathering in the parlor when Ian and Hanna announced their plan to Ian's parents. Of course, Hans had already talked to his wife about Ian's plans and even the yachts they had looked at.

For the show, both Hans and Susan looked surprised and excited for their children. And like always, Ian's sister, Sarah, must have had her radar up because she called fifteen minutes after the announcement and was told the news. She, as always, was happy and proud of her younger brother. The family enjoyed a bottle of champagne and agreed that the next day Ian and Hanna would start looking for an existing yacht or find a builder with a suitable plan for the yacht. It was September and they wanted to be underway by New Year's Day.

Weeks before, Hans had retained two of the best brokers in Holland to find the right boat for Ian and Hanna, so they were well into their research before it was official.

"Used or new, Hans asked as he tried to pin Ian down. Ian was more focused on the transit than the vessel itself. Hanna was sure there was something on the brokerage market that would allow them to buy and have a yacht ready to go on time. She still remembered her shipyard experiences and the problems, mess, and noise.

She wanted to stay in the brokerage market and buy a used yacht that had been gently cared for and properly maintained. She'd be the judge of the quality of the engineer and the owner's pride in the boat.

Soon the brokers contacted Ian with possible yachts positioned around the world. Ian and Hanna looked at the specifications and the attached pictures and some were worth a trip to see and most were discarded by Hanna for any number of reasons. Ian trusted her judgment and moved on without question. In time, the hunt for the perfect yacht became Hanna's job and Ian sat back and admired his wife's enthusiasm as she looked for the right yacht.

It was November when the broker called and told Hanna there was a yacht homeported in Dubai, United Arab Emirates that met the requirements they had described. He told Hanna on the phone, "Its two years old, built in Italy for a Saudi Prince. The vessel is one hundred and seventy feet in length and has two MAN slow speed diesel engines." Hanna's interest was piqued. She knew

MAN engines and they were reliable. The hull was traditional in appearance and had ample living and entertaining accommodations. The yacht complete with its crew were available for inspection and consideration in Newport, Rhode Island until January.

"Send us the portfolio, machinery maintenance logs, and an inventory of items of significance like expensive machinery, art, furniture, and tenders/watercraft. Send the resumes of the current officers and crew if they would be interested in remaining with the vessel. Lastly, contact the U.S. Coast Guard vessel documentation authorities and see if this vessel has been grounded, in a collision, or suffered damage. Check with the U.S. Marshall and ensure there are no liens on the vessel either. Why is the prince selling the boat?"

"He wants a larger one." The broker replied.

"Fine, what's the asking price?

"Twenty million US dollars, but I think that is very negotiable."

Hanna said, "I'll call you back after I talk with Ian."

She hung up the phone and realized she was really excited and at the same time realized … *she was considering a personal yacht for twenty million dollars. She was a simple girl from Northern California who wouldn't make that much money in a lifetime and she was considering a toy with as much horsepower as the ship she'd sailed as Chief Engineer aboard.* "Fate… its strange isn't it?" She said under her breath.

She called Ian and in five minutes they were planning an overnight trip to Rhode Island to see the yacht. Hanna called the broker back and told him of their travel plans and asked if he'd like to travel with them. He immediately agreed.

"Meet us at the corporate terminal at seven this evening. We'll take you from there to the hanger ourselves." She was excited about the trip and the possibility of the yacht. Ian came home early to pack. He came into the door and kissed his wife. She pushed him away and smiled, "Not now, silly. There'll be time on the flight for that." They smiled at each other.

Susan stuck her head in the room. "Hey, you two, please stop by Bristol and visit your grandparents and bring back a bushel of quahogs. Remember, Ian, I like the small size. Oh, and, could you bring a dozen lobsters too. I know Hans and the kids would love to have a fresh lobster. Now kiss your mother and you two be on your way, and be careful."

They walked hand-in-hand to the waiting limousine. Raul stood by the door patiently. He was now an old man, but the van der Waterlaans considered him part of their family and their 'go to' driver.

He took them to the corporate terminal and the broker was there standing on the curb. Ian opened the door and invited him to join them in the car. The three of them were then delivered to the awaiting jet in the corporate hanger. The captain, Fritz, and his crew had the jet prepped and ready to go. Ingrid had the champagne opened and she served it as soon as the three of them were seated in the cabin.

Ingrid and Bill had married three weeks before and had just returned from their honeymoon. The decision for the two of them to make a commitment to each other had been the right thing for both of them and their new and fresh love was wonderful for the van der Waterlaan family to see.

Fritz had the plane in the air in short order and soon it was at altitude and pointed west. Hanna and Ian talked with the broker for the first hour and they looked over the portfolio and pictures. After their second or third glass of champagne and a light dinner, Hanna and Ian excused themselves and retired to the stateroom. The broker found a comfortable chair in the cabin and he slept, too. It was a quiet trip for Ingrid and she spent much of the flight sitting in a jump seat in the cockpit with Fritz and Bill.

It was four in the morning when Fritz landed the sleek jet on Rhode Island soil. Ingrid let the passengers sleep until eight and by then she had everything prepared for breakfast. The broker was the first one up. He came around the corner into the galley where Ingrid had started to brew the first pot of coffee. "Ingrid, is there a place where I can take a shower and freshen up?"

"Yes, follow me." Ingrid took him to the forward staff space and there was a bathroom and shower.

It was nine o'clock when Ian and Hanna emerged from their stateroom. The three gathered around the dining table and Ingrid prepared breakfast. After the meal, they departed the jet and entered the waiting limousine. It was a short forty five minutes and they were at the Newport Launch and Ferry Terminal. The launch was waiting for them, and after a short and scenic trip, it approached the yacht lying on anchor in the harbor.

The yacht was magnificent. The hull was a dark blue with white topsides. There was a large door opened at the stern where the tenders and watercraft were stored. The hull was a traditional shape that endeared itself to a time long ago yet it was ultra-modern inside the engine room and the accommodations.

The captain waited for them in a crisp white uniform. Hanna and Ian took one look at the captain and smiled. It was Ian's old academy roommate from Plebe year. "Dave? Dave Tomily?" Ian said.

"Mr. van der Waterlaan? Sir, is that you?"

"Yes, it's me, old roommate. You remember my wife Hanna Horton. She was a year ahead of us."

"Holy shit, it's nice to see you, Ian, or would you prefer Mr. van der Waterlaan? ... Sir?" the captain said.

"I'll leave it to you to decide when it is appropriate and when it's not." Ian said with a smile.

"Fair enough, welcome aboard the *Dolce Vita*. Let me show you around." Dave took them through the living quarters and the large and open entertaining areas on the various decks. The interior was appointed with various types of granite, plush carpets, and fine furniture. The bulkheads were covered in tasteful finishes and adorned with exquisite art in the appropriate amount. It was neither underdone nor overdone. Everywhere there were crew and hotel staff busy keeping the vessel immaculate.

The staterooms were large and well-appointed. The master stateroom was the width of the vessel and nearly sixty feet fore and aft. Complete with a sitting room and incredible bathroom with a large sunken tub and enormous showers, a huge desk and several pieces of original art. "Sir, you probably already know this, but there is over one million dollars of fine artwork aboard which comes with the boat. These two paintings are but an example. Would you like to go to the wheelhouse or the engine room first?"

"The wheelhouse, please," Hanna said.

Up two flights of stairs and they entered the bridge. It was large and appointed with the same state of the art electronics and navigation equipment the van der Waterlaan fleet was provided. Ian recognized the equipment, but didn't know how to use most of it but there would be time for that later.

It was nice to be on a bridge again and he thought for a moment of his friends and mentors from the *American Spirit,* Joe Kelly and Captain Horne.

"Captain, I like it." Ian said. The captain smiled and bowed slightly and turned to Hanna. "Mrs. van der Waterlaan, or should I say Chief Engineer van der Waterlaan, would you like to see the engine room?"

"Of course, silly," she smiled. It had been years since anyone called her chief engineer.

From the bridge they entered the elevator and took it down to the control room in the engine room. It was an air conditioned and sound proof space where the watch engineers monitored the engine vitals.

The third assistant engineer was there and greeted the captain and the van der Waterlaans. He began to speak to Ian about the engine room and Ian stopped him. "Third … you should be telling my wife about the machinery. She's the licensed chief engineer, any horsepower, motor and steam," and he smiled at her. The third didn't miss a beat and continued, then took her on the tour.

Ian and Dave stayed in the control room where it was cool and quiet. Ian asked, "Dave, would you stay with the yacht if Hanna and I buy it? We're looking to travel the world for the next year or two. For the most part, I think it will be just the two of us, but we'll have family and friends spend time with us too."

"I'd be honored," the captain beamed.

"How about the rest of the crew, are they reliable and competent?" Ian asked. "Are you satisfied with them?"

"Yes, I hand-picked each one of them myself." Dave replied with pride.

"Good, then if the engine room is to Hanna's liking and there is nothing terribly wrong that comes up during the dry-dock, survey, and classification process, we'd like you to position the ship in Rotterdam – ready in all respects for us to board and sail to the Mediterranean with a short stop in Rome to visit my sister and her husband."

"Sounds great I know the yacht will pass inspection with flying colors. I hope your wife likes the vessel. I'd love to work for the two of you." Captain Tomily said.

Hanna returned to the control room and looked at Ian and he knew. He turned to the broker who had been following her through the engine room, "We like it. We'll make an offer. Thank you, captain, for your time and patience. I hope to be talking with you soon."

"I hope so too." The captain replied and then led them back to the waiting launch.

On the way back to the beach, Ian talked to Hanna, "Do you like it?"

"Yes, very much," she said.

Ian turned to the broker. "Make an offer eighteen as is with art and all equipage aboard. Sale is pending successful dry dock, sea trials, survey, and classification. Have the yacht brought to Rotterdam prior to New Year's and presented ready in all respects for a one to two year round the world voyage. I've mentioned the itinerary to the captain, any questions?"

"No, sir, let me go to work and get you the yacht. I'll make my own way back to the Netherlands when the business is completed here. Thank you, Mr. and Mrs. van der Waterlaan ... Thank you!" the broker said as he parted ways at the launch terminal.

He walked into town whistling like a sailor coming ashore after months at sea. He found a bar stool at the Mooring and had the first of four martinis.

In the meantime, Hanna and Ian met their limousine on the corner of American Cup Boulevard and headed to Bristol to visit with Ian's grandparents. Being back in New England was exciting for Ian and he stared at the scenery as the car moved north along the West Main Road. Ian noticed little had changed in Rhode Island since he'd left eight years ago. Over the Mount Hope Bridge and a few more minutes and the car stopped in front of his grandparent's small cape home.

Ellen and Stanley were sitting on the porch in their rocking chairs bundled up in their sweaters and sipping coffee when the car rolled up. Ian and Hanna jumped out and ran to the older couple as they rose from their chairs together and moved to the stairs.

"Welcome home, son." Stanley said and shook Ian's hand. "Welcome, Hanna, you're beautiful, my dear."

Ellen's eyes teared with joy at the sight of her grandson and his wife back in Bristol. The four of them came in from the cool air and sat around the kitchen table and talked for hours. It was only on the insistence of Ian's grandparents that Ian and Hanna discussed the purpose of their trip and the yacht they had just made an offer on.

"Son, how much did you offer?"

"Eighteen"

"Eighteen million U.S. dollars!" Stanley nearly fell off his chair. "Damn, that must be some boat. I hope your grandmother and I can see it someday."

"Of course you can, grandpa. We expect you to spend time with us as we travel the world."

After a short diversion to the fish monger to purchase quahogs and lobsters, Ian and Hanna left Bristol and went directly to the airport where the jet was waiting.

Exhausted after a long day, they retired to the stateroom and slept all the way back to Amsterdam. Ingrid went forward and sat in the jump seat with the pilots and the three of them kept each other company on the six hour flight home.

As the plane taxied towards the hanger, Hans called Ian. "Ian, seems you and Hanna have bought a yacht. Your broker called and the owner accepted your offer. Congratulations. The ship will transit to Virginia for dry-dock and inspection. I have asked Alex Saparo and Eirk Mauss, our best engineers, to oversee the dry-docking, survey and classification process."

Within the month the vessel was given a clean bill, the contract was signed, and money changed hands. In a brief ceremony the ship was renamed the *M/V Grand Madam* after Ian's grandmother who had been responsible for so much. It was a fitting name. The captain presented the ship in Rotterdam as instructed before Christmas and the van der Waterlaans hosted a number of parties on the yacht as they prepared to leave on their adventure. The yacht was magnificent and the holidays were memorable for everyone.

By that time Hans was comfortable running the dynasty with his loving wife by his side. The van der Waterlaan family threw a New Year's party that made the headlines and would be remembered by those who attended. On one January, while the rest of the world was hung-over, the *M/V Grand Madam* quietly and without notice, slipped her moorings and headed to sea. The vessel and her owners headed south in search of adventure and memories and Ian had found harmony with, and was no longer torn between, desire and destiny.

***

Trailing twenty miles behind the *Grand Madam,* there was a nondescript trawler. It discreetly left Rotterdam loaded with an unusual cargo including fast boats, weapons, and explosives. The men aboard were athletic, professional, and patiently followed their prey at a safe distance. They wore black clothing, their hair cut short, and they busied themselves as warriors do, cleaning weapons, sharpening knives and testing their equipment.

Three years ago, these men were part of a clandestine team employed by "a friend of the van der Waterlaans". He was gone, but the remaining team had stayed together and discreetly continued their very lucrative vocation …

The End

***

The van de Waterlaan Family story continues … pick up *Drawn to the Sea* and *The Gentleman Pirate*. Read all three!

275

Please turn the page for an exciting sneak peek of Rex Inverness' next novel:

The Gentleman Pirate

Book Three

The van der Waterlaan Dynasty

Rex Inverness

Chapter One
Adriaan

Adriaan van der Meer (from the water, in Dutch) was born to a minor aristocratic family in June of 1934. He was hailed into the world as the only child to Rogier and Anika, the Baron and Baroness, van der Meer.

The van de Meer family had made a large fortune in the 18th century through a lucrative shipping arrangement tied to the Dutch East Indies. But ever since, the banking journals recorded, the sun had been setting on the family's fortune ever since.

Over the last two hundred years a succession of dullards and poor businessmen, at the helm had squandered away virtually all of what was once the largest purse in Holland. By the time Adriaan was a young man all that was special about the family was their title, the facade of wealth his parents managed with great care, and the family address in Amsterdam, the family home on the Herrengracht in the center of town.

His parents like all the van der Meer's before them, lived beyond their means and played themselves off to be something they really weren't. The wealthy and landed families politely acknowledged them but discreetly kept their distance, whispering among themselves. Commoners and merchants were initially impressed by the way Adriaan's parents carried themselves, but when the bills came due and the money wasn't forthcoming, the working class were quick to throw darts at the fragile veneer the van der Meer's lived behind.

All the same … Adriaan had a memorable childhood in the heart of Amsterdam. His parents did their best to provide him with the opportunities and education commensurate with his family title and scrimped in other places where it was less apparent.

From as far back as Adriaan could remember, he was reminded of his family's history. His parents went to great length to ensure he knew about the family history and the successes that led to title. He learned the van der Meer's, in the day, owned one of the largest fleets of merchant ships in the world. The fleet in total had been cleverly chartered to the VoC, the Dutch East Indies Company, on twenty year contracts. Though the van der Meer's were technically the ship owner, the ships were leased for the hulls working life to the government subsidized company.

The VoC maintained and repaired the ships, provided captains and crews, and guaranteed full payment to the owner even if the ships should be lost to storm, enemy action or piracy. In short, the money came in like clockwork with little risk on the part of the family. As the VoC prospered, the van der Meer fortune grew quickly. Those were the days of glory his parents would say.

The darker side of the family history came later when competition became cut-throat and the British and French fleets began to sweep the Dutch from the sea. The van der Meer's, preoccupied in their wealth and blinded by excesses and distractions, did nothing to position themselves in the changing market and soon were wealthy but isolated from business opportunities and for the last two hundred years the sun was setting fast on the once prosperous family. All the time they lived off the interest and minor investment successes and money continued to slip through their fingers.

Such was the life of the fallen elite in Holland. That was until May 1940 when life for everyone, in Holland, changed overnight. In just five days the Nazis occupied the entire country. They came like locust over the borders, destroyed what they wanted and took the rest. All social norms in Holland vanished.

The Dutch, occupied and beaten were forced to resolve themselves to their fate.

Chapter Two
First Came the Nazis

Adriaan was 6 years old when he watched with curiosity from the third story window of his family home. There were airplanes with crosses on their wings, flying overhead. In the streets, he saw hurried activity as the Dutch citizens ran for cover, hiding inside shops, anywhere, clearing the streets seconds before Nazi trucks and tracked vehicles came down the narrow cobblestone roads. Adriaan thought, *the German's inside the vehicles must think the streets are deserted. It's strange how the people hide*.

The moment the vehicles moved on, life resumed on the streets and the citizens came back out into the light. Later the Nazi soldiers in gray uniforms were seen walking the streets in groups of six to eight with their weapons at the ready. As the days continued, Adriaan noticed the soldiers had their rifles slung on their shoulders.

At night, Adriaan worked on his homework or read a book. In the distance he'd hear the sharp report of gunshots and the yelling of Germans as they closed a snare around the neck of their prey. For the first two weeks, confusion and abrupt marshal law reigned supreme.

280

Adriaan's family remained safe within the walls of their home. Twice the Nazis came calling; entering the house without warning. They ran through the house turning it upside down looking for any sign the van der Meer's were doing anything they considered anti-Nazi. Satisfied there was nothing out of the ordinary the gray soldiers, with angry eyes and coats smelling of sauerkraut, vanished. Each time Adriaan could see the pure unadulterated fear in the eyes of his parents. His mother would cry and tremble while his father would cower and looked like a man beaten down, his head bowed, and hands shoved deeply in his pockets.

It was during the third week of the occupation the Germans came to stay. Adriaan was in his room drawing when he heard several trucks pull up to the front of the house, the diesel engines making a loud sound and emitting black smoke from their exhausts. Next, the report of the soldier's boots striking the cobblestones around the stopped trucks filled the air. Behind the trucks were two more vehicles. These vehicles were long and black.

From his window, Adriaan could see four Nazi officers sitting leisurely in the opened vehicles while the soldiers came quickly through the front door of the house. This time his parents were there to greet the soldiers.

After a few minutes Adriaan saw his parents escorted out of the house to the waiting car. Adriaan watched his mother and father climb into the first car with the German officers. After a few moments, his parents left the car and returned to the house with the four officers following behind.

Adriaan moved from the window to the door of his room so he could hear the voices inside the home. His father started by welcoming the Germans into their home and then his mother, who was dressed more nicely than Adriaan had seen her since the occupation, provided a tour of the home.

Adriaan didn't know with the occupation the economy had turned upside down and there was no credit and his family had no money. His parents quickly realized the only way they could survive was to collaborate with the Nazis and take their chances.

***

Two nights ago, Anika had discreetly left the house with the sole purpose of contacting a Nazi informer. It took her most of the night and she met many unsavory characters in her adventure, some of whom tried to solicit favors for their information. She was able to steer clear of most until she was directed to an older man in a full length leather coat.

His bald head was covered by a black hat. His round glasses sat on his sharp nose and focused his dark piercing eyes. His pock-marked face and pasty white complexion confirmed he was a creature of the night.

Without a word he led her to a back room. She had no option but to satisfy him, after which she made her request. She wanted to rent her home to the Nazis, preferably officers. She provided the address and a brief description of the old but well-appointed home and its central location.

He took the information down into his note book and placed it back in his jacket pocket, "I'll pass it along, Frau" and with that he faded into the shadows.

Later that evening she told her husband what had happened and the vulgar thing she had done to deliver the message. Rogier was a man of little courage and less honor. With a long gulp from the jonge jenever bottle he became numb to his wife's infidelity. She watched his indifference and took note.

Two days later four German colonels came looking for billeting. Certainly they had been keenly informed of the talents demonstrated by the landlord several nights before. Mrs. van der Meer walked the officers through the house. They were satisfied and the soldiers hurriedly moved the officer's personal belongings into their respective rooms. In addition, six enlisted men were billeted there to provide security and staff support for the officers.

As the officers took their leave from their hosts, the black sedans pulled up to the front door. The men climbed into the vehicles and sped away. The soldiers finished moving the personal belongings and the equipment into the house and they too returned to their trucks and soon disappeared around the corner. Left behind in the mansion were six enlisted men who busied themselves preparing the officer rooms and the three rooms on the third floor chosen to be their offices and billeting for the duration.

Adriaan's parents came into his room and sat down on his bed. They explained the Germans would be living in their home for some time. Adriaan was to be polite and he would move out of his room and into the attic so the soldiers could move into his room. His mother gently held his hand in hers and said, "You must be quiet and respectful and never discuss anything you may see or hear in the house to anyone, Dutch or German." For a 6 year old boy it was difficult to understand but on her insistence, he agreed.

They gathered for tea in the kitchen, enjoyed a quiet moment together as the enlisted men worked upstairs. When their tea was finished, Adriaan and his parents swiftly moved his belongings into the attic.

Later the officers returned to the house. They were greeted by their orderlies and briefed. Satisfied they turned their attention to their hosts and each of the officers greeted Adriaan and his parents politely. One even brought Mrs. van der Meer a bouquet of flowers. Then the stiff and formal officers made their way to their respective rooms to rest and change before dinner.

The orderlies retrieved food and cases of wine from the officer's sedans and brought a number of boxes into the kitchen. Anika was happy as she began to prepare the evening meal. There was plenty of food to feed the guests and her family. Possibly even more … She smiled, she hadn't seen this much food in years. *The war wouldn't be too bad after all,* she thought. *We have senior officers, they appear to be gentlemen and there is plenty of food.*

With that thought she rationalized the moments of disgust and humiliation at the hands of the Gestapo agent was worth it and she forced the memory out of her mind. She thought, *it could have been worse.* For the time being they were safe, fed and able to retain their title and position, albeit under the Nazi regime.

Time continued in war torn Holland and as the calendar moved through 1940, 1941, 1942, and 1943 little changed in the way the Dutch lived under German domination. Occasionally a Dutchman was publicly shot or hung by the Germans as a member of the underground.

From time to time there would be a German officer or NCO found with his throat slit. The Nazis would scurry around to gather up innocent Dutchmen and kill them in retaliation. It all blended into the daily life of occupied Holland and, especially, Amsterdam.

Adriaan's father was one of the lucky men who managed to stay employed. He worked long hours and it seemed like the money he brought home each month was less and less. Adriaan didn't understand why his father seemed to age so quickly during the war.

In part it was from the strain of housing Nazi officers and the looks he got from the Dutch who knew he was aiding the enemy that burned his soul and in part he'd just given up. Rogier and Anika tried to keep up the front of being aristocrats but their collaboration with the oppressive Nazis made them lepers in their community.

The Baron drank excessively and spent the evenings in his study while his wife spent more and more of her evenings in the parlor with the German house guests. She'd be heard laughing and carrying on like a young girl as she flirted with the older gentlemen in hopes of increasing the food and money they'd provided. As the war turned on the Nazi, she became more desperate, she knew what would happen to Rogier and her if the Nazis left.

For most of the war Adriaan was left to himself during the evenings. He'd sit in the attic looking out the windows at the city. His once comfortable and secure childhood was nothing more than a memory. Through the summer of 1943 the sounds and sights of war were contained in the German news reels shown in the cinemas and approved Nazi radio announcements made over loudspeakers throughout the city.

The demographics and population of Amsterdam had changed abruptly following the occupation. The Jewish communities disappeared. The older Dutch seemed to give up and pass away and the younger ones weren't having children.

One afternoon, when Adriaan was playing hide and seek on the street with his friend Fritz, a German soldier saw Fritz hiding and, thinking he was a terrorist, shot him through the head. It was an unfortunate mistake and it ended the days Adriaan was allowed to play on the street. His world closed in on him, he was only 10 years old.

His education had become nothing more than a place to go each day. The quality educators had all been transferred or arrested and replaced by pro-Nazi teachers who spent most of the day extolling the virtues of Nazism and the Third Reich. Adriaan no longer enjoyed school and spent the days daydreaming until 6 June 1944 when there was hope and excitement infecting the citizens of Holland. Word moved quickly albeit quietly. The allied forces had successfully landed on the beaches of Normandy. In hushed tones the population trembled with excitement and hope. They spoke under their breath, "Soon Holland will be free again."

In the winter of 1944 the war started going badly for the Nazis and the weather was especially harsh. Food, medicine and fuel became scarce in Holland. The cities were hit hard and Amsterdam was one of the worst. Citizens starved and froze to death on the streets. The few who prepared or made arrangements for food and fuel from the country kept quiet. If they fed one starving friend one meal there where twenty at the door for the next meal.

The collaborators who'd lived well under their German benefactors found even the occupying forces were unable to access food. The van der Meer home was no different. Where there had been ample food and wine early in the war, now they were hungry. The hushed voices of the senior Germans living in the home told of pending withdrawal to establish a front on the German border.

Anika and Rogier knew they were in serious trouble. When the Nazis retreated, the Dutch citizens would dole-out harsh vigilante justice to those who had collaborated. There were already stories of Dutch women who'd provided sex and comfort to the Germans being stripped naked, shaved, and painted orange for all to see. In humiliation, most ended their own lives. Men were being hung in the streets for collaborating with the Nazis. Anika and Rogier looked at each other and knew it was only a matter of time and they'd face a similar fate.

In April 1945, Anika asked if she could leave with one of the German officers. In desperation, she was ready to take her chances with the man she had been intimate with for the last two years. He wasn't interested, he had his own problems. His wife and three children lived along the eastern boarder currently being overrun by the Soviet army. The Soviet brutality was infamous and the Germans trembled at the thought of what Soviet soldiers were capable of doing to soldiers and civilians alike.

As he left he gave Anika his pistol in consolation which she carefully hid in the cupboard.

Several days later, without ceremony or even a 'goodbye', the house guests were gone, leaving much of their equipment and personal effects behind. That afternoon the planes overhead were adorned with a star and bars and circles of the Americans and British. The Nazi occupying forces assembled and withdrew from the city mere hours before the arrival of the allied forces. It was May 1945.

As the allied forces entered the city, the Amsterdamers, now emboldened, took it upon themselves to take out their frustrations and anger on collaborators. It was only a matter of time before they'd come looking for Rogier and Anika van der Meer. That evening Adriaan was sent to bed early with the last of the food in the house in his stomach. He was happy to be back in his bedroom since the soldiers had left. He climbed into his bed and slept soundly. As he fell asleep, he felt happy and almost giddy with excitement. As he fell asleep he spoke in a soft voice, "Holland is for Hollanders again!"

Down at the ground level of the house Rogier and Anika sat in the parlor of the large house. They sat beside each other facing a roaring fire they'd built in the fireplace. Rogier had broken up some furniture to fuel the fire and it burned bright and hot. Together they drank the last two bottles of jonge jenever and consoled each other. It had been years since they'd spoken to each other with honesty and intimacy. They spoke of what could/should have been and the mistakes and regrets they had and forgiven each other for their failures and short-comings.

It was later when the fire was nearly extinguished and both bottles of gin consumed, they knew their neighbors would be coming for them in the morning and it would be a humiliating experience. Anika got out of her seat and kissed her husband gently for a long moment then went to the cupboard and removed the pistol. Hiding it from him she walked behind his chair gently put the barrel of the gun against his head and pulled the trigger. He slumped forward in his chair. She took her seat and put the barrel in her mouth. Her final thought was of her now orphaned son, Adriaan. The life left her instantly as the gun discharged into her skull.

Adriaan woke abruptly to gunshots. He climbed out of bed and walked down the stairs calling for his parents. Walking around the corner into the parlor he saw by the waning light of the dying fire what had happened. He was in shock. He was too young to understand his parents had killed themselves, but he was old enough to recognize he was alone. He gathered a pillow off of the couch and sat down between his parents bodies looking at the glowing embers in the fireplace. His mind was blank and his heart empty.

He had no idea what to do or even who he would tell.

Chapter Three
Then the Americans

The next morning Adriaan lost his battle with fatigue and dozed-off. As he slept the local Amsterdamers came to the van der Meer house with the intention of gathering up the conspirators, haul them off to be summarily tried, sentenced, and punished within the hour. Hatred ran deep in the hearts of the Dutch who'd suffered at the hands of the Nazis and especially for their countrymen who had sold themselves to the Germans for a better lot in occupied Holland. Those who had kept warm and fed while playing the puppet or sleeping in Nazis beds would be harshly dealt with, was the consensus of the crowd as they approached the large estate in the center of town.

Wearing rags for clothes the angry crowd moved in a large group. There was blood in their eyes and the sharp taste of vengeance in their throats. The van der Meer sentences would be harsh and swiftly administered. The mob mumbled the sentences, Rogier would be hung slowly by the neck in front of his home with a sign around his neck "verrader nazi" (Nazi traitor). As had already been done many times elsewhere in the city, the crowd would cheer and spit as they watched him squirm, shake and his face turn bright red as he slowly suffocated. His wife's fate, no less horrible...

Anika would suffer the same fate as the other Dutch women who had provided comfort and intimacy to the Nazis. The crowd carried shears, razors and orange paint. She'd be stripped naked by the crowd and passed around and physically abused at the whim of the crowd. This abuse ranged from slaps across the face too much worse. She'd be shaved completely and painted orange and cast out into the streets to be humiliated by the community. She could have done better as a leper. No one would talk to her, help her or provide food, water or clothing until the allied forces occupied the city.

This time the crowd would be cheated of its sadistic pleasure. They burst into the house and the noise woke Adriaan. The angry mob poured in looking for the van der Meer's as they moved deeper and deeper into the mansion. They rounded the corner, looked into the parlor, and were confronted with a sight which stopped them in their tracks. Rogier van der Meer was slouched forward in his chair with the front of his face blown away and Anika was seated with her head laid back over the top of her chair, most of the top of her head removed from the self-inflicted gunshot ... a German luger lying on the floor beside her.

The site of the two dead bodies didn't affect the crowd, they had seen plenty of traitors who'd taken the coward's way out, but the young boy sitting on a pillow between his parents stopped them dead in their tracks. The boy was scared, cold and confused. Seeing this poor innocent boy sobered-up the crowd.

An elderly woman stepped forward and approached him, she gently kneeled next to him and began to carefully stroke his hair as she said, "Arme jogen … zign wel goed…(poor boy … it's going to be alright)" and she gently raised him to his feet, covered him with her shawl, and led him slowly through the silenced crowd. The mob parted for the woman and the child behind her.

Gradually the woman and Adriaan made their way to the street and as they walked away the sounds of the crowd ransacking the home and mutilating the bodies sounded like lions feeding. Adriaan was in shock and the memories seared his soul.

The older woman, Moira Prinz, was a war widow and lived alone on a boat on the Prinzengracht near the Runstraat Bridge. The old boat rested on the bottom of the canal and tilted slightly to one side. Moira and Adriaan walked down a narrow wooden plank to the uneven deck below. Moira had suffered at the hands of the Nazis and lost everything. She brought Adriaan into her simple and seriously neglected home with little food, but, it was a place to live, he was off the street, and for the time being, safe.

Moira fed Adriaan all she had, watered down soup, which he inhaled, he was so hungry. After the meal she led him to a small room forward in the boat with nothing but a bed. She encouraged him to lie down and get some rest while she went out for a while. Grateful, Adriaan was soon asleep under an old moldy blanket. She slipped off the boat to find clothes and food for the boy.

Moira, like most Dutch, had no money to bargain with and the city was in complete chaos. The Nazis had left and the Allied forces closed in but hadn't arrived. There were groups of people like those who terrorized the van der Meer home looking for revenge. Some were whipped-up into a wonton frenzy of blood lust and hysteria while others looted. Those who maintained their faith and moral grounding stayed home or at work and tried to make the days as normal as they could.

Moira returned a few hours later with some clothes and a few potatoes and a stick of celery. She thought, as she carefully hid the food, she and Adriaan would eat like royalty tonight on potato and celery soup. Moira had lived on much less. As she came down the plank and entered the cabin Adriaan sat at the table. He was scared and had been crying. She approached him and sat down.

Gently she reached across the table and took his hand in hers and he looked up confused and disoriented. Gently she squeezed his hand and began to talk. Her voice soft and calm, her callous hands were warm. "Young man, there is no need for you to be scared. I'll take care of you until we can find you a better home." She looked around the shabby, sunken boat with broken windows and rotting wood and said, "We're on the Prinzengracht near the Runstraat. We're only a few blocks from your old home."

She wiped her hand on the front of her worn dress then extended it towards the boy and said, "My name is Moira Prinz and this old boat is called the *Wolven* (Wolf). It was my late husband Erik's pride and joy. We have lived and sailed this canal boat for the last thirty years together. My dear Erik died during the war and I struggle to keep the old boat ..." she pulled her hand back and her voice tapered off and she began to cry.

After a few minutes she gathered herself together and continued, "You're welcome to stay with me as long as you need or want. I have no money and very little food but I'll share what I have with you, young man." Her kind and gentle eyes embraced his as he looked into her face searching for clues. He looked around the cabin and then back into her face and felt he could trust her.

He gathered himself together and began, "My name is Adriaan van der Meer. My parents Rogier and Anika are dead and I am all alone. I have no other family that I know of. I'm afraid ..." He looked down and started to cry. She reached over and held his hand again. Slowly he looked up and ran into her arms. He felt warm and safe for the first time in days. With that, Moira and Adriaan became friends. Safe off the streets with some food they stayed below – out of sight. The sunken abandoned wreck gleaned little attention from the passersby which was just fine – with both of them.

There were several more days of anarchy until the Allied forces arrived ... but they finally did. To the glee of the liberated Dutch the army brought a parade of military vehicles and soldiers from America, Canada, Britain and Poland that filled the streets. The Dutch lined the sidewalks to see the spectacle.

Young women dressed in their nicest dresses and the men wore their suits and ties. The victorious soldiers looked strong, powerful, well-fed, and healthy compared to the Dutch who'd just survived a horrible winter without food or fuel to heat their homes.

Moira and Adriaan made their way to the parade and watched with fascination as the 'supermen' liberators strutted through the streets. They didn't carry themselves with the arrogance the Nazis had when they entered the city. These men looked like boys and men who were determined but gentle. These men seemed approachable and honest, caring, and generous. Moira held the young man's hand as they watched the army arrive. Finally the parade ended, and as the citizens returned to their homes, the city took on a renewed sense of order and discipline.

There were no more open gangs of thugs roaming the streets. There were no more murders and violence on a mass scale as had happened only hours before. Moira looked at Adriaan and said, "Now we are going to be safe. People have returned to their senses. Thank God." They returned to the *Wolven* and warmed up the soup they'd been nursing for the past three days.

After dinner Moira reached under the seat in the cabin and pulled out a bottle of jonge jenever. She pulled out two small shot glasses, and looked at Adriaan. "Young man, I've been saving the last bottle of my late husband's gin for a special occasion. I guess the freedom of Holland is a good enough reason."

She opened the bottle and carefully poured out two even portions right to the rim of the glass and looked at Adriaan, "To a free Holland -- may we rebuild and be successful, and to you, Junger ... may you have everything you desire in this life. Prost!" She downed the drink in one gulp while Adriaan looked suspiciously at the glass. "Drink it. It won't hurt you." Moira said and laughed as she refilled her glass, "Prost" and this time she waited until he sipped the gin and nearly fell over.

She laughed, swallowed her drink, then leaned over, and took the glass out of his hand, "No reason to let it go to waste," and she threw it down her throat as well. She carefully placed the cork back in the bottle and returned it to its hiding place. The sting on Adriaan lips turned into a warmth that felt good and the minimal alcohol in his blood made him feel relaxed and his cheeks began to glow bright red.

Soon the sight of allied soldiers moving through the streets handing out candy to the children and flirting with the young girls became common place. Large trucks arrived at advertised locations to dispense food. Some trucks provided prepared food while others provided unprepared food for housewives anxious to make a home cooked meal for their families. Little by little the city returned to normal. People returned to work and the Dutch government began to exert control over the country again. The Allies gracefully backed away from the day to day running of the city and country governance. It was true; *Holland was once again for Hollanders and their Queen.*

Within the month American soldiers were walking through the streets without weapons and helmets. Their numbers and the quality of their clothing and equipment; their bright smiles and obvious individual strength and excellent health made them easy to see. Of course the minute they opened their mouths there was no doubt where they came from. Each one had his own story with one common thread. They all wanted to return to their home and their private lives. None were professional soldiers. They were citizen soldiers there to do a job with the expectation of returning to their own lives as soon as it was over.

The people of the city were full of hope and joy. The Allied forces for the most part conducted themselves professionally and politely and with great generosity and provided an endless stream of food, building materials, equipment and money to help the Dutch rebuild themselves and their beloved country.

***

During the winter of 1945, just months after the war had ended, Moira took seriously ill. Old and frail, the war years had been hard on her and now she had nothing left to fight the flu that wracked her body. She lay in her bed on the *Wolven* for two days as the fever drained the life from her. Adriaan stood by helplessly as she made peace with her life. She asked Adriaan to lean down to her side and she gently kissed him and spoke her final words, "Take care my son." She closed her eyes and left this earth peacefully.

Adriaan sat by her side as he had with his parents six months before. He found himself, once again, alone and afraid. After the better part of the day, he packed his minimal things in a small sack and left Moira in the *Wolven* as it sank deeper into the Prinzengracht soft mud. He walked away and didn't look back. He gazed to the sky and asked his God, "Why? First my parents and now Moira … what have I done to deserve this?"

As he wiped his tears with his soiled sleeve Adriaan decided he'd take Moira's advice and look out for himself. He found a bench in a small park and considered what to do. It was winter in Holland, he had no money, and he was only twelve years old with an incomplete education. There wasn't family to turn too and no friends to bring him out of the cold. With few options, he would get cold and hungry soon. Then the thought of Moira and the stories she'd told him of her life with her husband moving cargo through the canals. He remembered her telling him about a man who she said in hushed tones was a smuggler. His name was Hans van Zweden and he owned and operated a canal boat called the *Raaf* (Raven) he kept near the Keizergracht tucked out of site in the Leidsegracht.

Adriaan decided he'd find van Zweden and join his crew and cast his fortune to the wind. He started in the general direction of where he thought the boat and its captain could be found. It was 10pm, dark and cold by the time Adriaan found the *Raaf* sitting inconspicuously in a small side canal. The boat was black and a typical canal boat with red trim and the pilot house and living quarters aft. It was long and narrow and the cabin height, by design was low so the boat could pass through the city canals and under the low bridges spanning the waterways.

There were three dangerous men lounging on deck playing cards. Their clothes, bearded faces, and drunkenness alarmed Adriaan but he had made his mind up. He took a deep breath and proceeded down the plank and boarded the vessel. The three men jumped to their feet and approached him, "Hey, kid, get off now. You're not welcome here." The largest of the three said.

Adriaan stood his ground and said, "I'm here to see Captain Hans van Zweden. I'm a friend of Captain Erik and Moira Prinz of the *Wolven.*"

The leader cocked his head to the side and scratched his scalp for a moment and repeated, "Friends of Captain Erik? Get him boys ..." and the other two grabbed Adriaan and held him tight. The leader walked up to the boy and put his face right up into Adriaan's, "Captain Erik has been dead for three and a half years, kid. What do you want?"

Adriaan looked into the wild eyes of the man, "I want to speak with Captain Hans van Zweden. I was sent by Moira Prinz of the *Wolven*." As Adriaan made his request there was the sound of someone coming up on deck from the pilothouse. Everyone on deck turned to see. It was van Zweden walking forward to the group of men surrounding Adriaan.

"Unhand the 'junger', you dogs," van Zweden shouted and the men released Adriaan and gradually moved away like mangy cowering beasts under the glare of their brutal master. "Moira Prinz, hum," he held his chin in his left hand, looked at the boy and said, "how is my sister?" The captain asked.

Adriaan' eyes got the size of silver dollars ... "Sir, your sister?"

"Yes, my sister lad ... how is she?"

Adriaan thought quickly and saw opportunity ... "Captain, I am here to tell you that your sister has died just this morning from a winter illness. She is still aboard the *Wolven* and I was hoping you and your men would help me bury her. You see, sir, she took me in when my parents died and I was all alone. She protected me and fed me for the last six months. She was very good to me and told me I should find you if I ever needed help. Sir, I need your help to bury her ... I owe her so much, she saved my life."

Van Zweden took a long look at the boy as if to size him up. "Okay, junger, show me where the *Wolven* is and we'll retrieve Moira."

"Yes, sir, this way please ..." Adriaan walked over to the boarding plank and made his way back to the street above. Van Zweden gave some orders to his crew. He and two men followed Adriaan to the street and one man stayed with the boat. The man left behind pulled the boarding plank down onto the boat. Adriaan didn't understand at first then he realized it would keep people off as the four of them set off with Adriaan in the lead followed by the captain and his two mangy helots.

It was a short walk and Adriaan found the *Wolven* easily. Standing on the canal edge, looking down on the old boat, the captain looked at Adriaan, "Stay here lad." He and his crew moved swiftly down the plank and into the cabin to retrieve Moira. They gently brought her body on deck wrapped in the bedding under the careful supervision of her brother and placed her body on the street next to the canal. The captain came up on deck a few moments later with a picture of Moira and her husband Erick in his hand. In the boat cabin Adriaan could see a fire beginning to take hold. The fire grew and began to engulf the *Wolven*. Van Zweden came up the plank and ordered his men to pull it up and use it as a stretcher for Moira.

Van Zweden cut the mooring lines while the boat burned intensely and it somehow lifted itself off the bottom and moved into the middle of the canal where it burned to the waterline and the *Wolven* was gone forever.

The four of them moved away from the crowd gathered to watch the fire on the canal and the captain led them through back alleys and side streets until they were at the back door of the undertaker.

The captain's heavy fist rattled on the door and it was soon opened by an elderly man in an apron. The men addressed each other and the captain led Adriaan and his crew into the building. After a few minutes of hushed small talk, the captain spoke, "Herbert, this is my sister, Moira van Zweden-Prinz. She was born February 17, 1885 and she died today. Please prepare her and make all the arrangements to bury her properly. Send word to the *Raaf* when you bury her so her young friend," he looked at Adriaan, "and I will know where to find her. Understood?"

"Yes, captain …"

Van Zweden reached into his pocket and pulled out a purse and threw it at the undertaker. "This should cover the expenses."

"Yes, captain, and thank you very much." The skipper turned and walked back out the door with his crew behind him. Adriaan followed too. After a few yards the van Zweden stopped and looked over his shoulder and addressed Adriaan, "Junger, your job is done. Go home."

Adriaan with genuine sincerity in his face and voice said, "Sir, I have no home. I was hoping I could join your crew and work for you on the *Raaf*."

The captain rubbed his chin and considered the idea for a moment, "What the hell, if you don't work out, we'll eat you! Come along, you're part of the *Raaf* crew." Adriaan smiled and thought, *I've maneuvered myself into a place to sleep, with ample food, adventure, and a vocation – smuggling...*

***

Please purchase *The Gentleman Pirate* to continue the story of Captain Adriaan van der Meer.

Rex Inverness

About the Author

The author was raised in the rolling hills of Marin County, not far from the Golden Gate Bridge. He grew up on and around the San Francisco Bay and there he developed a keen passion for sailing, merchant ships, and the foreign ports they frequent. He pursued a career in the maritime industry where he spent 27 years between afloat and ashore assignments.

Most of the story is the product of his imagination. Others were influenced by his personal experiences. Readers, decide for yourselves which is which.

Today the author is semi-retired and living in New England where he and his wife explore the New England coastline, its harbors and inlets aboard their boat.

If you enjoyed *Torn Between Destiny and Desire,* please look for my other books available soon.

TORN BETWEEN DESTINY AND DESIRE

Drawn to the Sea / *The Gentleman Pirate* / *Two Warriors Collide* / *Bonnie Mae* / *The Cursed Seven* / *Lobsta* / *Leviathan* / *and Death of a Liberian Seaman* / *The Accidental Heir* / *and The Delivery Captain*

Contact me at rex.inverness@gmail.com

Rex Inverness

MV2

Maritime Fiction Novels
Bristol, Rhode Island
02809

Made in the USA
Columbia, SC
20 October 2017